More praise for Ellen Hart and ROBBER'S WINE

"[An] excellent novel . . . Details about each character as well as the crimes make a book that is not a formulaic mystery. . . . A quick, engaging read. Red herrings, a surprise ending, the usual twists, and fast action of a well-written mystery are here, as well as a cast of credible and likable characters."
—*Twin Cities Reader*

"Hart tackles personal ambition, marital relationships, and women's roles yesterday and today."
—*Publishers Weekly*

"Amateur sleuth Jane Lawless and her trusty sidekick, Cordelia Thorn, are the most refreshing, entertaining, and cerebrally stimulating duo since Rex Stout's unbeatable combo of Nero Wolfe and Archie Goodwin, and Robert B. Parker's Spenser-Hawk team."
—*Baltimore Alternative*

By Ellen Hart
Published by Ballantine Books:

The Jane Lawless mysteries:
HALLOWED MURDER
VITAL LIES
STAGE FRIGHT
A KILLING CURE
A SMALL SACRIFICE
FAINT PRAISE
ROBBER'S WINE

The Sophie Greenway mysteries:
THIS LITTLE PIGGY WENT TO MURDER
FOR EVERY EVIL
THE OLDEST SIN
MURDER IN THE AIR

ROBBER'S WINE

Ellen Hart

BALLANTINE BOOKS • NEW YORK

A Ballantine Book
Published by The Ballantine Publishing Group
Copyright © 1996 by Ellen Hart

http://www.randomhouse.com

Library of Congress Catalog Card Number: 97-95023

ISBN 0-345-40494-7

This edition published by arrangement with Seal Press.

Manufactured in the United States of America

First Ballantine Books Edition: July 1998

10 9 8 7 6 5 4 3 2 1

For my dear friend, Maureen Wells.
An inspiration, always.

Special thanks to the original creators of Robber's Wine:
Bethany Kruger and Shawna Kruger Gibson

Cast of Characters

JANE LAWLESS: Owner of the Lyme House Restaurant in Minneapolis.

CORDELIA THORN: Jane's closest friend. Artistic director of the Allen Grimby Repertory Theatre in St. Paul.

ANNE DUMONT: Belle's oldest daughter. Owner of Anne's Classic Catering in Minneapolis.

BELLE DUMONT: Anne, Lyle, and Melody's mother.

FANNY ADAMS: Belle's long-deceased mother. Anne, Lyle, and Melody's grandmother.

EDDY DUMONT: Belle's ex-husband. Anne, Lyle, and Melody's father. Retired high school teacher.

LYLE DUMONT: Belle's son. Manager of a real estate company in Earlton.

MELODY DUMONT: Belle's youngest daughter. Wife of Pfeifer. Part-time secretary.

HELVI SITALA: Life partner of Belle. Retired high school teacher.

QUINN FOSH: Gardener.

DENNIS MURPHY: Chief of police in Earlton.

PFEIFER BIERSMAN: Melody's husband. Salesman for Ringly Marine Outfitters.

JULIA MARTINSEN: Friend of Jane. Doctor.

JEFF WEINTZ: Son of Robert. The Dumont's lawyer.

ROBERT WEINTZ: Old friend of Fanny and Belle. Father of Jeff. Retired lawyer.

ANGELA MCREAVY: Old friend of Fanny and Belle.

" 'Tis the eye of childhood
That fears a painted devil."

—*Macbeth,* Shakespeare

PROLOGUE

Pokegama Lake
Early October, 1963

Something funny was going on. Annie Dumont could tell. Her mother had barely spoken during dinner. Her younger brother and sister had noticed it too, both attempting to catch Annie's eye, wanting her to explain what was going on. After all, she was the oldest, in first grade. Lyle was in kindergarten, and Melody was the baby, just three and a half. Annie was supposed to help them understand the world—that was her job. But this time she couldn't. She couldn't even figure it out herself.

Even worse, no one had bothered to light a fire in the fireplace before dinner. Annie loved the smell of wood smoke, especially when the leaves were turning fairy colors outside and the air was chilly and damp. Tonight, the house felt as cold as the tree house her dad had made for her before he went away. Last spring, Mom had talked to the three of them about something called a separation. She said that she and Daddy weren't going to be married anymore. All Annie knew was that she missed him. Even though he came and took them on Saturdays, sometimes out to the island to go swimming, sometimes to go fishing or to lunch in town, it was never enough. She cried at night wishing he could be home again just like before, but Mom said he was going to live in town

1

now. One thing she knew for sure, if Dad had been here tonight, there would have been a fire.

Yesterday, Annie's Grandma Fanny had come home from the hospital in Earlton. Except she hadn't gone to her cottage, the one she'd had a bunch of men build closer to the lake. Instead, she was staying in one of the downstairs bedrooms at the main house. Annie's house. Annie had been sitting in a tree when her mom drove up. She'd watched her help Grandma up the stairs into the screened porch. Grandma didn't want to go inside right away. Annie figured she must have sat on the porch until close to dark. She was in her bedroom now, resting. She didn't always eat with the family, so Annie wasn't surprised she wasn't at the dinner table. But Mom was upset about something. As Annie thought about it, she decided it was probably about Grandma.

Annie studied her mother's face. She seemed so sad tonight. She'd been sad a lot lately. Sad before Dad left. Sad after. And now sad again. But this was worse. She hadn't eaten hardly anything. When Annie was sad, she didn't feel like eating much either.

"Anne?" said her mother, her hands folded in front of her face, elbows on the table. "I need you to help me tonight. I want you to take Lyle and Melody upstairs and see that they get their baths. You need to take one too."

"But—"

"Don't put much water in the tub—I want it to be really shallow. And no roughhousing, is that understood? If you have any problems, just call me. I'll be downstairs with Grandma. When you're done, I want you to all get ready for bed. I put a clean sleeper in Melody's drawer. I'll be up to say good night later."

"But aren't you going to read us a story?" asked Lyle, his voice indignant.

"We'll see," said Mother, rising wearily from the table. "Your grandmother is very ill. Remember we talked about it the other night? I told you then that when she came home from the hospital I was going to need help from each one of you. We have to take care of her now. And of each other. We must always take care of each other. That's what families do." She wiped a tear away from her eye.

The tear silenced Lyle.

"Now, when you're ready for bed, I'll come up. One of you can come down and get me."

Annie watched her mother turn her back and leave the room. All the food was left sitting on the table. She'd made no attempt to clear it away, or to ask Annie and Lyle to do it for her.

This *was* a strange night.

"I'll go down and get Mom," said Lyle, pulling on his pajama bottoms.

All the kids still slept in one room. Mom said that Annie would be moving into her own room soon. Probably the one Grandma was sleeping in right now. Lyle would get this room, and Melody would move closer to Mom. The house was very big and made of logs. It was the only log house Annie had ever seen.

"No," said Annie. "I'll go. You stay here with Melody."

"I will not!" he said indignantly. Lyle was usually indignant about something.

"I go," said Melody, skipping out of the room.

Lyle and Annie looked at each other, then bolted for the door themselves.

Once downstairs, they crept quietly toward the bedroom. Something about the stillness in the house made them feel the need to be still themselves.

Annie put a finger to her lips. "Shhh!" she commanded, inching closer to the open doorway. She crouched down.

Lyle and Melody crouched behind her.

Inside, her grandmother was speaking:

"I acted rashly, Belle. I'm afraid you and the kids are going to have to pay for it someday."

"Don't concern yourself about that now," said Annie's mother. She was sitting next to the bed, a pile of papers in her lap.

"But I have to talk about it. I'm dying. You have an enemy in this town because of me, Belle, and I can't leave this world without warning you. You have to take this seriously. You're all in danger. The only one protecting you now is—"

Annie's eyes opened wide. *Danger?* What did her grandmother mean? She looked over her shoulder at Lyle. His eyes were wide and fixed intently on the two grown-ups. Glancing down at Melody, Annie saw that she was examining a snap on her sleeper top.

They listened for a few more moments and then Annie motioned for Lyle and Melody to follow her. They raced through the darkened house to the kitchen on the other end. As they passed through the dining room, Annie saw that the food was still sitting out on the table. Nothing had been put away.

"What did she say?" demanded Lyle. "I heard Grandma say that the only thing protecting us was . . . and then I didn't hear it right. I want to know!"

So did Annie. She could tell Lyle was scared.

Melody had started to cry.

"What did Grandma *say*?" pleaded Lyle.

Annie climbed up on a stool, trying to think. She'd heard the words too, but like Lyle, they didn't make sense. She squeezed her eyes shut and tried to remember. She could hear her grandmother's voice saying, *The only one protecting you now is—* Her eyes popped open. "Robber's Wine!" she announced.

Lyle cocked his head. "Huh?"

Annie wasn't absolutely sure, but she had to say something. It was her job. And Robber's Wine was almost right. She was sure of it.

"What's Wabbu Wine?" asked Melody.

"Yeah," said Lyle indignantly, a hand rising to his hip.

"Well," said Annie, not having the faintest idea, "I'll tell you." She had to think fast.

She jumped off the stool and ran to the china cupboard in the dining room. Melody and Lyle followed. Opening one of the lower cabinets, she removed a wineglass and then marched back to the kitchen.

"Now," she said to Lyle, "you hold the glass while I go get the wine."

First she ran to the bathroom and brought back several bottles. Next, she dragged a chair over to the cupboard above the refrigerator and, on her tiptoes, removed several more bottles from her mother's supplies. Assembling it all in front of her on the kitchen table, she asked Lyle to hold the glass steady while she poured dandruff shampoo into it. Next came some creme rinse, then a bit of hydrogen peroxide, caster oil, Calamine lotion, Bactine, and finally she topped it all off with a sprinkling of Ajax cleaning powder and a tiny bit of Mom's favorite perfume.

"There," she said, smiling proudly at her creation. "Robber's Wine."

"But what's it for?" asked Lyle. "I'm not drinking that gunk!"

"Yeah," said Melody indignantly. She was learning indignation from Lyle.

"I didn't ask you to. Just listen. See, it's not really wine, it's poison. But it looks like wine 'cause it's in a wineglass. If a robber comes in here to try and hurt us, he'll see it on the counter and drink it. And then he'll die."

Lyle thought about it for a minute. His face finally brightened. "Right," he pronounced.

"Wite!" agreed Melody. "Gimme some."

"No!" said Lyle, grabbing her hand before she could touch it. "You must *never* drink it. Never, ever ever. Otherwise you'll be dead. You don't want to be dead, do you?" He made a strangling sound and stuck out his tongue.

Melody shrank back, shaking her head gravely.

"We'll leave this on the counter tonight," said Annie.

"Do we have to do it every night?" asked Lyle.

Annie thought it over. "No, I don't think so. Just on the weekends, like tonight. Robbers only come on the weekends."

"I knew that," said Lyle indignantly.

"Me too," said Melody, punctuating her statement by plunking down on the kitchen floor.

1

Minneapolis
The Present, Late June

Jane Lawless was in her front yard emptying grass clippings into a lawn bag when she saw the car pull into her driveway. It was a Friday evening and it was about as hot and humid as it ever got in Minneapolis. She was glad she was going to be driving north tomorrow for ten days of well-earned vacation. Along the north shore of Lake Superior, where she and a friend were headed, it was always cooler, even in the dead of summer.

Jane waved a greeting and then switched off the power mower as Anne Dumont got out of the car. She was a small woman with the kind of thick, raven black hair Jane had always admired. Even though she was approaching middle age, it was still as shiny and black as the day they'd first met. At forty, Jane's hair—long, chestnut brown, usually done up in a French braid—was beginning to show signs of gray. Anne had worked for many years as a sous-chef at Jane's restaurant, the Lyme House. After Anne's divorce, about five years ago, she'd left to start her own company, a catering business. Now a successful businesswoman herself, she radiated a kind of confident well-being.

Jane had always enjoyed spending time with Anne. Their personal friendship had been a natural outgrowth of their

7

professional one. And since Anne's mother was a lesbian, and had been in a relationship with a woman for sixteen years, they shared another common link. Jane too was gay. She'd been invited to the family home on Pokegama Lake in northern Minnesota many times over the years and had grown to care about Belle Dumont and the rest of the Dumont clan every bit as much as she did Anne.

As a matter of fact, after Jane's partner, Christine, had died many years ago, Jane had spent several weeks staying with Belle and her partner, Helvi. They'd offered her a room, keys to the house and to the boat, free run of the kitchen, and then left her alone. Every evening, from midnight well into the wee hours of the morning, Jane had sat in one of the old rockers on the front porch and listened to the crickets, finally allowing the pain she'd kept so tightly bottled up during Christine's long illness to pour out. Sometimes she woke with the morning sunlight in her eyes, realizing a blanket had been placed over her during the night. It had been a terrible time, and yet because of Belle and Helvi's quiet love and concern, she looked back on it with an odd sense of peace. That log house had been her safe haven away from home, a private space in which to grieve, and to come to terms with her loss and begin the healing process. Belle and Helvi had been like mothers to her then, and they'd stayed close ever since. She'd never forget their kindness.

Tonight, as Anne approached with a big smile on her face, she carried a briefcase. "Where's the happy couple?" she asked, glancing toward the house.

She was referring to Jane's Aunt Beryl and her fiancé, Edgar Anderson. The two had first met at a bridge club about a year ago. Romance followed soon after. The wedding was scheduled for September 10, and Anne's Classic Catering was providing the food. It was Anne's wedding present.

"Beryl's doing some gardening in the backyard," said

Jane. She reattached the grass catcher to the rear of the mower. "And Edgar should be here any minute. Why don't you come inside and I'll pour us each a glass of iced tea while we wait."

"It's a deal." Anne smiled. "You look like you could use something tall and cold."

Jane pulled the power mower over to the porch steps. "That and a brief visit to the north pole and I'll feel like a human being again." She held the screen door open while Anne entered the house.

"I've got my menu book with me. And lots of ideas. I hope Beryl and Edgar are ready to get down to business and plan the meal."

"I think they've been ready since about ten minutes after they first met." Jane grinned and ducked into the kitchen. As she looked out the window over the sink, she could see her dogs investigating the flowering almond bushes near the south fence. On the opposite end of the yard, her aunt was bending over a rosebush, doing a little pruning. Thankfully, the hepatitis that had flared up last winter was now under control. Beryl was once again her old, energetic self.

Over the past two summers, ever since Beryl had moved here from her home on the southwestern coast of England, she had turned the backyard into a proper English garden. This summer, she'd even begun a small herb patch. Knowing that the house, and especially the garden, would be hard for her to leave after the marriage, Jane had proposed a solution. And just last night Beryl and Edgar had agreed. They would live here after the wedding. There was more than enough room, far more than the small apartment Edgar had rented for the past ten years. Because of Jane's work schedule, she was rarely home. And when she was, she loved their company.

Moving over to the refrigerator, Jane took out a pitcher of iced tea and some sliced lemons. She poured them each a glass. After handing one to Anne, she leaned back against the counter and took a long sip. "This is going to be an awful summer," she said, wiping the back of her hand across her forehead. "I'm more of a winter person myself. At least you don't have to mow snow."

"But you don't have to shovel grass."

"Cute, Anne. You should work for the Minnesota Department of Tourism." She took another sip, holding the glass against her forehead. "Have you been up to the lake to see your mom and Helvi lately?"

"Not this month," said Anne, pulling out a kitchen chair and sitting down. She set her briefcase on the table-top and flipped it open. "June's been kind of bad for me. Problems at work. Normally, I try to get up at least once a month. I love it up there. I suppose it will always feel like my real home."

Jane understood. She often felt the same way about her childhood home in England, the place she'd lived until she was almost nine years old. "Pokegama Lake, especially in the summer, is really beautiful. Since you love it so much, I've always wondered why you live in Minneapolis."

Anne leaned back in her chair and folded her arms over her chest. "Oh, I'll probably move back one day. I can't imagine retiring and staying here. But you know Mom. She always wanted Lyle and Melody and me to make it on our own. Not rely on the Dumont money." She laughed, a hint of bitterness in her voice.

"What's so funny?"

"Oh, nothing really. It's just that it's played such a small part in our lives, it feels like a fairy tale. None of us knows how much the estate is worth."

Jane sat down opposite her, squeezing more lemon into her tea. Anne had never talked much about her family's money. Jane had always assumed the subject was off-limits. "You know, I've wanted to ask you something, but I haven't wanted to pry."

"Of course you wanted to pry, but you're too polite. Go ahead. What's the question?"

"Well, I mean, how did your family make all that money? I've heard gossip around Earlton that it's over a million dollars."

"Many millions," said Anne, gazing at Jane languorously over the rim of her glass. "To be fair, Mom has put a sizable chunk in the bank from the real estate company she started back in the late Sixties. But the bulk of the money came from my grandmother, Fanny. All I know is that she invested wisely during the war. She left Earlton when my mom was pretty small, and when she returned, she was a rich woman. Lyle thinks she swindled someone."

Jane couldn't help but laugh. "Lyle would think that."

"Oh, Mel agrees. But unlike Lyle, she's got nothing against swindling."

Jane shook her head.

"Me, I tend to lean more toward homicide."

"Annie!"

"Oh, you didn't know Grandma Fanny. She was a feisty old goat. Occasionally, I even thought she was a little crazy. But I adored her. She died when I was pretty small." She ran her fingers along the edge of her briefcase. "I guess you could say that Mom always wanted her kids to learn the value of a dollar. That's why she made it clear we shouldn't expect much financial help from her. We got our college paid for, and then we were on our own."

"Is everyone happy with that arrangement?"

Anne's smile was guarded. "Happy? No. Resignation is the order of the day. Then again, Mom doesn't live like an heiress either. But you know what? I think she and Helvi live exactly the life they want. And how many people can you say that about? I'm happy for them, I really am."

Jane glanced at her watch. It was nearly seven. Edgar

should be here any minute. As she got up to fetch more tea, the phone rang. "I better get that," she said, moving to the end of the counter. She grabbed the receiver before the answering machine could pick it up. "Hello?"

"Jane? Is that you?"

"Yes?"

"It's Belle Dumont."

"Hi! What a coincidence. Anne's here and we were just talking about you."

Anne mouthed the question, "My mother?"

Jane nodded.

"No wonder my ears were burning," said Belle. "Or is it itching?" She laughed. "You know, Helvi and I were just talking about you and Cordelia the other day too."

Cordelia Thorn was the artistic director for the Allen Grimby Repertory Theatre in St. Paul. She was also Jane's best friend and her traveling buddy on tomorrow's trip to the north shore.

"And what were you and Helvi saying about us?" asked Jane. "Nothing libelous, I trust."

"Actually, we were just wondering when the two of you were going to visit us again. We had so much fun the last time, we were hoping for a repeat performance. Tell Cordelia that strawberry season is nearly over. If she wants to sample some of my famous shortcake, she better get up here. You know, I can still see the look on Cordelia's face when you pushed her off the end of the dock."

"She had it coming."

"I agree. If you hadn't pushed her, I would have." Her laugh was deep and hearty. "You think about it, Jane. Our door is always open."

"Thanks."

"Say, I don't mean to cut our conversation short, but can I talk to Anne?"

"Sure. Give my love to Helvi." She handed over the phone.

"Hi," said Anne, giving Jane a wink as she pressed the receiver to her ear. "How did you know I was here, Mom? You're having me followed, right?"

Jane sat down at the table, pouring herself another glass of iced tea. The first one went down so fast, she needed a second.

Anne bit her lower lip and listened. "Yes, I understand, but I've got an appointment tomorrow morning for my car at the garage. Something's wrong with it. I don't know for sure, but my mechanic said he'd need it most of the day."

As Jane sat at the table and watched, she could see the conversation was serious. Anne was a very controlled person, guarding her thoughts and emotions carefully. In that, they were much alike. And they had something else in common too. Both Jane and Anne were firstborn females. They'd talked about the effects of birth order more than once over the years. Each felt a certain pressure to take care of the family, to be the leader of the pack, so to speak. Anne had always been protective of her brother and sister, and also of her mother. Watching Anne now, listening so intently, always mindful that she had to do the right thing, be the good, levelheaded kid, Jane couldn't help but wonder what was being said.

"Sure, Mom," said Anne, staring straight ahead. "I guess I'll bus up then. I'll see you tomorrow afternoon."

Jane waited until Anne had returned to the table before she asked, "Problems?"

"I don't know. Mom wants the entire family present for some big powwow. We used to have family meetings all the time when I was a kid, but we haven't had one in years."

"She didn't give you any clue what it was about?"

"Nothing. Except that it had to do with our future,

Lyle's, Mel's, and mine. I'm going to have to take the bus up tomorrow." She picked up her glass but before she took a last sip, she asked, "Listen, just say no if it's not possible, but since we're on the subject—would you con-sider taking me to the Greyhound depot in the morning?"

"What time?"

"Around ten."

Jane and Cordelia had planned on getting an early start. To Jane that meant seven or eight A.M. To Cordelia, it probably meant anytime before dinner. "You know, I've got a better idea."

"What's that?"

"Why don't Cordelia and I drive you up?"

"Oh, I couldn't ask—"

"No, really. We're leaving for a vacation tomorrow anyway. Ten days up on the north shore without a care in the world. No work problems. No phone calls. Just peace, relaxation, and lots of hungry gulls to feed. Earlton's a straight shot up Highway 169. It's hardly even out of the way."

"You're sure Cordelia wouldn't mind?"

"Mind? She'll be snoring in the backseat until we hit Hill City. I suppose after that she might notice you're in the car. But by the time she's fully awake, we'll have dropped you off and will be standing in front of the Dairy Queen in Grand Rapids. While she's ordering her mega-death-chocolate-triple-dip cone, your presence will have faded to a dim memory."

Anne laughed. "Sounds like a good plan to me."

"Great," said Jane, hearing the front doorbell chime. It had to be Edgar. "It'll be fun to see your mom and Helvi again. Cordelia and I were just going to take a leisurely drive up to Tofte tomorrow. We don't have to be to Bluefin Bay until late evening." She rose from the table and started for the front door, calling over her shoulder, "And besides, what's a small detour among friends?"

2

Cordelia sat propped against several pillows in the backseat of Jane's new used car, a 1992 four-wheel-drive Trooper. She was fanning herself madly with a magazine. "I feel like I'm in a scene from *The Grapes of Wrath*."

"Why's that?" asked Jane, slowing and turning right onto a dusty, gravel road. It was nearly three in the afternoon.

"You need to ask? Just look at all the stuff we've crammed into this vehicle. Everything but the kitchen sink."

"*Your* stuff, you mean?" said Jane.

"Don't use that holier-than-thou I'm-a-real-pioneer-and-you're-just-a-pathetic-city-creep tone on me," grumped Cordelia. "And by the way, can't you crank that air-conditioning any higher?" She took the last drink from her can of cream soda.

"We can probably open the windows now," said Anne. "I'm sure it's cooler up here than it was in Minneapolis."

Cordelia rolled down the rear window, stuck her finger out, made a sour face, and then rolled it back up. "Dante would feel right at home." She yanked impatiently on her silk turban.

"If you didn't insist on dressing like Norma Desmond in *Sunset Boulevard*, you'd be a lot happier," observed Jane.

Cordelia glared at her in the rearview mirror. "I dress as *any* theatrical diva would."

"I'll buy that," said Anne under her breath.

15

Jane looked over at her with a secretive smile. "Does that mean you brought your matador outfit too, Cordelia?"

"None of your damn business," she said, flicking a popcorn kernel off her lap. "And anyway, the costume shop wanted it back."

"Then how about your Dracula cape from that show you directed a few years back? Say, it's wool, isn't it? That should be a nice, cool addition to your summer wardrobe."

Cordelia leveled her gaze. "My wardrobe is no longer open for discussion. Period."

Jane glanced up at the hot June sun beating down on Pokegama Lake in the distance. She was a bit disappointed herself. She'd also hoped for a respite from the heat.

After strong-arming Cordelia out to the car shortly before eleven, Jane and Anne had popped in a vintage Judy Garland CD—in honor of the new Judy Garland museum in Grand Rapids, her childhood home—and had driven north out of the city. They'd stopped near Mille Lacs Lake for lunch. Cordelia had awakened from her slumber long enough to down a burger and fries. Then, crawling back into the rear seat, she'd dozed off again until just a few minutes ago. To be fair, Jane knew Cordelia had been putting in some long hours at the theatre. Jane had lived through a pretty hectic spring herself. Still, even if Cordelia hadn't been exhausted, she loved to sleep in the car. Jane was glad for Anne's company, at least for a few hours.

"Look, there's Helvi's Jeep," said Anne, pointing to a dark green vehicle parked in front of the garage. "But I don't see Mom's."

Jane pulled in behind the Jeep. After turning off the motor, they all got out and stretched their arms and legs. Even though the air was hot, it smelled sweet and damp, with a woodsy freshness. A welcome breeze drifted off the lake.

Anne didn't bother to get her suitcase. Instead, she hurried up the stone steps and entered the screened porch. "Mom?" she called. "Helvi? Anybody home?" She disappeared inside.

Jane stretched a moment longer and then walked around behind the car and opened up the rear door, lifting out Anne's overnight case.

"Kind of quiet up here," said Cordelia, leaning against the fender. She looked up, watching the wind rustle the leaves in the trees. She'd already plucked a long blade of sweet grass and was chewing contentedly.

"Yeah. It's nice," said Jane. "I sort of wish we were staying for a couple days."

"Well, I suppose we could see what Belle and Helvi have to say."

"I don't know," said Jane. "This family meeting sounded serious. I'm not sure she'd want visitors right now."

As they continued to talk, Anne poked her head out the front door and called, "Come inside for a minute, will you?"

Jane couldn't help but notice the worried look on her face. It hadn't been there a minute ago. "Come on," she said to Cordelia.

Once inside, she found Anne and Helvi seated at the dining room table. Except for the sound of a wind chime tinkling softly from the back deck, the house was quiet.

"What's up?" asked Jane, smiling hello to Helvi and then giving her a hug.

"I'm all ready for that strawberry shortcake!" announced Cordelia, sweeping into the room carrying Anne's overnight case. Her grin faded as she saw Helvi's grim look.

Sensing that the older woman was close to tears, Jane bent down next to her and took her hand. "What's wrong?" she asked gently.

"It's Mom," said Anne, rising and moving restlessly over to the bay windows.

"What about her?" prompted Jane, her eyes moving from Anne back to Helvi.

Helvi rubbed her forehead. She seemed almost frantic. "I don't know where Belle *is*."

"I don't understand," said Jane.

"She left this morning shortly after ten. While I was getting dressed, she went downstairs to make us a breakfast tray. She was in a great mood—looking forward to everyone being here tonight. Planning the dinner. But when she came back up, she was upset. I asked her what had happened—what this mood change was all about—but she wouldn't discuss it. She just mumbled something about a mother never being too old to take care of her children."

"What did she mean by that?" asked Anne, a perplexed look on her face.

Helvi shrugged. "I guess I thought she was referring to the dinner she was planning. As she was dressing she said I shouldn't worry. Everything was fine. Then she gave me a quick kiss and left."

"Did she say where she was headed?" asked Anne.

"She mentioned something about going for a walk. And then into town to buy groceries. But if that's all she was going to do, she should have been back hours ago. We've always had a deal. If we're going to be gone more than a few hours, or if our plans change, we call and let the other person know. She should have called! I can't tell you how many times I've looked out at that drive thinking I heard her car!"

Helvi Sitala was the same age as Belle Dumont, midsixties, yet her hair had gone completely white. Belle's was still black, with only a few gray streaks. And while Belle looked much like Anne, small, wiry, and full of nervous energy, Helvi was plump, with a soft, kind face, a cheerful disposition, and a can-do approach to life.

"Where specifically did she say she was going?" asked Cordelia, sitting down next to her at the table.

Helvi briefly eyed Cordelia's silk turban, then shook her head and looked down at the lace tablecloth. "That's just it, she didn't say *anything* specific. She often goes for walks in the woods, but that could be anywhere. As far as the groceries, the local market in Earlton isn't so hot anymore, so I assumed she'd drive to Grand Rapids. I know she wanted to find fresh asparagus—and steaks."

Jane thought about it. "Did the phone ring while she was downstairs?"

"Not that I heard," said Helvi.

"Or the doorbell?" asked Cordelia.

She shook her head.

"Can you hear the phone and the doorbell from upstairs?" asked Jane.

"Yes," said Anne, pushing away from the windows. "Easily."

Helvi put a hand up to her throat, clutching her thin cotton blouse tightly around her neck. "This isn't like her. She would have called if she'd been delayed. I phoned Lyle at the real estate office around one, but he said he hadn't seen her. If she came by, he said he'd have her call. I didn't want to pass on my fears because I didn't want to worry him unnecessarily."

Jane wasn't sure what to make of this. It might not be time to hit the panic button, but she understood Helvi's concern. "Maybe she had car trouble and hasn't been able to get to a phone?"

"I thought of that," said Helvi, "and about a half dozen other scenarios, none of which I like."

Jane looked at her watch. It was nearly four. "What time are Lyle and Melody supposed to get here?"

"Around six," said Helvi. "Lyle is driving over from work. And Mel, well, you'll all find out soon enough." She turned to Anne. "She left Pfeifer at the beginning of

June. It just wasn't working. She moved in here about three weeks ago."

"I had no idea," said Anne, her tone a mixture of surprise and curiosity. "Is she here now?"

"No, she drove up to the Prairie River Dam to take some pictures. You know Mel and her photography."

"Say, I've got an idea," said Anne. "Where are your car keys?" She looked down at Helvi.

"On the kitchen counter."

"Great. Jane, what do you say we drive around and look for my mom? You and Cordelia can go in your car. I'll take Helvi's."

"Good thinking," said Jane.

"I'll take the road toward Fosh Lake. Why don't you two head toward Earlton?"

"I'd thought about doing that myself," said Helvi. "But I was afraid to leave the house just in case she called and needed me."

"You did the right thing," said Jane. "Come on, Cordelia. Let's get going."

Cordelia raised an eyebrow. "Ah, actually, instead of being part of the posse, I think I'll stay here with Helvi. Keep her company." She gave Jane a veiled nod.

Cordelia was right. Helvi shouldn't be left alone. She'd been alone all day with her fears, no doubt imagining the worst. At least now someone was here to help. And, if by some awful set of circumstances the worst had happened, Cordelia would be a strong shoulder.

For now, Jane refused to consider it. She waited while Anne found Helvi's keys and then together they dashed outside.

3

Jane drove around for the next few hours looking for Belle's Volvo. She checked every winding back road she came across, but with no luck. Around six-thirty, she stopped at a gas station near Grand Rapids and phoned Helvi for an update. Belle had neither called nor returned. Anne had also phoned, but with no news. Helvi was beside herself with worry, insisting that the police be notified immediately. Since it would be dark in a few hours, Jane felt she was probably right.

Returning to her car, Jane sped back onto the highway and headed south to Pokegama Lake and the Dumont house. As she pulled into the wide drive in front of the garage, she saw that another car had arrived while she was gone. It was Lyle's Lexus. She was glad that another family member was on the scene. As she got out, the Jeep came bumping down the dirt and gravel access road, kicking up a cloud of dust as it came to a stop directly next to her.

"No luck?" asked Anne, scrambling out of the front seat. She looked hot, her cheeks flushed, her clothes damp.

Jane shook her head.

"Damn it all, where could she be?" As she looked up at the porch she said, "Come on. Lyle's here. Let's see what he's got to say."

Wiping the sweat from her forehead, Jane followed her inside, wishing with a kind of blind hope that Belle

21

would just drive up with some innocent or even silly excuse for her daylong disappearance. At the same time, an inner sense told her that wasn't going to happen.

The front room was deserted. The entire house had always reminded Jane of a northern Minnesota resort lodge, circa 1950. The rooms were spacious, with knotty pine walls, old-fashioned braided rugs, and woodsy leather furniture. Jane stopped for a moment next to the family portrait centered above the stone hearth. Belle's quick, dark eyes stared back at her. Jane felt herself willing the likeness to speak, to tell her what was going on, but it was useless. The painting, one that seemed to capture the humor and affection in the young Dumont family, remained mute. It was Belle's inexhaustible energy that dominated the mood of the picture. For a moment, Jane wondered what it must have been like to have Belle Dumont for a mother.

Continuing on into the kitchen, she saw that everyone was gathered on the back deck overlooking the lake. She crossed to the patio doors and stood for a second, listening.

"Why doesn't she call!" demanded Anne, her voice full of frustration.

Lyle turned around. He'd been standing at the railing, gazing toward the distant dock, hands in his pockets. He was dark and small, like his sister. And if possible, he had even more nervous energy than she. "I don't know, sis," he said, giving her a quick hug. He stood back, loosening his tie.

Jane had known Lyle Dumont for years. He was friendly and talkative, the kind of guy who would give you the shirt off his back if he thought you needed it. Most everyone in town had some story about how Lyle had helped them in one way or another. He seemed to know everyone, and in turn everyone counted him as a friend. Jane had met his wife on several occasions and gone fishing a couple of times with his two boys when they were younger.

"I called the police a few minutes ago," said Lyle, pouring himself a Scotch from a cart that served as a makeshift bar just outside the kitchen's patio doors. "Talked to Dennis. He said it was too early to treat this like a formal disappearance, but he's going to send out a couple of cars."

"Dennis?" repeated Anne, making a question out of her face.

"Dennis Murphy. You remember him from high school, don't you? Big guy. Curly red hair. He was on the wrestling team. Good buddy of mine. Anyway, he's the new chief of police over in Earlton."

"Really." Her voice held little interest. She stepped over to the railing, turning her back on everyone.

Jane sat down next to Cordelia. The cool evening breeze did little to ease the tension. Even Cordelia's usual humorous exuberance was noticeably absent. The bottom line was that speculating about what had happened was too frightening, yet talking about anything else seemed pointless.

Cordelia pushed her can of beer over to Jane. "Sustenance," she whispered.

Gratefully, Jane took a sip.

After another tense few minutes, Jane caught Anne's eye. "I think Cordelia and I should run into Earlton and see if we can find a motel room."

"We can't leave without knowing what's happened to Belle," agreed Cordelia. Her turban had been removed, her auburn curls drooping like satin ribbons around her face.

"I won't have that," said Helvi firmly. "There's plenty of room here."

"I'm not sure you need houseguests right now," said Jane.

"You can stay at the cottage. You'll be perfectly comfortable out there. I just changed the sheets in both bedrooms last week. Everything's fresh." The look in Helvi's eyes told everyone she wasn't going to take no for an answer.

Jane had no doubt that they would be comfortable. The cottage, the small house Anne's grandmother had built for herself the year after Belle had been married, was cheerful and cozy, with the same kind of Northwoods charm as the main house. The exterior was wood and stone. Inside was another stone fireplace. The structure sat closer to the lake than the big house, with a screened porch facing east to catch the morning sun. Everything smelled of pine and wood smoke. Jane had been in it a couple of times, but never to stay.

"Are you sure you don't mind?" said Jane.

"It's settled," said Helvi.

Anne moved over to the cart and poured herself a glass of mineral water. She downed it and then said, "I wonder where Melody is? It's nearly seven-thirty. I thought you said she was going to be here around six." She looked over at Helvi.

"I've been so preoccupied with Belle, I never thought—" The sentence was left unfinished. Helvi looked at everyone, unable or unwilling to say what she was thinking—or fearing.

"Shit," said Lyle, sitting down in one of the deck chairs. "Now we've got to worry about her too."

Jane knew he didn't mean it the way it sounded. He was just upset and impatient, as they all were.

"She's late a lot," said Helvi, her voice hopeful.

"Tell me about it," grunted Lyle.

Jane had heard from Anne that Melody had begun working part-time as a secretary for Fosh Lake Realtors, the real estate company Belle had started in the late Sixties. After learning the business from the ground up, Lyle had taken over as manager about eight years ago.

"I need a couple aspirin," said Anne, running her hand through the back of her damp hair. "Do you remember where I put my overnight case?" She looked at Cordelia.

"I put it in your old room," answered Helvi.

"Thanks." As she passed through the patio doors, she nearly bumped into Melody, who was on her way out to the deck.

"Hey, sis," said Melody, giving Anne a brief hug as she breezed past, "watch where you're going. The life you save may be mine." She gave everyone a big smile.

Helvi sat forward in her seat. "Mel, you made it. We were worried about you."

"You were?" She set her camera bag and tripod down and then sank wearily into a redwood chair next to Lyle. "Well, I guess maybe you should have. I nearly died of heatstroke out there today." She picked up a magazine and began fanning air onto her flushed face. "Say, you all look like you could use a drink. Me too." She got up and walked over behind the cart, picking up an olive and popping it into her mouth. "Since I used to be a bartender, let me do the honors." She bent down and cracked the lid on the cooler. "Hey, there's no Coke. Do we have any inside?"

"I'll get you one," said Anne coldly, retreating into the kitchen.

Melody stared after her. "She got a flea up her butt, or what?" Her eyes came to rest on Jane and Cordelia. "Hi! I hear you two brought Anne up. Are you staying for dinner and the grand announcement?"

Jane noticed that Lyle seemed to grow sullen at the mention of the evening's agenda. "I think we may, yes."

When no one else spoke, Melody asked, "Jeez, did I miss something? You all look like someone just died."

Anne returned and handed her the Coke. "You have such a way with words sometimes, Mel."

"Hey, lighten up."

"It's Mom," said Lyle. "We don't know where she is."

Melody appeared confused. "What do you mean?"

In an attempt to clarify, Helvi explained what had happened earlier in the day.

"You mean you haven't heard from her since breakfast?" she asked.

Helvi nodded.

Anne leaned her back against the railing. "When did you see her last?"

"Well, I guess it was when I left this morning. She was sitting . . ." She stopped, her eyes dropping to the bottles of liquor on the cart.

"What?" prompted Helvi.

Mel said nothing. She seemed to be thinking. After a moment she said, "Mom just said . . . 'See you tonight. Don't be late.' "

"That's all?" said Lyle.

She nodded.

"Where was she sitting?" asked Helvi.

"On the front porch steps."

"Did she seem upset?" asked Lyle.

Melody shrugged. "I didn't notice." Again, she seemed to turn inward.

Jane was positive Melody wasn't telling everything she knew. Yet she couldn't imagine why she'd hold something back.

"Say, I need to wash up," said Melody. "I'm pretty dusty. I'll just be a minute."

As soon as she'd disappeared into the kitchen, Jane rose from her own chair. She had a hunch. She wanted to see what Melody was up to. "I think I'll grab one of those Cokes too. Anybody else?"

Cordelia raised a finger.

"Great. I'll be back in a sec." Stepping quietly inside, Jane saw that Melody was nowhere in sight. She glanced toward the bathroom door and saw that it too was open, the room empty. Next, she crept quietly into the dining room. Still no Melody. Inching her way toward the living room arch, she found the young woman bent over the wastebasket near the front door. She was searching through the contents so intently, she didn't even notice Jane enter the room.

Placing the wastebasket soundlessly back on the floor, Melody darted onto the screened porch.

Jane slipped up behind her and watched as she rummaged through the contents of another wastebasket, this one larger and much deeper. "Did you lose something?" asked Jane finally, seeing Melody jump at the sound of her voice.

"What? Oh . . . you startled me." Her tone was casual, but her body language was full of guilt.

"Sorry."

"Yeah, well, I just remembered a piece of paper I wrote an address on yesterday. Like an idiot, I tossed it in the trash as I left this morning. I thought I had it written down somewhere else, but it turns out I don't."

"An important address?" asked Jane.

"Yeah. I guess you could say that."

Melody didn't look very much like her mother, or her brother and sister. From what Jane could tell, she took after her father's side of the family, both in appearance and temperament. Jane had never actually met Eddy Dumont—he'd been living in Florida for the past seven years—but she'd seen pictures. Even in her stockinged feet, Melody was taller than Lyle. Her coloring was fair, her hair a dark gold with reddish highlights. And she was far more laid-back than the rest of the clan. She didn't seem to be driven by the same endless Dumont energy. In fact, she often made a joke of it.

Melody shook her head. "I'm really worried about Mom."

"Me too," said Jane, feeling that the subject had just been switched on purpose.

Mel studied Jane openly for a minute. "You know, you look good. Really good."

"Thanks."

"Have you lost weight?"

Jane shrugged. "No, not really."

"Then you must be in love."

Jane felt her cheeks burn. The fact was, there was someone in her life right now. Someone very special.

"It's all right." Melody grinned. "You don't have to explain—at least, not right now. I'll get the whole story out of you before you leave."

"Oh, you will, huh?" Jane shook her head and smiled.

"Where do you think Mom is?" Melody asked, walking over to the front door and looking out through the screened porch at the woods.

"I don't know," said Jane. "But I have to be honest. Unless something serious was preventing her, she'd be here."

Melody turned around. "You think she's hurt? Or being held hostage? Maybe someone wants money!"

"Why would you say that?"

"Oh—" She gave an apologetic shrug. "It's just my morbid imagination. Too much TV. Don't listen to me. If this really is serious, I guess it hasn't sunk in yet."

Jane nodded. A couple of hours ago she'd felt the same way.

"It's like, nothing can happen to Mom. She's . . . you know, *Mom*. She's always here, always will be."

It was a very young, naive attitude, thought Jane. One which, because of her own past—losing her mother at the age of thirteen—she'd never had the luxury of indulging.

Melody put her arm around Jane's shoulder. "Anyway,

come on. Let's go back out on the deck. See what the family elders have to say."

"All right."

"Oh, hey, I forgot. I want to wash up first. I'll meet you out there in a minute, okay?"

"Sure," said Jane. As she watched Melody retreat into the house and shut the bathroom door behind her, she had the distinct sense that she was being handled. And she didn't like it.

4

Lyle put the phone back on the hook. It was just after midnight. He and his two sisters had just returned from a frustrating three-hour search for their mother. Shrugging his shoulders to relieve some of his tension, he said, "There's no news. Dennis is out too, looking around. The cop I spoke to said he'd call as soon as he knows anything."

"I can't believe we couldn't find the car," said Anne. "How could it just disappear?"

Lyle shook his head. "I'm sure as soon as the sun comes up, Dennis will have every officer in the county searching for her."

Anne was sitting in the living room, sipping from a glass of wine. The alcohol had done nothing to mellow her agitated state. She was glad the family was all here tonight. Whatever happened, they would face it together, as they always had. Still, with every passing hour, the hope she'd felt earlier in the day was dimming. A depression had settled over the house and everyone in it. No one dared say the words out loud, but Anne knew that each of them was wondering silently if Belle Dumont would ever be seen alive again.

With her rational mind, Anne resisted such a melodramatic scenario. Lots of things could have happened. And yet, even on this warm summer night, the house felt curi-

ously cold, as if the presence of death was already float-
ing through the rooms.

Lyle glanced up the stairs. "I wonder if Helvi's asleep?"

"I doubt it," said Anne. "I'm glad Melody went up to
sit with her. They seem like they've become pretty close
this past year." She set the glass down on an end table
and turned off the lamp. Pushing out of her seat she said,
"Come on. Let's go out on the screen porch. I need some
fresh air."

Lyle led the way. Before he took a seat, he removed a
lighter from his pocket and lit the kerosene lamp his
mother kept on a low table between two wicker rockers.

Anne felt warmed by the soft glow. She knew her
mother and Helvi spent many summer evenings on the
screened porch, enjoying the darkness and the quiet. "I
wonder if we should call Dad in Colorado," she asked,
shivering at the thought.

Lyle made himself comfortable next to her. "He'll be
home from his vacation in a couple of days. Let's wait
until we know something specific."

"God, I'm glad he moved back here. I missed him so
much."

"Me too," said Lyle, rolling up the sleeves of his light
blue oxford shirt. "Say, did you get Jane and Cordelia all
settled into the cottage?"

She nodded. "They said if we hear anything to give
them a call. I doubt any of us will sleep much tonight."
She stared at the flickering shadows the firelight threw
against the screens. Was this the moment she'd been
waiting for? She'd been wanting to speak to her brother
for weeks but felt a phone call wasn't right. When her
mother invited her up last night, she thought that this
weekend might provide her with the perfect chance. She
wanted to talk to him face-to-face, wanted to see his reac-
tion, to convince him that she was desperate for money
and he was her last hope. But with everything that was

happening tonight, bringing the subject up now might seem crass. She decided to wait.

Lyle lifted a pack of cigarettes out of his pocket and offered her one.

"No, thanks," she said. "I quit." A bit sheepishly, she added, "Again."

He smiled. "Is that right? When?"

"Yesterday."

He held the pack steady while she pulled one out. After lighting hers, he lit his own, took a deep drag, and blew smoke into the damp night air. "I just feel so helpless. Maybe—"

"Maybe what?"

"Oh, I don't know. Maybe we should make some Robber's Wine."

Anne caught the twinkle in his eye and they both laughed. "What on earth made you think of that?"

"Melody mentioned it before she went upstairs. Isn't it what we always did when we felt scared? And look, it must have worked. No robber ever got us."

"Until now?"

He flicked some ash into an ashtray. "I don't know *what's* got us now."

They sat in silence for several minutes, listening to the crickets.

Finally, Anne said, "Lyle?"

"Uhm?"

"Do you . . . know what this family powwow was supposed to be about?"

He took another deep drag. "Not exactly."

"What's that mean?"

"That I don't know for sure, but I have a hunch."

"So, give. What is it?"

He stared at the burning tip of his cigarette. "I think Mom wants to sell the real estate company."

"Seriously?"

He shrugged. "That's only my guess."

"But why would she do that? She loves it so much. Isn't that what she always says?"

"I don't know. The housing market's taken another downturn, but we're holding our own. Oh, we've lost a couple of good agents. I know Mom was upset. But what can I do? I can't sell the freaking houses for them."

"What about your job?"

"Yeah, good point. I'm not exactly interested in looking for another one."

"Have you said anything to her about any of this?"

He shook his head. "If that wasn't her reason, I didn't want to plant the idea in her mind. The job base around here isn't all that fabulous. I'd like to keep mine, thanks very much. Also—"

"What?"

He flicked more ash into the ashtray. "Well, I was kind of toying with the idea of running for state representative two years from now. I'm already on the local tourism board. I've gotten to know some of the movers and shakers in the area. I think it's fair to say they like me a lot."

Anne wasn't surprised. Everyone liked her brother. Yet, over the past year, she'd begun to notice subtle changes in the way he lived his life. Gone were the casual jeans, chinos, and sport shirts. Slowly, Lyle had turned into Mr. Corporate Corporate, as Melody had begun calling him. He rarely wore anything other than suits and ties now. And last winter he'd joined the Fosh Lake Country Club, where he hung out most weekends when he wasn't working. Networking, he called it.

What Lyle seemed to care most about these days was his image. He wanted to be seen in the right circles. The less kind members of the social community probably pegged him as a climber, though the Dumont name did carry a certain amount of clout by itself. It was just that the Dumonts had rarely claimed any of that clout, political or otherwise. "Winning public office could take a lot of money," she offered, turning to look at him. In the intimate glow of the kerosene lamp he looked older and somehow more weary than he'd ever seemed before.

"I know."

"Would Mom help?"

"I haven't asked. You know the rules. We make it on our own, no help from her or the Dumont largesse, whatever the hell that turns out to be."

The sight of headlights in the drive caused them both to jump. A squad car, lights flashing, pulled in behind Lyle's Lexus. The driver turned off the motor and got out.

"It's Dennis," said Lyle, jumping out of his chair and bolting for the door.

Anne stubbed out her cigarette and rushed after him.

"What do you know?" he called, clenching his fists as he came to a dead stop. He looked like he was steeling himself for a blow.

Anne moved up next to him and slipped her arm through his.

Dennis was a big man, nearly six three. Even though the night had cooled down considerably, his shirt was wet with perspiration. "We found the car."

"Where!" demanded Anne. "Is she all right?" She could feel Lyle's body tense beside her.

Dennis shook his head. "Just off the highway before you get to Benning Road—on the other side of Fosh Lake."

"By the railroad tracks?" asked Lyle.

Dennis nodded. "It's densely wooded around there. And there's a steep drop-off."

"But where was Mom?" pleaded Anne.

Dennis looked at Lyle, then at Anne. "I don't know. I called for backup. Me and six other guys have been looking around there for the last hour and a half. It's a rough spot, and in the dark, it's nearly impossible to track her—that is, if she walked in toward the lake. We're going to have to wait until morning. There's nothing more I can do tonight."

"But she could be hurt!" pleaded Anne.

"We found no evidence of that. We opened up the car—it started just fine, so unless she flooded it, it wasn't car trouble. It's nearly one. The sun will be up in four hours. That's the best I can do." His gaze returned to Lyle. "I'm sorry, buddy."

"I understand," said Lyle, squeezing Anne's hand reassuringly.

"We don't even know for sure that she's out there," added Dennis. "She could have walked in any direction, could be miles away. Maybe tomorrow morning we'll find her sitting on the side of the road somewhere, cursing her carburetor."

Anne stared at him. She knew he was just trying to make them feel better, but the attempt fell flat.

"Again, I'm sorry I can't bring you better news."

As he was about to leave, Lyle stopped him, placing a hand on his arm. "I want to go with you in the morning."

"I don't know—"

"I'm driving back to my own home in a little while. Both my kids have the flu, or I'd spend the night here. I don't want to leave my wife alone."

Dennis nodded.

"Anyway, pick me up in front of my house on your way back to Fosh Lake tomorrow. Come on, Dennis. You owe me."

Dennis rested a hand uneasily over his gun. He looked at the log house behind them, then squinted up at the moon high above the trees in the distance. "All right. Five A.M. Your place."

"Good."

Dennis tipped his hat good night. "I guess I'll see you

both tomorrow." His gaze lingered for a moment on Anne, and then, returning to the squad car, he backed it up, turned around, and sped out of the drive.

"Four hours," whispered Lyle, folding his arms around his sister and holding her tight. "Then we'll find out what's going on—and we'll deal with it."

5

"I think you should take the bedroom with the nautical motif," said Cordelia, draping a red and white gingham dishtowel over the moose head on the wall in the living room. "You love the sea."

"I do?" said Jane, walking out of the cottage's kitchen carrying a bottle of brandy and two glasses.

"Sure. You like . . . you know, tartar sauce. Tuna sandwiches. All the earth's natural aquatic bounty. And I'll take the Brontë room. I'm in sort of a *Wuthering Heights* mood myself."

Jane poured them each a glass, handed one to Cordelia, and then stepped out onto the porch facing the lake. The moon's reflection spread across the water in glittering ribbons, casting a weak light on the Dumonts' dock in the distance. A pontoon and a speedboat were moored near the far end. As she stretched out on a chaise longue and stared into the darkness, she marveled at what a lovely, peaceful night it was. Water lapping lazily against a sandy beach was just the sort of sound she'd come north to find. And yet, any calm this scene might normally have engendered was completely lost on her tonight.

Jane could hear Cordelia banging cabinet doors and metal pots around in the kitchen. After another minute she could smell popcorn being popped. These were all ordinary sounds, comforting in their own way. Jane decided that being away from the tension of the main house was allowing her to gain a certain perspective. Maybe matters weren't so bleak after all. Even so, it had been the right decision to stay close, just in case. And Helvi was right. The cottage was far more comfortable than a motel.

They'd eaten very little for dinner. Jane had prepared a Caesar salad, but nobody showed much interest. Now, sipping her brandy, she realized she was ravenous.

Hearing the phone ring, she cocked her head and listened. Cordelia had answered it in the kitchen. She spoke briefly, then grew silent. Jane figured it had to be Anne. She said she'd only call if there was news.

A few moments later Cordelia appeared in the doorway, brandy and bowl in hand. "They found Belle's car," she said, making herself comfortable on the chaise next to Jane. She set the popcorn between them on a small table.

"And?"

"It's somewhere on the other side of Fosh Lake."

"But what about Belle?"

Cordelia shook her head. "Nowhere around. They're sending a search party out as soon as it gets light."

Jane took a deep breath. "Well," she said, exhaling slowly, "I guess that's progress."

"I guess," agreed Cordelia. She waited a second and then said, "Janey?"

"Uhm?"

"What are we going to do about our reservations at Bluefin? When I called, I told them we had an emergency and couldn't make it until tomorrow. But what if we can't make it tomorrow either? They said that if we have to cancel altogether, the sooner we let them know, the better. If they can rent out our condo, we might get some of our money back."

Jane took a sip of brandy and thought about it. "Let's wait until we hear what the police have to say in the morning."

Cordelia nodded. "Okay. You know, this may sound crazy, but I got the distinct impression that Helvi wasn't telling everything she knew."

Jane turned to look at her. "Meaning what?"

Cordelia held her hand high above her head and dropped popcorn kernels into her mouth. "Well, while you and Anne were out looking for Belle, we had a pretty good chance to talk. At least five times during those few hours she sidled up to the subject of the family meeting Belle had called, but when I pressed her on it, she got cold feet and clammed up."

"Because it was a secret?"

"I'm not sure. Maybe I'm way off base, but she seemed frightened. Or at the very least, extremely uneasy. After Lyle arrived, and you and Anne got back, she never brought it up again."

"And you think the family meeting had something to do with Belle's disappearance?"

"Maybe. It's pretty apparent Helvi's holding something back."

"She'd never do anything to put Belle's life in jeopardy," said Jane.

"I know that," snapped Cordelia.

"Then what are you saying?"

"I don't know! But something isn't right."

Jane wasn't sure how to respond, and yet she knew better than to dismiss Cordelia's instincts. "You know, I can't help but wonder about that comment Belle made before she left the house this morning. The one about never being too old to take care of her children."

"Yeah, she always did seem like a pretty hard-core mom to me. But I didn't buy Helvi's explanation. I highly doubt Belle was referring to her kids' *nutrition*."

Jane had to agree. She finished her drink. "You want another brandy? The bottle's in the living room."

Cordelia shook her head. "I'm beat—too tired even to look for the popcorn kernels with the most butter."

"Poor dear."

"Yeah. Normally, this time of night I'm just getting started. I think sleeping in the car really tired me out." She yawned. Then, flopping on her side, she tucked her hands under her cheek and closed her eyes. Barely moments later, she began to snore.

The night had turned cool. Jane got up and found two quilts resting on the back of the couch in the front room. She covered Cordelia with one and then sat back down on the chaise and pulled the other one up over her bare arms. It felt good just to lie here in the open air. The heavy, sweet scent of peony drifted in through the wide screens. Turning her head to the side, she saw a long row of bushes just outside the porch. They were thick with pink and white flowers. She had no desire to go inside on a night like this. She closed her eyes and let her senses float to the sound of the lapping water.

A beam of light woke her. Rubbing a hand over her eyes, Jane sat up straight and looked outside at the water. A large cabin cruiser, its engine running, sat just off the end of the dock. Whoever was on board had switched on a bright searchlight and was scanning the shore, the cottage, and the main house. As the beam moved away from her, Jane could make out a figure standing on the rear deck. It looked like a man, though she couldn't be sure. She watched the light wash over the woods near the boathouse and then come to a stop.

"Cordelia," she whispered. "Wake up."

Cordelia brushed a hand over her face. "Go away. I'm busy."

Jane threw off her covers and rushed to the far end of the porch. The beam was moving back toward the cottage. As it swept over the base of the dock, the side of the boat was illuminated. If it was a police craft, it would have been marked. This boat was unmarked. She crouched down. "Cordelia!"

"What!" Cordelia pulled the quilt away from her face and sat up, her nose twitching like a prairie dog who'd just come out of her hole. "Hey, what's that?" She pointed to the beam as it moved toward her.

"Get down!" called Jane.

"What the hell," she muttered, diving to the floor. "What's going on?"

Jane crawled toward her. "Just wait until it moves away. Then we'll go outside and look around."

"What do you mean *we*?" Cordelia reached up and brushed popcorn kernels out of her hair. "I'm having a bad dream."

"Do you have popcorn in your hair in your dreams?"

"No, I'm usually bald."

"How trendy. Come on." The light had moved farther up the beach. Jane scrambled to her feet and shot out the door. Her eyes darted toward the main house, but no one seemed to be stirring. Dashing behind the nearest tree, she waited a moment and then crept deeper into the woods.

Cordelia puffed up behind her a few seconds later. "Slow down."

The light passed several more times over the beach, lingering on the cottage and the main house. Thick fingers of cloud covered the moon, making identification of the man on board almost impossible.

"Do you realize how many wood ticks are probably out here?" said Cordelia, eyeing the foliage around her feet suspiciously. She settled her bulk down on a rock and examined her ankles.

"No one will ever mistake you for a lumberjack."

"Good. The only creature I'd care to meet in the woods

is a hobbit," she sniffed. "And you can't even trust all of them."

Jane kept her eyes on the boat. "What *is* that guy looking for?"

"Well, whatever it is, the show seems to be over." The light was switched off and the boat began to move away.

"Damn," said Jane, spinning around, her eyes searching the woods behind them.

Cordelia turned too. "What are you looking at?"

"I thought I heard a noise."

"Define *noise*."

"I don't know. Maybe a raccoon or a bear. Or Bigfoot."

"Oh goody. Do I get to pick?"

Jane listened, easing cautiously behind a tree. "There it is again."

It was the sound of breaking twigs. Someone or some-*thing* was coming toward them in the dark.

Jane felt a shiver of anticipation. She couldn't see anything in the blackness, but whatever it was, it was almost on top of them. "Let's get out of here."

"Good thinking." As Cordelia shot to her feet, a tall blond man stepped into a clearing about ten feet from them. The moonlight was enough to illuminate the binoculars around his neck and the rifle in his hand.

"This is private property," he said, his voice low and angry. "What are you doing here in the middle of the night?" He pointed the rifle at Jane.

When she didn't answer quickly enough, he swung the barrel toward Cordelia, flipped off the safety, and pumped a shell into the chamber.

"Looking for hobbits?" she answered weakly.

"What?"

"Come on." A sarcastic hand rose to her hip. "Do you really think we're some kind of criminal element? I mean, *pulease*."

Jane moved out from behind the tree. "We're friends of Anne Dumont. We're staying in the cottage right now."

The information left him unmoved.

"My name's Jane. And this is Cordelia. Anne's mother is missing and we're staying to see if there's anything we can do."

He stared at her a moment and then said, "Belle's missing?"

She nodded. From the concerned look on his face, Jane assumed he was a neighbor. "They found her car over near Fosh Lake, but not her." As the moon came out from behind a cloud, she could see that he was older than she'd first suspected. His skin was leathery hard and tan, and his hair wasn't blond, but gray. He was wearing a rumpled T-shirt and jeans and looked as if he'd just gotten out of bed. "Who are you?" she asked, keeping her eyes on the rifle.

He lowered it to his side. "Eddy Dumont. I'm Anne's father. Belle's ex. That," he said, pointing to the boat, which had just about disappeared in the distance, "woke me up. I saw the light from my cabin. Wondered what the hell was going on."

"Your cabin?" repeated Jane.

"It's an A-frame about a quarter mile down the beach. I lived in Florida until a couple of months ago when I moved back here. Actually, I've been on vacation for the past few weeks. I just got home from Colorado late today. I haven't been up to the main house yet to say hello. Thought that could wait until tomorrow." He walked a few paces closer. "I'm sorry if I frightened you."

"No problem," said Jane. She recognized him now. She'd only seen photos of him before—pictures of him as a much younger man. He had to be a good ten years older than Belle. Anne talked about him a lot. He'd been a high school English teacher in Earlton until he retired.

He and Helvi had been good friends while they were on the teaching staff together.

Jane nodded to the binoculars. "Did you get a look at the guy on the boat?"

Eddy scratched his prickly face. "Yeah, it was Pfeifer."

"Melody's husband?"

"That's the one."

"Why would he be out on the water at this time of night?"

He crossed in front of her and walked over to the edge of the water. Gazing up at the moon, he said, "The guy's a nut case. I warned her not to marry him. So did everyone else. But she's stubborn—a lot like me."

"I still don't understand," said Jane.

"Ever since she left him, he's been following her around, spying on her. God knows why. I think it's jealousy. He figures she's found someone new and he's damn well going to prove it." He turned to face her. "Is Anne here?"

Jane nodded. "And Lyle and Melody."

"I see. And you don't know anything more about what happened to Belle?"

"Just that the police are sending out a search party at first light."

He looked up at the main house, running a hand over his stubbly chin. "I wonder if I should run up there and see what I can do?" He seemed truly upset.

"I can't believe they didn't see the lights on that boat," said Cordelia, slapping a hand against her neck. "Maybe they were too busy swatting mosquitoes. You know, if we don't get inside soon, we'll all come down with yellow fever. Could we continue this discussion in the cottage?"

Eddy stuck the rifle under his arm. "I think I'll just head back to my cabin. If no one's awake up there, I've got no business bothering them."

"Maybe we'll see you tomorrow," said Jane. "I'm sorry to be the bearer of such . . . uncertain news."

He gave a short nod. "Thanks." As he turned to go he stopped. "Hey, what'd you say your name was again?"

"Jane Lawless."

"Are you Anne's friend, the one who owns the restaurant?"

"That's me."

He looked over at Cordelia. "And you're the crazy theatre director, right?"

Cordelia stiffened.

"Sorry, I didn't mean to offend you. It was a poor choice of words."

"It was."

"Your theatre did *She Stoops to Conquer* this spring. I drove down to the Twin Cities just to see it. It was a great show."

"Thank you," she said, her voice oozing sarcastic formality.

"Really top notch." He hesitated. "Actually, I was the drama coach at the high school where I taught English."

"No kidding."

"Yes indeed, I love the theatre. Always have. Earlton High mounted a production of that same play the last year I was there. It was my idea, and if I do say so myself, it was a smash."

Cordelia raised her hands to her hips. "Do you realize how surreal this is? I'm standing here in the woods. It's two in the morning and I'm having a discussion about Restoration comedy with a man holding a shotgun."

"It's a rifle."

"Whatever."

He stared at her. "Well, I guess I'd better get on home. I'll see you two tomorrow."

"I shall look forward to it, Eddy. One might even say breathlessly."

Tucking the gun under his arm, he trudged back through the woods calling, " 'Night," as he disappeared into the darkness.

Cordelia waited a moment, patting her chest and waving air into her face. "For a second there, I actually thought he was going to shoot us," she whispered.

"Yeah," said Jane. "You can't be sure with ex–English teachers. They can get pretty violent."

Cordelia did a double take. Then, turning toward the cottage, she slung her arm over Jane's shoulder and said, "The fact of the matter is, I'm positive I'm still asleep back home in my bed in Minneapolis. None of this is real, not even the mosquito bites. Belle's fine, Eddy Dumont and his rifle don't exist, and tomorrow, you and I are going to drive up to the north shore and boogie—calmly—for the next ten glorious days."

"You think so?"

"Have I ever been wrong?"

"Frequently."

She glared down her nose. "Did you bring any insect repellent?"

"Sorry."

"You know, Janey, I have a bad feeling about all this. A premonition, if you will. I don't think this vacation is going to be quite the ten days of sun and fun we expected."

6

Helvi sat and looked out the window in her bedroom. It was nearly five A.M. and the sky was turning light. She'd always found dawn the loneliest time of day. Unlike yesterday, the morning was overcast and gloomy. Maybe it would rain later. That was probably good. Belle's garden could use a soaking. Helvi's eyes dropped to the empty driveway directly beneath the window. Lyle must have left sometime during the night.

She had tried to sleep, tossing and turning until after three, but it was no use. She couldn't turn off her feelings. Every few minutes her body would tense in a cold panic. It was as if her senses were on automatic. No matter what she was thinking about, the terror seized her. What if something awful had happened to Belle? How could she go on? How did someone survive something like this? She had no answers, only more worry that turned quickly to fear, and then to horror.

She got up and walked over to the unmade bed, sitting down on the edge. She and Belle had been together for sixteen years. They'd first met when Belle had come to Earlton High for a teacher's conference. Helvi had been one of Anne's favorite teachers.

For most of her life, Helvi had known she was a lesbian. In her early twenties it had been a hard truth to deal with, hard for her to understand what it all meant and where she might fit in the world. But she'd survived her self-doubt and attained a certain self-acceptance. She was lucky. She never thought of herself as sick or bad, never bought most of the shame society tried to lay on her. She was simply different. But different was bad enough in a small town, and she'd learned to guard her privacy carefully.

She'd had one four-year relationship early in her life. Just like Helvi, the woman had been Finnish, her father a miner. Yet before Belle entered the picture, she'd lived alone for almost fifteen years. She knew, having grown up in Earlton, that small towns could be narrow and vicious. Small-town life, while embodying many of the values Helvi cherished—values such as self-reliance, hard work, and concern for your neighbor—also contained the classic roots of American prejudice.

Since she felt small-town life embraced both the best and the worst in the American character, Helvi learned quickly to monitor what she said and did. Being *different* in Earlton was virtually the same as being bad, wrong, deviant, diseased, or possibly even evil. Early on, Helvi learned to hide her sexuality. Oh, she could have left Earlton, gone to a large city, dissolved into a certain anonymity. By the Seventies, the world outside her small community was changing. Gay liberation had finally begun to happen. Stonewall had drawn a courageous line in the sand, making the world a different place forever after. But even though she had less of a chance of developing a personal relationship in Earlton, Helvi knew that in most ways she was a small-town girl at heart. She was happy here. Perhaps it was hypocrisy, or even cowardice, but she felt she was dug in. Perhaps somewhere down the line she could even be an agent for change. For good or ill, she would live the life of a small-town teacher—a gay small-town teacher. There were others.

She found out later that Belle had made some of the very same decisions, hiding her sexuality and on occasion, even her opinions. Then again, Belle could hide much more easily. She'd been married and had three children. That meant she could pass, even under the closest small-town scrutiny. Narrow-minded people often saw only stereotypes, and Belle didn't fit the stereotype. Helvi had never connected with a man, which meant she was always under a cloud of sexual suspicion. It wasn't said out loud, but the implication was there: You aren't one of *those*, are you? But, since no one had proof, and because she was well liked by her students, her professional peers, and her neighbors, she was pretty much left alone.

At Anne's graduation reception, Belle and Helvi talked personally for the first time. Helvi guessed Belle was gay almost immediately. It took a while, but eventually the subject was broached. Over the next few years, the two of them grew close, going for walks, antique shopping in some of the other small towns in the area, starting a book group together in Grand Rapids. Their friendship was very public, but in private, the friendship had turned into something much more. Belle and Helvi had fallen in love.

When Melody, Belle's last child, moved out to attend college in Illinois, Helvi and Belle were left with a question. Could they finally live together? How open could they be with their relationship? It was 1980. Belle's real estate company was well established. Helvi would be able to retire in a few years, even sooner if she allowed Belle to support her, a notion she consistently rejected.

The turning point came in 1981 when Belle fell down the back stairs and broke her leg. After spending several days in the hospital, she moved back home. But she needed help. Lyle had just married—he couldn't be asked to come back and nurse his ailing mother. Anne was living and working in Minneapolis. Her job would be in jeopardy if she took several weeks off. And Melody was away at school. Helvi, the most logical choice, was packed and on her way out to the lake in a matter of hours. She left her apartment in Earlton and, as fate would have it, never returned.

It just seemed so right—even to the neighbors. Both were older women. Belle was suffering from empty nest syndrome—her kids had all gone. Everyone understood what *that* was like. And both women were in their fifties. Nobody considered women in their *fifties* to be *sexual*. Heavens! They were completely over the hill—much too old and unattractive for any hanky-panky to go on. No, Belle and Helvi were good friends who moved in together. Nothing more. They were assigned an asexual status by the community. They were aging and manless. A sorry state, but there it was. Or so everyone thought.

In reality, Helvi and Belle were happier than they'd ever been. They loved living together—taking care of each other, buying new things for the house, talking and loving late into the night. That was the same year they had the new deck built onto the back of the house off the kitchen. As some sloganeer said, wasn't happiness the best revenge? It certainly seemed so.

Helvi and Belle told the kids a year later. Helvi was amazed at how well they took it. They didn't have many questions, which surprised her, but she was grateful for the generous way they accepted her into the family. Even Eddy Dumont, Belle's ex, had been wonderful. He and Belle had remained close over the years, keeping in contact initially because of the children, but later because they realized they genuinely liked and respected each other and enjoyed each other's company. Eddy and Helvi had been professional friends for many years, but his warmth and understanding when she and Belle told him of their relationship had touched her deeply. It meant so much, especially because it paved the way for the kids' acceptance.

Helvi felt that she was an incredibly blessed woman. Her life was so good, for the next few years she tried even harder as a teacher to encourage her students to be themselves, even if they didn't fit the small-town mold. It struck a chord in nearly all of them. The year she retired, students from her thirty-five years of teaching came back and threw her a huge party. Earlton declared Helvi Sitala Day. She was honored by the faculty and the entire student body by being voted teacher of the year. During the summer she found out the new school auditorium was going to be named after her. The love and appreciation was immeasurable, and she knew it was a reflection of what she'd tried to give over the years. Perhaps remaining in Earlton hadn't been such a mistake after all.

And yet, here she was, sitting in an empty room, wondering where the love and center of her life had gone. Could all the happiness be wiped away in a matter of moments? Where *was* Belle? Helvi knew the family meeting she'd called for last night was important. But why hadn't Belle confided in her more completely? Why had she never told her the full story? The awful Dumont family secret. She couldn't believe that Belle's mother had done something so hideous that the details had to be locked up inside Belle for over sixty years.

Whatever it was, Helvi knew she had to be strong, not just for herself, but for the kids. She loved Anne, Lyle, and Melody as if she'd given birth to them herself. She would do anything to protect them, just like Belle. If the worst happened, if Belle never came home again, what could she tell them? What did she know for sure? And what had Belle meant by that last comment yesterday morning? *A mother's never too old to take care of her children.*

Helvi rose from the bed and walked over to the dresser where a framed photo of Belle was resting. As she stroked the cold glass, imagining the softness of her lover's skin, she whispered, "Come back to me. Please, sweetheart, just come home."

7

"Morning," said Melody, shambling into the kitchen. She was wearing an oversize T-shirt and a pair of gray jogging shorts, her shoulder-length blonde hair uncombed and pushed behind her ears.

Anne was scrubbing out the refrigerator. "Did you get any sleep?" she asked, nodding to some fresh-baked muffins on the center counter.

"Not much." She put a hand over her stomach, turned her back to the muffins, and took down a mug from the cupboard. "I think I'll just have coffee."

"Suit yourself." Anne lifted one of the crisper drawers over to the sink and began rinsing it out.

"How can you be so energetic?"

"I have to have something to *do* or I'll go crazy with this waiting." She stopped for a moment and leaned her arms against the counter, lowering her head and shutting her eyes. Then, turning around she said, "Lyle went out with the police search party. Dennis Murphy said it was all right."

Melody sat down at the center counter, pushing the muffins as far away from her as they would go without falling on the floor.

"Hey, I thought you liked my cooking."

"I do, but not this morning."

"Sure. I understand." Anne watched her sister briefly,

then returned to the crisper, scraping at a sticky patch near the bottom.

"Have you seen Helvi this morning?" asked Melody.

Anne shook her head. "But I know she's up. I went out for a walk around four and I saw her sitting at the bedroom window, just staring outside."

"God, I feel so sorry for her."

"Me too," said Anne. She checked her watch. It was nearly nine. "We should know something pretty soon."

Melody stirred sugar into her coffee, but let it sit on the counter untasted. "You make me feel like a complete lump, you know that? Everyone in the family does—except Dad. You're like machines—constantly in motion."

Anne could hear the edge in her sister's voice. She returned the crisper drawer to the refrigerator and pulled out the next one, emptying the contents into the other side of the sink. "Right, Mel. I remember now. Lyle and me, our job is to make you feel like shit. Your job is to believe it."

Melody rubbed the back of her neck. "Well, just look at the mess I've made of my life. I'm thirty-five, married four years, and already about to be divorced."

"If you recall, I won the prize for the shortest marriage and the earliest divorce. Mine started when I was thirty-two and *ended* when I was thirty-four."

Melody lowered her eyelids and gave her sister a veiled smirk. "If you're trying to make me feel better, it's not working."

"It's not?"

"No, but thanks anyway. Honestly, it just seems that . . . no matter what I do in this family, I can't win. You've all done it first or better, even if it's just screwing up." She gazed into the coffee mug, her hand rising to her eyes to cover the tears that were forming. "I thought my one chance to do it right was with Pfeifer. And look at the mess I made."

Anne felt like a complete ass. With everything that had happened, she'd failed to sit down with her sister and talk about the separation. Melody had to be in terrible pain. Anne wiped her hands on a towel and pulled out the stool next to her. "Are you all right?" she asked, taking hold of Mel's hand.

"No," she sniffed. "I'm a mess, just like always."

"You've got to stop all this blaming, Melody. All this self-criticism. We're not in a race."

"Sure we are. We always have been. Belle Dumont's kids had to be the best and the brightest. Shit, we could have been poster children for the U.S. Marines."

"That's not fair."

"No? You were the academic whiz. Lyle was the social and athletic superachiever. What did that leave me?"

"I can't believe you're still thinking about high school after all these years."

"But it wasn't *just* high school. You and Lyle did great in college. I hated it. You both have successful careers. What am I? A part-time secretary. Big fucking deal."

"But you're a beautiful young woman. You have so much going for you."

"Right, drumroll please. Melody Dumont's pretty. Dumb, but pretty."

"Mel! Where's this all coming from?" As Anne thought about it, she realized it had to be the separation. From her own experience she knew the process of divorce sent everyone's self-esteem into the dumper, and Melody didn't have much to begin with. "Are you and Pfeifer sure you want to call it quits?"

"Oh, Pfeifer thinks I'm just being childish. He never wanted me to leave in the first place. When I filed the legal separation papers last week, he was pretty surprised, but he rationalized it all by saying this was just a phase I was going through and I'd get over it. In the meantime, everywhere I go, he's there watching me, just to make sure I'm not cheating on him. He's really getting on my nerves. I suppose that's the point. He probably sees it as psychological warfare. He's good at that. I feel like I'm living in a fishbowl."

Anne had to admit she was curious about what their problems were. Melody had never confided any specifics to her, or to anyone else in the family, although everyone had known for years she wasn't happy. "Look, sis, all I can say is that it gets better. I've lived through it. Staring a potential divorce in the face isn't the happiest of times, but you'll get through it. And then you'll move on."

Melody wiped a hand across her eyes. "You bet I will."

"That's the spirit."

"Nobody may believe this, but I'm going to make this family proud of me one day. It's time for a change. It may take a while to get myself together—" The sound of a car pulling into the drive interrupted her thought. "I'll bet that's Lyle!"

They both jumped up and rushed through the house to the front door. As they looked outside, they saw a gold Cadillac El Dorado come to a stop in front of the double garage.

"Who the hell does that belong to?" asked Anne, a hand rising to her hip. She remained inside next to the door watching a man get out and walk around to the trunk. It was partially open, tied shut with cord. "Hey, is that Quinn Fosh?"

Melody heaved a sigh. "Damn, I thought this might be the news we were waiting for. Yeah, it's Quinn. He's been mowing the grass for Mom and Helvi this year."

"He's never been here when I was."

"That's because he isn't very consistent. When he doesn't show up, Mom just gets someone else to do it. Usually me."

"But mowing the grass?" Had Anne heard her correctly?

"Yeah, I guess that's what he does for a living now. That and raise glads in his backyard. He sells them to florists around the area."

"Can't be much money in that. How can he afford those wheels?"

Melody shrugged and leaned against the door frame. "Jeez, but he gives me the willies. Always has. He's been around here a lot the last few weeks. Mom had him put a bunch of new strawberry plants out in the garden. As I think about it, doesn't he seem like the kind of guy who probably molests four-year-olds in his spare time—or tortures animals in his basement?"

"Yuck, what a thing to say."

"Well, that's how he strikes me. I don't like him."

Anne had known Quinn Fosh since she was a child. For want of a better term, he was the "town loser." His father was Herbert Fosh, a well-respected physician who'd been instrumental in getting the hospital in Earlton built in the early Fifties. He'd died a few years back. Fosh Lake had been named after Quinn's grandfather, Isaiah Fosh, another eminent physician. Quinn was the childless end of the Fosh dynasty, such as it was.

Years ago, Quinn had been a strikingly handsome man. Long before gym bodies had come into fashion, Quinn looked like a body builder. He had beautiful reddish blond hair, much like Melody's, and smooth golden skin.

Quinn clearly fascinated the locals, and that included Anne. Even though he was considered a real dud, or occasionally even a fast-talking slicker, he had a certain charisma, probably derived from his looks and his family's celebrity status. Anne hadn't seen him in years.

As she watched him remove the hemp cord from the trunk, she realized he had to be in his sixties now—probably around the age of her mom. But unlike her mother, Quinn had gone to pot. He'd gained weight, and instead of looking strong, he just looked lumpy. He had virtually no neck, merely a thick head resting on equally thick shoulders.

"Who's out there?" asked Helvi, coming down the stairs that separated the living room from the dining room. She was dressed in a light blue sweat suit, her white hair done up in a tight bun.

At the sound of her voice, Anne whirled around. "Gee, you scared me." She steadied herself on the doorjamb.

"I'm sorry," said Helvi, stepping over to the window. "What's *he* doing here?" she demanded, a frown forming.

"He's come to cut the grass," said Melody. She flopped down on the couch in the living room. "You know him. He just shows up when he feels like it."

Helvi stared out the window, her lips tightening into a thin line. "No more. I want one of you to go outside and get rid of him. I don't ever want to see that man around here again, is that clear!"

Anne had rarely seen Helvi so agitated. "You want us to fire him?"

"Yes!" Her face flushed a deep red.

"Why?"

"Because he's loathsome. I don't know why. I just want him to leave!" She turned and marched out of the room.

Anne and Melody exchanged glances.

"Don't ask me," said Melody after they'd both heard the door to the downstairs study slam shut. "She's never gone ballistic over him before. At least, not that I know about."

Anne scratched the back of her neck. "You want to talk to him?"

"Not particularly. You're the big sister. You do it."

Anne nodded. "Right."

"If you need me, I'll be in the kitchen. I think I'm going to try one of those muffins."

Squaring her shoulders, Anne walked out through the porch and trotted down the stone steps. Quinn had already started the mower and was halfway down the grassy slope between the house and the lake. Just as she was about to head in his direction, another car came barreling down the entrance road and pulled to a stop behind Quinn's Cadillac. It was Lyle's Lexus.

Anne could feel her muscles tense. She glanced back toward the house just as Melody charged out the door. A second later, Helvi rushed out as well.

Lyle slid slowly from the front seat.

Anne studied the look on his face. He wasn't smiling, so the news wasn't good.

Helvi crossed quickly to the drive, her arms held stiffly at her sides. "What's happened?" she asked, standing very still, gazing up into his eyes.

Lyle put his arms around her and began to sob. "I'm so sorry," he said, hugging her close. "She's dead."

Anne felt her body shiver and grow weak. She would have fallen except for Melody's strong arm, which had slipped quietly around her shoulders. She saw that her sister's face was red and streaming with tears. Lyle came past them, helping Helvi back up the steps into the house.

Ever since yesterday afternoon, this had been their worst nightmare. But it was a nightmare no longer. It had moved into the full light of day. Their mother was gone and nothing anyone could do would bring her back.

8

Two days later, Belle Dumont's funeral took place. It was a hazy Tuesday morning, the sun filtering through low clouds in long golden shafts. Several of the attendees commented that the light was reminiscent of a Renaissance painting—God in heaven spreading His glory over the assembled crowd. By the time the service at the church was over, the clouds had closed and darkened.

After the gravesite ceremony was completed and the coffin lowered into the ground, nearly fifty people gathered at the Dumont house on Pokegama Lake for food and conversation.

Jane and Cordelia spent most of the early afternoon in the kitchen, helping Lyle's wife, Carla, take care of stocking the buffet table.

Around four, feeling the need for a breath of fresh air, Jane stepped out onto the back deck. Cordelia and Eddy Dumont were sitting on the couch in the living room discussing the ins and outs of modern theatre. Jane knew everyone felt ill at ease talking about anything today other than Belle and the transitory nature of human existence. Sadness and the need for some sort of philosophic resolution always followed in the wake of death. It seemed horribly inappropriate to move on so quickly, to resume everyday life and normal conversation, though some, like Cordelia and Eddy, were attempting it. Yet no one could eat or drink or sit or stand without the heavy realization that a life, only days ago vital and strong, had now ended. Nothing felt normal today. Everyone, in his or her own way, experienced the emptiness.

Jane sensed someone move up next to her. As she turned, she saw Anne, her face pale and drawn, step out of the patio doors, two cans of Coke in her hand.

"You want one?" she asked.

"Thanks," said Jane, taking it gratefully.

"I've got to get out of here for a while. I can't stand any more sympathy. Care to come along?"

"Sure," said Jane.

"You've got to promise not to be sympathetic."

"My word of honor. Where do you want to go?"

"Just follow me."

A few minutes later, Jane found herself in Belle and Helvi's speedboat, so far from the house that it had almost disappeared from view.

Jane relished the feel of the wind in her hair. She'd taken apart her bun and let her hair hang loose around her shoulders. Even though the day was cloudy, the temperature and humidity were high enough to make it uncomfortable. Out on the lake it felt much cooler. The water was choppy, but the movement felt invigorating after she'd been cooped up in the kitchen most of the afternoon.

After a few more minutes, Anne cut the motor and then climbed out of the driver's seat, making herself comfortable on a padded bench near the rear of the boat. She held the can of Coke to her forehead. "Thanks for coming," she said, pulling off her shoes and socks and then rolling up the legs of her cotton slacks. "Actually, I suppose I should say, thanks for staying. I know this has totally wrecked your vacation."

"I hardly think that's of much significance," said Jane, sitting down across from her. "Besides, you were more than generous to offer Cordelia and me the use of the cottage for the next week. Although, I'm not so sure you and your family really want guests around that long."

Anne removed a pack of cigarettes and a lighter from her pants pocket. As she lit one, she said, "Don't be silly. We're all delighted to have you stay. There'll be a Fourth of July celebration in town on Friday night. That might be fun for the two of you to see. And then there's always the fireworks on the lake. I haven't missed that in almost twenty years." She took a deep drag. "Oh, and don't forget, you've got use of the boats whenever you like. The water skis are in the boathouse. And come up to the main house whenever you want. I think I'm going to stay through next Wednesday too."

Jane nodded her thanks.

Anne leaned back and blew smoke out of the side of her mouth. "Boy, that was some funeral, wasn't it? Especially Helvi's short but sweet eulogy. I never expected her to spell out what her relationship with my mother really was, especially not in front of ninety or so of their friends, business associates, and neighbors."

"Some of them already knew, didn't they?" asked Jane. "Your mom and Helvi weren't completely closeted."

"They were pretty close to it. Mom has always been super private about her personal life. I think my grandmother taught her to be that way, and Mom in turn passed it on to us. Family and personal matters were off limits to anyone outside the immediate family." She took another deep drag. "Brother, would I have loved to get that eulogy on videotape. When Helvi announced that she and my mother had been partners and lovers for over sixteen years, didn't you hear the collective gasp?"

Jane had, and she'd silently cheered her on.

"What a great moment," continued Anne. "Helvi was probably sick of hiding. I don't blame her. Neither does Mel or Dad. But Lyle . . . I'm not so sure how he took it."

"You think he's upset?"

"I haven't had much of a chance to talk to him since we got back to the house, but I was sitting next to him during the service. He didn't look happy. At the cemetery all he said was that he wished she'd talked to him about it first."

"Maybe she didn't say anything because she didn't want anyone to stop her."

Anne flicked some ash into the water. "Maybe. But I'll bet she expected more than fifty people to come back to the house."

"You think her announcement wasn't so well received?"

"By some, I know it wasn't. Did you see how fast Lyle was tap-dancing, doing damage control with several of his political cronies who happened to show up?"

"I didn't notice. Do you think Helvi did?"

"I hope not. He was behaving like an ass." She glanced up at a bird flying over the sandbar that jutted out from Pumpkin Seed Island. "You know, not to change the subject, but I just don't understand why my mother picked that spot to go for a morning stroll. I mean, it was all the way over on the other side of Fosh Lake. There are plenty of places around here she could have picked, most of them every bit as beautiful. The drop-off next to those railroad tracks is treacherous. I'd never just go wandering around out there alone."

Jane had a lot of unanswered questions about the manner of Belle Dumont's death. She hadn't wanted to upset the family with her fears, but she couldn't help but wonder if the death had really been a simple accident.

From what Jane had been able to find out, Belle's body had been found Sunday morning, around seven-thirty. She'd fallen down the steep ravine next to the railroad tracks. The coroner had listed the cause of death as severe head trauma. Nothing but large boulders and scrub brush would have prevented her from falling all the way to the bottom. Even with her head bleeding, the police determined that she'd tried to climb back up. She'd made it about thirty feet before collapsing. The most tragic part of all was, she'd probably lived for a few hours. Still, even if she'd been found, the prognosis wouldn't have been good.

"Did the police ever find her purse?" asked Jane. This was one of the loose ends she felt needed to be tied up before her doubts would go away.

Anne shook her head. "If you remember, it rained cats and dogs all that afternoon. There's a lot of mud and sand around the tracks. It probably got buried somewhere."

"You really think so?"

"Don't you? What other explanation is there? It wasn't in the car. She always carried that same small purse over her shoulder—has for years. I suppose maybe Lyle and I should take a run out there and see if we can find it."

"Or . . . I could," said Jane.

"Oh, you don't want to spend your vacation doing something like that."

Jane shrugged. "I suppose the police will continue with some sort of investigation."

"I doubt it," said Anne, dipping her hand into the cool lake water. "Dennis Murphy was at the funeral, but he didn't come back to the house. He told Lyle he felt it was a pretty clear-cut accident."

"But, I mean, are you comfortable with that?"

"I'm not comfortable with anything that's happened since I got up here," she snapped, a hard edge to her voice. "But what can I do? Dennis has a lot on his plate right now. He's getting pressure from the mayors of Earlton and Grand Rapids to find out what's behind some recent thefts in the area."

"Thefts?"

"Yeah, I guess for the past year or so, there have been almost a dozen houses burglarized around the lake. Expensive houses."

"What was stolen?"

"Money, or whatever could easily be turned into money, like jewelry or guns."

This was the first Jane had heard of it. "Has your mom's house had any problems?"

"Not that I'm aware of." She took a last drag from the cigarette and then pushed the butt into her now empty cola can. "I'm glad Melody's going to be staying on out here. I hate to think of Helvi being alone—at least right now." She paused, lighting another cigarette with a nervous, jerky movement. "To be honest, I'm kind of worried about Mel. She's taking Mom's death pretty hard. I caught her in the bathroom this morning after breakfast. It was the first time I've seen her eat a good meal in days—but she lost it all. When I asked her what was wrong, she just brushed it off. Said it hit her stomach wrong or something. I can't help but wonder if she's ill. Does she look like she's lost weight to you?"

"Actually, she does seem thinner."

Anne shook her head. "I'm going to talk to Lyle, see what he thinks. Except, right now he's all wound up about the reading of the will tomorrow afternoon."

"That soon?" said Jane.

"Yeah, he said there's no reason to wait. I suppose he's right. It's time we all finally find out what the Dumont fortune is really worth."

Jane could tell from the tone of Anne's voice that she was every bit as eager as Lyle.

Off the end of the island, a boat sailed into view. Both women turned to look.

"Oh, no," groaned Anne.

"Who is it?" asked Jane. She watched as it chugged straight for them. As it got closer, she saw that it was a rather dilapidated hand-built houseboat, made to look like an outhouse. The front of the structure was screened and a man sat in a bright orange La-Z-Boy, waving with one hand and steering with the other.

"Why do I have all the luck?" said Anne, breathing smoke out of her nostrils.

"Who is that guy?"

"His name's Quinn Fosh. He's the town ex–golden boy turned deadbeat. He's been mowing the lawn for my mother. Helvi wants me to fire him, but I haven't had a chance to talk to him about it yet."

"Does he live on that boat?"

"He's got a small house outside Earlton, but in the summer he often stays on the lake—at least he used to. I haven't talked to him in years."

The boat slowed and drifted alongside them.

"Afternoon, ladies," called Quinn, stepping out onto the front deck.

From the looks of him, Jane decided that he was probably the boat's architect. There was about five feet of open space on the front of the craft, and a little less on the aft. Two cheap plastic deck chairs rested next to him, along with several clay pots containing large cactus plants. Christmas lights had been nailed all the way around the rectangular cabin. Inside, across the far right side, she could see a small kitchenette. The other side probably contained a bed.

"Hi, Quinn," said Anne, her voice something less than friendly.

"It certainly is a small world. I was just thinking about you and your family." His voice was deep. Authoritative. Officious.

"Really?" She flicked more ash into the water.

"I, ah, just wanted to say that I was sorry to hear about your mother."

"Thanks."

He bent over the rail, raising a suggestive eyebrow at Jane. "Who's your friend?"

"Her name's Jane Lawless. A buddy of mine from Minneapolis."

"Always nice to meet a pretty lady." He tipped his rather silly nautical cap, one that was loaded with official-looking gold braid. "Anybody ever tell you you look like Natalie Wood?"

Jane grimaced. "No, not that I recall."

"Well, you do. You should wear your hair in a flip. That's what I like."

"Is it?"

"Yup. You booked in at some hotel around here?" he asked, attempting to keep his tone casual.

"No, I'm staying at the Dumonts' cottage."

"Well, I'll probably see you around then. The name's Quinn Fosh."

"Nice to meet you."

"Likewise." He bent down, flipped the cover off a cooler, and grabbed a beer. After taking a long sip he said, "Anyway, see you tomorrow, Annie."

"Are you coming to mow the grass again so soon?"

Quinn had already returned to the driver's seat inside the cabin. "Nope," he called, gunning the motor—such as it was.

As the boat moved off, Jane could see the words *Half Moon* and a small outhouse painted in primary colors on the rear. "Jeez, but that guy is tacky."

"I wonder what he meant by 'See you tomorrow'?" asked Anne, a perplexed look on her face. She sat forward and stared at the wake of his retreating boat.

9

Melody paused on the front steps, watching the last car move slowly up the dusty gravel road on its way back to the highway. She was exhausted, glad the day was almost over. It had been about as hideous as she'd expected it would be. All she wanted was to go upstairs, crawl into bed, and pull the covers up over her head. She would have done it too if it hadn't been for Anne and Lyle. They insisted she stay downstairs and mingle with the guests. It was only for a few hours. Surely she could do that much in memory of her mother.

Oh well, thought Melody. She supposed they were right. At least Pfeifer hadn't shown up. She was sure he was planning some grand scene for the benefit of the family. The wronged yet patient husband, always willing to forgive, pleading with his uncaring wife for one more chance.

What crap.

She wandered over to the garden and stood looking down at the rows of corn her mother had planted a little over a month ago. Corn and tomatoes, peas, green beans, Swiss chard, onions, and as always, the perennial strawberry patch. As a child, she vividly remembered her summer weeding chores. She hated weeding. She hated her mother's perfectionism. And she especially hated tedious, repetitive work. Poor Lyle. He'd been more than patient with her at the office as she struggled with her secretarial duties, but his patience had worn thin. Now, at last, she could quit that asshole job. With what she would inherit, she'd be independently wealthy for the rest of her life. That is, if she was smart and didn't blow it all on something dumb. And Melody intended to be smart.

Pfeifer was probably having a silent fit somewhere, or more likely, breaking furniture and slamming his fists into the walls. He was so close to finally getting his hands on the Dumont money he could probably taste it. Well, too bad. She had a good lawyer who'd cut him out of any play he'd make for her assets, and that would be the end of that.

Her mother had never liked Pfeifer. The feeling was mutual. Pfeifer had positively loathed Belle Dumont for her decision not to help them financially. In her darker moments, Melody often wondered if Pfeifer had married her for her money. Silly boy. He simply didn't understand the Dumont dictum: Wealth spoils children, therefore children need to make it on their own.

Melody had met Pfeifer five years ago at Bigalow's Bar in downtown Minneapolis. She'd been bartending at different places around town for the last two years. It was mid-August and her first night at a new job. Pfeifer was working at an electronics store across the street, repairing VCRs. He'd just gotten out of prison, although she didn't find that out until after they were married. He came in, ordered a beer, and they struck up a conversation. Three nights later they slept together for the first time. Melody couldn't quite believe it herself. It had never happened that way before. In a period of days, she'd fallen head over heels in love with the guy. Pfeifer felt the same way. In late September she took him home to meet the family.

Big mistake.

As far as her mother and Helvi were concerned, it was instant dislike. The rest of the family felt the same way. Oh, they were all nice enough. Everyone was *always* pleasant. It must have been in a rule book somewhere. All the smiles and controlled tones drove her crazy. Why didn't they just come out and say what they thought? Pfeifer, with his unfailing *in*ability to read people, didn't pick up on any of the negative vibes. He thought the weekend had gone swimmingly and that he'd be welcomed into the family with open arms.

Mistake number two.

Even after their less than enthusiastically received announcement the following month that they intended to marry, the marriage had started out great. She'd felt closer to him in that first year than she ever had to any other human being. She'd confided in him, expressed all her insecurities about life, and found that, surprisingly, he shared many of them. He made her feel special, and at the same time, no different from anyone else. How could she explain to her family how liberating it was? Even though he had trouble keeping a job, he kept her happy and made her feel loved unconditionally, no matter how much she screwed up. He screwed up too, so it didn't seem so bad. They had each other, and they had love, and that seemed enough.

Yet as their money problems grew, so did the irritations, the frustrations, and ultimately, the confrontations. By the end of the second year, Melody was looking for a way out. Pfeifer knew it, and that knowledge fueled even more fights. He was committed, he'd given her everything, tried to make her happy in every way he knew how, so why *wasn't* she?

She tried harder.

She tried to ignore his drinking.

She tried to tune out his words when he screamed at her.

And finally, she tried to believe him when he said he was sorry for beating her up. She tried and tried until she couldn't try any more. The fists, the tears, the bruises and the apologies all blurred together. And eventually, she stopped thinking at all.

Yet, through it all, she never once said a word about any of her problems to her family. How could she? She was failing again. The silent *I told you so*'s would come so fast and thick, she'd be buried by them. She'd dropped out of college. Taken whatever dirtball job she could find just to keep from coming back home to Earlton. She knew her perpetual negativity was boring—she even bored herself. She loathed whiners, but so far she hadn't found a path away from that part of herself.

Sure, Anne may have already been divorced, but everyone had complete confidence that Anne would also get it right one day. Melody had no confidence she'd ever get it right, with relationships or anything else.

Pfeifer said the problems in their marriage were mainly her fault. Deep down, she knew he was right. If only he hadn't insisted on moving back to Earlton. A lot of their problems had started right there. For one thing, neither of them could find a good job. Pfeifer was a city kid, not a miner or a farm hand. And living near the Pleasant Family with all their unspoken criticism wasn't much fun either. For some reason she was never able to figure out, Pfeifer thought living in a small town would be cool. He wanted to get away from all the problems in his past and get "back to nature."

Right. Maybe they should have started a commune.

Melody crouched down and picked several ripe strawberries, popping them into her mouth. She'd eaten too much this afternoon after the funeral. She hated herself when she did that. Eating thoughtlessly, nervously. As a matter of fact, she hated her entire life. But that was going to change. It had to now. Her inheritance would make all the difference. Not that she had wanted to see her mother die. She'd never wanted that. But she had to concentrate on her new life now, her new responsibilities.

Even if her mother wouldn't be around to watch, she was going to make her proud.

Standing up, she heard a rustling sound in the woods behind her. She turned, trying to determine the location of the noise. Everything looked quiet enough. As her eyes passed over the birch trees nearest the entrance road, a lanky man with dark brown hair and a goatee emerged from the brush.

Damn. It was Pfeifer.

As he made straight for her she could feel her body tense.

"I've been waiting to talk to you alone," he said softly, his hands pressed into the back pockets of his jeans. His blue eyes looked hurt, concerned.

She'd seen the act before so she didn't buy it.

"I didn't think you'd want me at the funeral this morning."

"You thought right." She backed up several steps, nearly tripping over a wire tomato support.

He reached out to steady her, his face coming very close to hers.

"Don't," she said, squirming away. Her arms closed over her stomach. Even the smell of his breath was enough to nauseate her.

He returned his hands to his back pockets. "I just wanted to tell you how sorry I am about your mom."

"Right." More crap. He wasn't sorry at all.

"I'm ah . . . not clear on how she died. Someone said she fell off that railroad bridge near Fosh Lake."

She kept her distance, also her footing. She didn't want to give him another reason to come close again. "You heard right."

"Do you know why she was out there?"

"She went for a walk."

"Oh."

Was that a smirk? "What's so funny?"

"Nothing," he said, defensively.

"Really?"

"Yeah, really."

He was such a liar. "Then I got a question for *you*."

He clamped one hand over the opposite wrist and stood there, looking uncomfortable. "Like what?"

"Like did you see her that morning, Pfeifer? Did you meet her out there in the woods?"

He reared back, his expression startled. "Hey! Don't try and pin her death on me."

Melody glanced at the lake and saw her mom's speedboat returning to the dock. It looked like Anne was in the driver's seat. "The morning she died, I saw her reading something. As I was heading out the door to my car, she looked at me funny. I can't explain it."

"What was she reading?"

"A note. Maybe a letter. It kinda looked like the one you sent me two weeks ago. You know what I'm talking about? Your zillionth apology for the abuse?"

"Hey, I don't like that word. I just got a little rough, that's all. Don't make me out to be something I'm not."

"Just answer the question, Pfeifer." Her voice was cold.

He lowered both hands to his sides. "No," he said firmly. "I haven't talked to your mother in over a month. That's how much she loved her son-in-law. She didn't give a shit what problems I had."

This was pointless. "Is that all you came to say? Because if it is, I've got stuff I've got to do."

He rubbed his hands nervously against the sides of his jeans and looked around. "How come you're making this so hard? You know what I want." He lowered his voice even further. "You've got to stop all this craziness and come home with me. You know I'm sorry."

"Oh, right."

"Look, you've done the legal separation thing now.

Haven't you gotten that out of your system yet? I love you, Melody."

"You could have fooled me."

He grabbed her arm. "Don't give me this shit. I've got my car parked on the highway. I want you to come with me. Let's just get out of this town once and for all. You know, like in our song."

Springsteen's "Thunder Road" had always been their special song. Pfeifer loved Springsteen's music. It captured all the itchy blue-collar restlessness Pfeifer felt so keenly himself. It was true. He'd never gotten any breaks in his life. Early in their relationship, she'd wanted to help him—maybe even thought her love could save him the way she hoped his love could save her. But it hadn't happened. She tried to twist her arm away. "The only reason you're interested in me now is because you think I'm going to inherit some money."

"What do you mean, *think*?" He let go, glancing over his shoulder at the house. When she didn't respond, he said, his voice growing cheerfully eager, "Hey, really? Are you? Do you know how much?"

"You're so fucking transparent."

"Don't use that kind of language with me." He grabbed her roughly by her shoulders, then thought better of it and let her go again. He took a gentler tack. "Maybe you're right. I did figure if your mother was ever out of the picture that you'd finally get what was coming to you."

"You know, Pfeifer, it would serve you right if all the talk about my family's wealth was just that. Talk. Maybe I won't inherit a dime."

"Do you know something I don't?"

God, he was dense. "Just go, okay?"

His eyes traveled slowly down her body. "Who're you sleeping with now?"

"Oh, jeez." She started to walk away.

He grabbed her and spun her around. "You've found someone else, haven't you? Is it the same one?"

"What *same* one?"

"The one who broke up our marriage. The one you left me for."

"Is that why you've been following me around, spying on me? Oh, you didn't think I saw you, but I did. At the post office. In the grocery store. Dad even told me you'd rented a boat so you could check out what was happening here at night from out on the water. Clever, Pfeifer. Did you rent a telescope too? So you could get the full view of my bed?"

"I didn't rent the boat," he said indignantly. "I got a new job."

"Your jealousy is out of control, Pfeifer! You're not listening to me."

"Don't you even want to know where I'm working?" After a suitable pause and another smirk he said, "Ringly Marine. They started me two weeks ago as a mechanic. But I'm gonna be selling boats too."

"What the hell do you know about being a salesman?"

He looked hurt. This time it was real. Before she could say any more, he slapped her hard across the face.

At the same moment, Lyle burst out the front door and hit the ground running. "You lousy shit," he screamed, tearing across the lawn. About ten feet away he took a flying leap and slammed Pfeifer to the ground. Even though the younger man had several feet and a good thirty pounds on him, Lyle was clearly the athlete with all the right moves. They struggled together in the grass. Finally, when both of them had scrambled to their feet, Lyle took a heavy swing at Pfeifer and sent him reeling back into the strawberry patch. "You ever touch my sister again and you're *history*."

Pfeifer didn't get up. Instead, he just lay in the dirt and rubbed his jaw.

"And if I ever catch you around here again, I'm going to call the police."

"You don't own this town," snarled Pfeifer, brushing himself off.

"Don't be so sure."

"You Dumonts think you're such hot shit. Well, you're not. You're flesh and blood, just like the rest of us. Just look at what happened to your mother."

Lyle made another move toward him. "Get up and get out of here before I do something I'll regret!"

"You don't think I'm good enough for your sister, right? Well, welcome to the real world, Lyle. Contrary to the rumors around town, you couldn't get elected dog-catcher—especially when I charge you with assault."

"Just leave, Pfeifer," said Melody, holding Lyle's arm.

He brushed more dirt off his jeans and then stood. Melody read it as a taunt. He was saying he wasn't afraid. He was taking all the time he needed. "I'll go," he said finally. "But not before I tell Mr. Corporate Corporate here something he doesn't know."

"And what's that?" demanded Lyle.

"Your sister's a slut, man."

Lyle swung at him, but missed this time and fell awkwardly into the corn patch.

Pfeifer pointed at him and shrieked with laughter. Then, backing away quickly, he bolted for the gravel entrance road.

Melody walked over and helped her brother up, relieved that her crazy husband had finally gone.

"That guy's a lunatic," said Lyle, wiping a hand across his mouth.

"Don't let him get under your skin. That's what he wants."

"Are you all right?" He touched a small welt on her cheek.

"Fine."

"I don't want an argument on this, Mel. I'm calling our lawyer first thing tomorrow morning. We need to get a restraining order slapped on that guy. Has he ever hit you before?"

She shook her head.

"Good. If I've got anything to say about it, he never will again. Come on." He put his arm protectively around her shoulders and together they walked back to the house.

10

Jane stood on the railroad tracks and gazed down into the ravine where Belle Dumont had fallen to her death. It was a hot, humid Wednesday morning, the kind of day that could easily end in a storm.

"Let's check out the Fosh Lake Country Club when you're done playing Hercule Poirot," said Cordelia, punctuating her statement by snapping her gum and then blowing a bubble.

She was behind Jane, jumping from one railroad tie to the next. Today, in addition to black tennis shoes and socks, her ample frame was packed into a pair of baggy, red and black striped pedal pushers. An oversize University of Minnesota T-shirt and a baseball cap completed the ensemble. Cordelia was nearly six feet tall and tipped the scale at well over two hundred pounds. Even with those robust dimensions, she was a stunningly attractive woman, although today, at least in Jane's humble opinion, her attire did nothing to further her normally captivating image.

Jane turned to answer, but instead, stopped and stared. When you saw someone dressed in something so ridiculous, something you wouldn't even wear on a dare, it truly amazed. Jane dressed rather conservatively herself. She usually wore tailored blazers and slacks when she had to dress up. Her everyday clothing consisted of jeans, white high-top tennis shoes or boots, and a shirt, or in the winter, a sweater. Clothes were not high on her list of interests. Cordelia, on the other hand, ran the gamut from this morning's atrocity to gold lamé evening gowns and military uniforms.

"Where'd you get those clothes, Cordelia? Toys 'R' Us?"

"You like it?" she asked eagerly. "It's what *all* the tenth graders are wearing this season. You wouldn't want me to be left in the fashion dust, would you?" She flapped her eyelashes innocently.

Since Jane couldn't think of a response that wouldn't end their friendship, she returned her attention to the ravine. "Okay, here's the plan. The purse we're looking for is tan. It's going to be hard to see it, but we've got to try. Now, we'll cover the territory in a grid. First, we'll climb down—"

"I beg your pardon," interrupted Cordelia. "I'm not climbing down *anything*. I am not a goat, mountain or otherwise." She gave an indignant sniff.

Jane glared at her. "If you're not going to help, why did you come along?"

"To see where Belle died, of course. What else?"

Jane closed her eyes. "I don't believe it."

"Look, I'm not a voyeuristic sicko just because I wanted to see the spot for myself."

"No?"

"No." She yanked on her T-shirt. "Well, maybe a little, but no more than you."

"I'm here to help find out what happened."

"We know what happened, Janey. She fell down that abyss and died."

"But why was she here in the first place?"

"She went for a walk!"

"But why here!"

Cordelia gave an exasperated squawk. "You're going

to have to consult a crystal ball for that information, Janey. I left mine back in Minneapolis."

Actually, Cordelia did have a crystal ball at home, although it was a cheap one with lots of bubbles and flaws in it. Even though Jane knew her friend was probably right and there wasn't much hope of finding any answers out here, she still had to try. She couldn't just lie around the cabin and do nothing. "Okay, listen. You stay here and I'll do the search by myself."

"You're pouting."

Jane clenched her teeth. "You take the binoculars and scan the area visually."

"Good plan." Cordelia pulled a pair of binoculars out of her sack purse and sat down on a boulder.

"Are you comfortable?" asked Jane, not bothering to hide the sarcasm in her voice.

"Reasonably."

"Swell."

Her tennis shoes slipped on the damp earth as she started down. The incline was steep, far more treacherous than it appeared from the top. Holding on to brush, tree limbs, and exposed tree roots, she began to examine the ground. It was rocky, even muddy in spots. One false step and she might end up exactly where Belle had.

After about fifteen minutes, Cordelia called, "Want to take a bubble gum break?"

"No thanks," answered Jane, not terribly politely.

"Suit yourself."

Half an hour later, Cordelia hollered, "Say, move down a little to your right."

"What?" Jane straightened up. She'd been searching under some of the brush near the base of a far pine tree.

"Just move down a bit and look to your right. I see something that looks like thick string, about five inches long. It's probably nothing." Under her breath she added, "Just like this wild goose chase we're on."

Jane spied what Cordelia was talking about. Moving closer, she could see a cord sticking out of the ground, both ends buried in the dirt.

Taking a pen from her shirt pocket, she carefully slid it underneath the object and pulled up. A tan strap emerged from the dirt. The attached purse came next.

"I found it," she yelled, her voice full of the thrill of discovery. She quickly scrambled back up to the top of the hill. "It looks like it was buried under a mud slide." She sat down next to Cordelia.

"One correction, dearheart. *I* found it. Little ole me. Just sitting here like a lump." Cordelia blew kisses all around, then swatted a deer fly away from her face. "Now can we go have lunch?"

Jane opened the clasp and checked inside, then thought better of it and stopped. "This might be evidence. We should probably give it to the police. Let them decide how to proceed."

"Nonsense," said Cordelia, snatching it out of her hand. "We found it. Besides, we don't even know if it belonged to Belle. We better check."

Before Jane could stop her, Cordelia's hand contaminated the contents as she rifled energetically through the purse. Sure enough, it was Belle's. Her pocketbook was still inside, so were other essentials. Car keys. Several pens. Even a small case filled with family photos. None of the cash or credit cards had been touched.

"What's that?" said Cordelia, pointing at a piece of yellow notebook paper near the bottom.

Their eyes locked.

"Better leave it," said Jane. She was at war with herself. She desperately wanted to see what it was even though she knew she had no business tampering with evidence.

Again, Cordelia showed no such reticence. She whipped

it out and opened it up. It was a note written in longhand. Jane looked over her shoulder as Cordelia read out loud:

> "We have to talk. I've got some
> information about one of your kids
> you'll want to hear. If you don't
> call, you'll regret it.
> —Q"

She looked up. "Who's Q?"

"I have no idea," said Jane.

"Let's see," said Cordelia, placing a finger against her cheek, "I know a few Quentins. One Quigly. Even a Daniel Q. Erickson."

"I suppose we shouldn't jump to conclusions. This may have nothing to do with why Belle was out here."

"Of course it has something to do with it," erupted Cordelia. "Didn't Helvi say the last thing Belle said before she left was that a mother was never too old to take care of her children? Somehow or other, 'Q' must have slipped her this note. She found it that morning, read it, maybe called 'Q' to agree on a time and a place to meet, and then she went back upstairs and made that rather cryptic little statement to Helvi before she left."

Well reasoned, thought Jane, her eyebrows knit together in thought.

"We've got company," announced Cordelia, tossing another lump of bubble gum into her mouth.

As Jane looked up, she saw a gray-haired man and a lively golden lab emerge from the woods. Both had red bandanas around their necks. The dog raced ahead, scampering up to Cordelia with the kind of ridiculous enthusiasm only a dog could muster.

Cordelia patted his head, wiped her hand surreptitiously on her pants leg, and then tossed a stick.

The dog tore after it.

"Nice day," said the man as he got closer.

"If you like deer flies and humidity," muttered Cordelia.

Jane stood up as the dog came bounding back. She scratched his head and then tossed the stick, this time much farther. "He's got a lot of energy," she smiled.

"We go for a walk every morning," said the elderly man, stopping for a short breather. His face was red with the heat. As he glanced down at the purse in Cordelia's hand he said, "The name's Melvin. I'm on social security." He extended his hand.

Jane shook it with an amused grin. This guy was a character.

"Yup, I live in Grand Rapids, but I've got a cousin with a cabin not far from here. We have breakfast together a couple times a week and then Jolly and I go for a walk. I don't usually see many folks out this way."

"I don't doubt that," said Cordelia. "Unless you want to hop a freight train. Ah yes," she said wistfully. "The idea of riding around in a poultry car really appeals on a day like today."

He cocked his head. "It does?"

The dog returned and dropped the stick at Jane's feet. "Have you seen anyone around here lately?" asked Jane, patting the dog and then throwing it one more time.

He eyed her thoughtfully. "You asking if I saw anything the day that woman died? I read about it in the Grand Rapids paper."

"I don't suppose you were out walking that morning."

"Sure was. But all I saw was a couple of cars. Both were parked out on the highway. One was a foreign make—probably an Audi or a Volvo."

"Do you remember the color?"

He scratched his chin. "Blue, I think. Yeah, blue."

It was Belle's car, no doubt about it. "And the other one?"

"It was a gold Cadillac. Pretty flashy if you ask me.

You know, I kind of wondered if those cars had something to do with it."

"You should report what you know to the police,"
said Jane.

"You really think so? I don't like to get involved."

"It could be important information."

He nodded. "I'll think about it." He whistled for Jolly.
The dog bolted out of the woods wagging his tale. The
stick had been discarded somewhere along the way.
"Well, I guess I better be off. Nice meeting you folks."
He stared at Cordelia's clothing for a moment and then
nodded to her as he continued on down the tracks.

11

"You can put your minds at rest. It's not going to be a problem to get a restraining order," announced Jeff Weintz, the Dumonts' lawyer and longtime friend. He sat at the head of a long conference table in the Detrich & Weintz Law Office on Pokegama Avenue in Grand Rapids.

Melody sat on one side of Helvi. Anne sat on the other, gazing out the window at the old Central School building where she'd attended grade school as a kid. It was late Wednesday afternoon. The entire family had been summoned to the office for the formal reading of the will.

Jeff continued. "If Pfeifer comes within fifty yards of you, he can be arrested."

"Good," said Lyle, glancing at Melody. "Maybe I'm overreacting, but I think that guy's dangerous. I don't know what he's going to do next. We saw his van following us when we drove in from the lake. And he called Mel a good five times this morning before Helvi'd finally had enough and took the phone off the hook."

Jeff shook his head. "You better be careful, Mel. Don't go out alone until some of this gets resolved. We can start on the divorce papers tomorrow if you'd like."

Melody nodded but said nothing.

"That's what you want, isn't it?" asked Lyle. He seemed frustrated by her lack of enthusiasm.

"Yes, it is," she said, leaning forward and folding her

hands on the table. "It's just not as simple for me as you'd like it to be."

Lyle gave her a hard look then dropped his eyes to the manila folder in front of him. "I suppose not," he said, some of the intensity leaving his voice.

"What about his claim on her assets?" asked Anne. She thought it was a fair question since Melody was about to inherit a sizable sum of money.

Jeff sat back and crossed his arms over his chest. He was a weedy-looking man in his late fifties. Thin, gray-brown hair was brushed forward to cover a hairline that had not only receded, but had vanished completely. "This is a community property state, but we'll see what we can do. You *are* legally separated. That's in your favor. My advice to you now is not to worry. I'm a good lawyer. I'll protect your interests in every way possible."

Anne could see that the advice and the reassurances fell on deaf ears. She knew Melody was furious that Pfeifer might be able to get his hands on even a dime of her inheritance.

"Now," said Jeff, opening up a blue envelope and removing the will, "I think it's time."

Before he could continue, the partially open door at the back of the room opened all the way as a man stepped inside and moved quickly toward the conference table.

Everyone turned to look.

"What's *he* doing here?" asked Lyle's wife, Carla. Their two teenage sons sat bored and twitching next to her.

"This is a private meeting," said Jeff Weintz with great firmness, standing and addressing the man.

It was Quinn Fosh.

"I'm sorry to hear you're having troubles with your husband," said Quinn, a concerned look on his square face as he stared down at Melody.

"I'm going to have to ask you to leave," said Jeff, step-ping aggressively away from the table.

"Not so fast," said Quinn, standing his ground.

Anne saw the unmistakable hint of a smirk. From what she remembered, Quinn was like that. He enjoyed being tasteless. In her mind, there were few acts more crass than smirking at the family of the recently deceased.

Sensing that he had everyone's rapt attention, Quinn pulled out a chair and sat down. The smell of his sweat filled the room.

Lyle shot to his feet. "What the hell's going on? Don't you know Earlton's police chief is looking for you?"

Quinn raised an eyebrow. "For me?" He was inno-cence incarnate.

"You're goddamn right!" said Lyle, tightening his fists next to his sides. "Your car was spotted near my mother's the morning she died. You were there with her! For God's sake, man, why didn't you say something?"

Anne watched Quinn digest this information. He didn't seem particularly surprised by the unspoken accusation. Or upset. She wondered what he had up his sleeve. What-ever it was, she doubted they'd get the truth. Not that anyone was likely to believe him, no matter what he said.

In the space of a few hours, ever since Jane and Cordelia had returned to the lake with the purse and the note, everyone in the family had pegged Quinn as their mother's murderer. He must have *pushed* her down that ravine. What other explanation could there be? If he hadn't tricked her into going there for some evil purpose, he would have come forward.

Quinn took off his navy blue and white captain's hat and set it down on the table. Up close, Anne could now see that his blond hair hadn't exactly turned white; it was more of an icky yellow. "Yes," he said slowly. "We did talk that morning. First on the telephone, and then we met out near my lake." He always referred to Fosh Lake as *his*, not that he owned even a square inch of the expensive property surrounding it.

Sensing the drama of the moment and perhaps wanting to prolong it, Quinn took out a pipe already primed with tobacco and struck a match. Sucking in the pungent smoke, he sat back and gave them all his most winning smile. "I have every reason to be here, you see. I'm part of the family."

For several seconds, the only sound in the room came from a buzzing fly.

Lyle was the first to erupt. "What are you trying to pull?"

Quinn lifted an envelope out of his pocket and handed it to Jeff Weintz. "Maybe you'd like to read this and explain to everyone here what it means."

Jeff sat back down and studied the document. "This is a note written and signed by your father, Herbert Fosh, and notarized by my father." Jeff's dad had also been a lawyer.

"That's right." Quinn's smile was serene.

"It says here that Belle Dumont's natural father was Herbert Fosh."

There was a collective gasp.

"What that means, dear family," said Quinn, removing the pipe from his mouth with a flourish, "is that Belle and I were brother and sister. Half brother and sister, to be exact, but related by blood nonetheless." He said the words with a kind of repellent grandiosity.

"Let me see that thing," said Lyle, grabbing it out of Jeff's hand. He turned it over and then back again to the front. "This is just a piece of paper. What does it prove?"

"It's a legal document, signed by my father, and dated seven years after Belle was born. If it wasn't true, why would he sign it?" He let the question hang in the air. "Also, I can produce canceled checks paid to Fanny Adams, Belle's mother. Belle even admitted to me that her mother was paid child support for six years—from the time Fanny returned home to build her house on the lake until Belle turned twenty. That's how Fanny maintained her rather expensive lifestyle."

"Mom *knew* you were her half brother?" asked Anne, dumbfounded.

"Certainly. *I* was the one who didn't know. Not until last Saturday morning."

The room grew silent.

"The day she died?" said Anne.

He nodded. "My father never told me. I was lied to my entire life." His anger seemed genuine.

"But . . . why did Belle pick that moment to tell you?" asked Helvi.

He shrugged. "You'd have to ask her that. All I can say is, she dropped her little bomb and a few minutes later I left. As you might expect, I had a lot to think about. But," he added, stuffing the pipe back into his mouth and biting down hard on the stem, "she was alive when I left her. I'd swear that on a stack of Bibles."

Anne was trying hard to put it all together in her mind. By the looks of her family's faces, they were too. "Look," she said after a few seconds, "the note found in my mother's purse said you wanted to give her some information about one of her children."

Quinn's eyebrows knit together. "You found that, did you?" He sucked on his pipe. "Well, that was nothing really. I was just trying to save her some money."

Helvi snorted at the absurdity.

"What was the information?" asked Melody, her voice carefully neutral.

"Oh, well," said Quinn, eyeing Lyle with amusement as he sat back in his chair and folded one leg over the other, "I wanted to pass on some private information I'd found out about your brother's political future. I knew Belle was thinking of supporting her son's candidacy

with a large donation. I thought she should know it
would be a wasted effort."

Lyle glared at him.

"Can I see the piece of paper Quinn brought with
him?" asked Helvi, holding her hand out to Lyle. Her
face betrayed nothing other than coldness.

Lyle handed it over.

Quinn gave her a minute and then continued. "As
much as you kids may not want to admit it, I'm your
uncle. And," he added, his tone losing all its lightness,
"as your uncle, I expect a certain amount of respect."

Anne felt as if someone had just hit her over the
head with a two-by-four. She could almost see stars.
Quinn Fosh her uncle? It was not only impossible, it was
ludicrous.

Yet, as she thought about it, she realized her mother
had never talked much about her father. Since she'd
never known him, or at least she maintained she never
knew him, there wasn't much to say. All Anne knew was
that Fanny had met him in 1929, and that he'd died about
a year later, before they could be married. She had the
baby, and when she came back to Earlton in 1932, she
wouldn't talk about any of it. She said it was water under
the bridge and she wanted to get on with her life. When
she'd left Earlton again in 1938, she moved to Chicago.
Sometime during the war, she met another man, they fell
in love, and several weeks later he shipped out. He promised her that when he came back, they'd be married. But
he never came home. He died in France several months
later.

This second mystery man—again, Anne couldn't even
remember his name—had been quite wealthy. He'd left
Fanny and her small daughter, Belle, well provided for
until he returned. After Fanny found out he'd been killed,
she invested the money. Anne had no idea what the
investments were, no one did, but they were apparently

lucky and lucrative. The war made a lot of people rich. When she again moved back to Earlton in 1945, seven years later, Fanny Adams was a rich woman. Yet something about both accounts had never rung true to Anne. Perhaps it was the way her mother told the stories— quickly and with little interest. And now here was Quinn saying it was all a lie. That all along her mother knew it was a lie.

"Why would your dad admit fathering a child seven years after the fact?" asked Melody. Helvi had passed the paper on to her. "If Fanny could prove he was the father, why did it take her seven years to get him to sign that document? It's dated May 23rd, 1938. That was the same year Grandma Fanny left Earlton to move to Chicago."

Quinn shrugged. "Just because I'm not burdened by a conscience doesn't mean my father didn't have one. Even so, I'll lay you odds old Fanny was a blackmailer. An illegitimate kid back in 1938 was a pretty big deal, especially for someone in my father's position."

Anne knew he was right. Still, why wait seven years to admit paternity, and another seven years before paying any child support? It didn't add up.

"Besides, Dad already had a family," said Quinn, his voice full of pride. *"Me."*

"This is all bullshit!" said Lyle, slamming a pen down on the table.

"Now now," said Quinn. "You better watch your language. Not that you'll have much hope of a public career when all this comes out. Your grandmother a blackmailer?"

"You have no proof of that!"

He made a clucking sound with his tongue. "What about your mother living in sin with another woman? What *are* we to think?" He slapped a hand to his cheek, his voice growing snotty and mocking. "By the way," he said, winking at Helvi, "your lesbian ménage is *the* topic of conversation around town, in case you didn't know."

Lyle's face had turned bright red.

"Are we related to that guy?" asked Brad Dumont, Lyle and Carla's oldest son. He said the words with youthful distaste, just as if someone had asked him to eat an entire bowl of lima beans.

"Shhh," said Carla Dumont. She held a finger to her mouth.

"Can we go outside now?" asked Tom, the younger son.

Carla shook her head for him to be quiet.

"This is *such* a bummer," grumped Brad, slumping in his chair.

Lyle gave them both a stern look and then returned his attention to Quinn. "My political career is none of your business."

"Just trying to point out some political realities," said Quinn, puffing on his pipe. His eyes darted to Jeff Weintz. "So, let's get this show on the road. I don't have all day."

"What do you mean?" asked Melody.

"What do you think? I'm here for the reading of the will."

"Hey, just a minute," said Anne. "I don't feel comfortable with that." He'd already turned the meeting on its ear with his surprise announcement. "None of this has been authenticated. I, for one, refuse to let this proceed until you leave."

Quinn's expression turned angry. "I thought you people were better than that. You're just trying to cut me out."

"Cut you out of what?" asked Helvi.

"My inheritance!" said Quinn, his voice rising to a shout. "What's due me!"

"I can assure you that you're not mentioned in Belle Dumont's will," said Jeff Weintz.

"So what? I'm her natural half brother. That gives me rights."

"That gives you *nothing*," snarled Lyle.

They held each other's eyes for several long seconds, neither blinking.

Finally, Quinn pushed away from the table and got up. "Fine. If that's the way you want to play it, so be it. You'll hear from my lawyer in the morning." With that, he grabbed his hat and stomped out the door.

Everyone sat for a few moments in dazed silence.

Lyle was the first to recover. "Can he do that?" he asked, his voice deadly serious. "Does he have any claim on my mother's estate?"

Before Jeff answered, he crossed to the back of the room, shut the door, and then returned to his seat. "Probably not," he said, shaking his head wearily. "But—"

"What?" demanded Melody. "What!"

"Well, since Belle doesn't actually close the door completely by mentioning him by name and saying he's to receive nothing, he might be able to tie you up in court with legal maneuvers for a while."

"That's ridiculous!" said Lyle.

"I'm afraid that whether it is or not, it's possible."

Everyone in the room was silenced by the news.

Finally, Helvi spoke. "Can we dispense with all the legalese and just get you to synopsize the terms of the will for us?"

"Sure," said Jeff, laying his hands flat on the table. "You each have a copy of the document in front of you. You can take it home and read it later. If you've got questions, just call. The bottom line is, after fees and taxes, the estate is worth approximately three million dollars. It was to be divided four ways—with Helvi retaining rights to the family house on Pokegama Lake."

Three million, thought Anne. A lot of money. "But now you're saying that we have to wait until all the legal wranglings are settled before we can inherit?"

"Possibly." Jeff turned his palms up and gave them all a bewildered look. "I wish Belle had said something to me. We could have handled Quinn Fosh very easily. As matters stand now—I won't lie to you—we could have a mess on our hands."

It wasn't what they wanted to hear.

"Hey, Dad, does that mean we can get jet skis?" asked Brad Dumont. His boredom with the proceedings had changed into cautious interest.

"We'll talk about that later," said Lyle.

"But—"

"Later," he said, this time more firmly.

Anne's eyes returned to the window, watching the flag next to the old Central School building flap in the late afternoon breeze. The sky looked angry, as if a thunderstorm was brewing. Inside the room, the storm had already broken.

12

The next afternoon, Quinn's Cadillac screeched to a halt just outside Ringly Marine Outfitters. Yanking his captain's hat down over his eyes to protect them from the sun, he got out and looked up at the sign above the door. He'd gone to high school with the owner, Tim Ringly. Who knew such a bozo would end up with such a lucrative business? Just three months ago, thanks to Belle Dumont's need to keep his mouth shut, Quinn had bought a new speedboat from him, the one he docked at the Fosh Lake Country Club's main marina. Tim hadn't given him much of a deal. Quinn expected more from an old friend. But, what the hell. He'd get even one day. One day this entire town would pay for laughing at him behind his back. Quinn believed firmly in retribution.

Today, however, he had other business on his mind. Taking a handkerchief out of his back pocket and wiping the sweat from his neck, he hopped up the steps and entered the front door. Inside the cool building, his eyes swept the showroom floor. Most of the larger boats were outside. Stepping up to the counter, he leaned across the glass and stared at a woman sitting behind a computer screen until she looked up at him.

"Can I help you?" she asked.

Quinn smiled easily. She was pretty. Not fabulous, but sexy in a tough, been-around kind of way. He liked blondes, real or fake—it didn't matter. This one was fake.

"I don't know. Can you?" He flexed a muscle in his right arm. He could tell she caught it and that she liked what she saw.

"Are you looking for someone?" she asked, her voice growing cool.

Quinn figured the businesslike manner was just in case old Tim Ringly was lurking around somewhere, spying on the employees. Oh well, he didn't have time to play anyway.

Quinn considered himself an old-fashioned American patriot and tomorrow was his favorite day of the year. The Fourth of July. He had to get to the grocery store and stock up on chips and beer before the rest of the town cleaned out the supply. He planned to spend the entire day out on Pokegama just drifting around in his houseboat. Thank God the weather was cooperating. There was nothing worse than rain for the fireworks.

"Is Pfeifer Biersman here?" he asked in his most commanding voice.

"Pfeifer?" repeated the woman. "Yeah, I think he's working today. He's probably checking over the new sailboat we just got in. It's at the end of the west dock. Just go back out the door you came in and turn right."

"Thanks, honey." Another grin. He removed his beefy arms from the top of the counter and sauntered away.

Once outside, he quickly spotted the new boat. Even though he'd spent a lot of time sailing as a kid, he'd never enjoyed it. His father had owned a boat for most of his young life. Yet to Quinn, messing with the sails and tacking here and there across the lake was like riding a horse instead of driving a car. Motors made life easier. Besides, he'd never been a good enough sailor to please his old man. Even now, every time he set foot on a sailboat all those nervous, inadequate feelings came back. Quinn wasn't one to overanalyze, but he knew what he liked and he didn't like sailing. End of story.

Childhood had not been a happy time for Quinn. Even so, he hated people who whined about their past. All these idiots bleeding all over the radio and TV made him want to puke. If it was dead and gone, why dredge it up? As far as he could tell, it had no bearing on the here and now. What he'd done with his life he'd done of his own free will. Quinn absolutely refused to blame his father, or give his childhood even a moment's thought. Well, except that sometimes, late at night when he looked up at the stars from the deck of his houseboat, he could still hear his dad's voice telling him that he wasn't man enough to cut it, that he'd never make anything of himself, that he'd always be a disappointment.

That was a laugh. In the end, Quinn knew he'd given the old man exactly what he wanted. His father prided himself on his infallible ability to understand and predict human behavior. Quinn's life had been the fulfillment of that early prophecy. Herbert Fosh expected disappointment from his son, and that's what Quinn had given him.

Rounding the end of the dock, Quinn's ears were assaulted by a blaring radio. He hated rock music. At this moment, all he wanted to do was find the damn thing and switch it off. He jumped on board the boat and followed the obnoxious racket.

Pfeifer was below deck sprawled on a small bed, beating time to the music with the knuckles of his left hand against the side wall. He didn't even notice he had a visitor until Quinn snapped off the song.

"Hey," said Pfeifer angrily, jumping to his feet. Then, looking a bit disoriented, he added, "Oh, sorry, Mr. Fosh. I, ah . . . was just taking a break." He smoothed back his dark brown hair and then attempted a salesmanly smile. "You in the market for a sailboat?"

"I thought you were the mechanic around here."

"I am. But I'm starting to do some sales too."

Quinn leaned back against the kitchen counter, eyeing

the amenities. Sailboats had come a long way since the old tub his dad had owned. His eyes came to rest on the fully stocked liquor cabinet. From the smell in the cabin, it appeared Pfeifer had already helped himself. "I came to talk to you."

The lanky young man was almost too tall to stand upright in the small cabin. He hunched slightly as he said, "What about?"

"My niece."

Pfeifer seemed at a loss. "Sorry, Mr. Fosh. I didn't know you had a niece. What's her name?"

"Melody Dumont."

A scowl formed. Smoothing the small hairs in his goatee, he said, "Is this some kind of joke?"

"You tell me. I hear you two are getting a divorce."

As Pfeifer's back stiffened, his head hit the ceiling. "Not if I've got anything to say about it."

"You may not."

"Meaning what?"

"Meaning, Melody's already got herself a lawyer."

He shoved his hands into his pockets. "Fuck." Then, looking Quinn up and down, he said, "She never said anything to me about you being her uncle."

"No? Must of slipped her mind." Suddenly, Quinn pushed away from the counter and shoved Pfeifer back onto the bed. Even though the kid was younger, Quinn had a good seventy pounds on him, and most of it—he liked to think—was still muscle.

As Pfeifer tried to right himself, Quinn jammed him backward against the pillows and then dropped heavily on top of him, pinning his arms to the mattress, his right hand at the kid's throat. "Now, let's have a chat, shall we?"

"Get off me!" snarled Pfeifer, thrashing to get away. After a few seconds he realized any attempt was useless. He stopped, eyeing Quinn warily. "What do you want?"

It was just about what Quinn had expected. He'd

pegged him for a bully and a coward the first day they'd met. Not that cowards didn't have their moments. But when face-to-face with strength, they usually caved in pretty fast. "Well, I suppose you could say I want your attention." He tightened his grip around the young man's throat. "Do I have it?"

Pfeifer looked terrified. He gave a stiff nod.

"Leave my niece alone," said Quinn, his voice taking on an almost amiable quality.

"But—" He coughed.

Quinn brought his face down very close, smiling as he realized he'd eaten garlic at lunch. "I don't like what I'm hearing about you, kid. And believe me, you don't want me for an enemy."

Pfeifer turned his face to the side to get away from the foul breath. "I love her," he choked.

"You can do better than that."

"What do you want me to say? It's the truth!"

"Right. That's why you're following her. Calling her for hours on end. Destroying any peace of mind she might have. There's a law in this state against stalking, Pfeifer. Did you know that?"

He shook his head, his eyes fixed on Quinn's face. A drop of the older man's sweat fell on his cheek.

"I don't like what you're doing, Pfeifer. I don't like it at all. If you upset my niece, you're upsetting me." He felt a certain pride in handling this family problem so promptly. He'd never had a family to take care of before. As he thought about it, he was going to like being an uncle.

"I'll stop," gulped Pfeifer. "Okay?"

Again, Quinn tightened his grip. "I don't believe you, Pfeifer. And that upsets me. You're not a liar, are you?"

"No, really. You have my word of honor!"

"Honor? Now there's a concept you don't hear much about these days." He knew the kid was full of shit, but he also knew he'd scared him. If he didn't stop, Quinn could always beat the crap out of him later. "You know I could hurt you real bad, right?"

Pfeifer nodded.

"So if you don't back off, you'll see me again. And next time, I'm going to break something. Your arm, your leg. It doesn't matter to me. But I'll make you sorry you ever messed with me or my family. Got it?"

"Absolutely," gushed Pfeifer.

Quinn held on to him for a second longer and then climbed off.

As Pfeifer lay dazed on the bed, Quinn reached inside the liquor cabinet and grabbed a bottle of Johnny Walker Red Label. This year's Fourth of July celebration was looking better all the time.

"God Bless America," he called over his shoulder as he bounded up the steps. And, he thought to himself with a private grin, God bless Uncle Quinn.

13

It was nearly two A.M. Pfeifer sat at the worktable in his basement, tinkering with the old front door lock. Springsteen's "Hungry Heart" played softly from a tape deck in the corner. Pfeifer had always been a night owl. Around midnight, he'd replaced all the locks on the house with new dead bolts. If Melody wanted to leave him for another man, then screw her. She wasn't going to come and go here as she pleased when he was away. He threw the screwdriver he was holding against the far wall, watching it fall into a chair and then bounce onto the concrete floor.

So what if Mel's mother had helped them find a decent place to rent? That tightfisted old biddy could rot in hell for all he cared. He'd be damned if Melody'd force him out of here without a fight—lawyer or no lawyer. Hoisting a beer to his lips, he became aware of a creaking sound somewhere upstairs. Must be the cat. By the smell of the litter box, it was about time it got changed.

Melody had just walked away from their life together and never looked back. Oh, she'd come by a couple of times to pick up some clothes, but never to talk. He hated her for that—and he missed her. He needed her, wanted to protect her, wanted to touch her the way only he could, but he also wanted to hurt her bad, to teach her a lesson. It was all mixed together inside his head. But one thing he knew for sure. She was going to come back to him.

One way or the other. He wouldn't let the Dumont family stand between him and his wife. No way.

Trust had always been a big deal to Pfeifer. Ever since he was a kid he knew the world was a treacherous place. He'd been raised by his grandparents after his mother took off for points unknown right after his eighth birthday. He'd never seen her again. From that moment on, he'd always felt like an outsider.

His grandfather didn't like him much, and didn't mind showing it. He remembered asking the old man for two bucks so he could go see a movie once, when he was ten. It was Saturday and he was bored and wanted to have some fun. Gramps had said no. He didn't have the cash. He never had any when Pfeifer needed a little spending money. Pfeifer had run outside and crawled under a bush next to the open porch. He'd hidden there, nursing his frustration, until two of his cousins arrived a few minutes later. His grandfather had come outside to sit so Pfeifer was able to hear the entire conversation. One of his cousins asked for five bucks to go buy a new record he'd seen at the local record shop. The old man produced the cash instantly.

From that day on, Pfeifer knew he was alone in the world. He never completely trusted another human being again—not until Melody. He did, however, learn one vital lesson from the experience, and that was the importance of getting even. Nobody was ever going to mess with Pfeifer Biersman again and get away with it. After that fateful Saturday morning, his grandfather never knew what hit him. Pfeifer smiled as he thought about it. Poor old guy. Who would have thought some hoodlum would smash all the windows in his new car?

Crushing the can in his hand, he reached for another, snapped the cap, and and took a deep pull, laughing out loud as his thoughts turned to Quinn Fosh. That old bag of wind must've really thought he was tough today.

Thing was, he didn't know squat about the kind of tough Pfeifer knew. Running a hand along his soldering iron, Pfeifer thought he might just have to arrange a little accident for Uncle Quinn. He wasn't going to put up with that guy's crap ever again.

The sound of footsteps upstairs caused Pfeifer to jump. This time, he knew it was no cat. Grabbing a .45 from the drawer next to him, he slid off the stool and rushed to the base of the stairs, peering up into the darkened kitchen. He could see the back door. It was closed. The shade was pulled over the window, just the way he'd left it. Everything seemed quiet.

Still, he'd heard what he'd heard. Someone was up there all right.

Holding the gun in both hands, he started up. As he reached the kitchen, he eased around the doorway and glanced into the living room. Nothing.

Turning quickly to the hallway, he saw the cat trot out of the master bedroom. Then a noise. A thunk. Then scraping.

Gripping the gun tightly, he flattened himself against the wall and inched toward the half-open door. His breathing grew shallow and heavy. Sweat beaded on his forehead. He'd cornered the guy all right.

Feeling a sudden thrill, he spun around, slammed the door back flat against the wall, and then pointed the gun into the room, waving it from side to side.

The window was open, the curtain fluttering in the breeze.

Pfeifer plunged inside. Cracking open the bathroom door with his free hand, he kicked it all the way in with his boot. The bathtub was empty.

Bursting back out into the room, he checked the closet. Still no sign of life.

His eyes darted to the door and then back to the window.

As he studied it, he saw that someone had cut the screen and then just pushed the window up and climbed through.

Damn.

He'd opened it last night to get some fresh air and then had forgotten to close and lock it this morning before he left for work. He was a big-city kid. He never left doors or windows open. It was just asking for trouble. As he stuck his head outside, he saw a car speeding down the street. It was too far away to get a make.

So, he thought, his body relaxing as he leaned against the wall, had they gotten what they'd come for? His eyes took in the room more carefully this time, noticing that one of the dresser drawers was open. Walking over, he drew it back all the way and looked inside. It was mostly Melody's fancy underwear. It hardly seemed likely that she'd break into the house in the middle of the night just to steal a pair of panties. So, if not Melody, then who?

And more important, what the hell did they want?

14

The Fourth of July dawned hot and humid, with the lake bathed in mist. By evening, the sky was clear, but the temperature had risen into the nineties.

Jane sipped from a can of lemonade as Lyle piloted the Dumonts' pontoon—on happier occasions often referred to as the "party barge"—toward the section of the lake where, in less than ten minutes, the fireworks display would begin. Cordelia sat next to her, munching contentedly on taco chips and bean dip, compliments of Lyle's wife, Carla. The entire Dumont clan, minus Helvi and Eddy Dumont, were on board. Lyle's two teenage sons sat toward the back of the boat, staring sullenly into the dark water.

Jane had spent a good part of the day trying to locate Quinn Fosh, unfortunately, with little success. She wanted to talk to him in person, get a feel for the kind of man he was. She had no doubt that he knew more about Belle's death than he was telling. Ever since his surprise appearance at the reading of the will two days before, he'd become the hot topic of conversation around the Dumont house. Not only had they convinced themselves he was their mother's murderer—though they had no proof—they were also furious that he might have some legal claim on her estate. Emotions were at a pitch.

"Unless they start late, we aren't going to see the opening display very well," grunted Lyle, standing at the wheel and watching the light fade in the west. The comment was directed at both Melody and Anne, who'd arrived late for the ride over to Drumbeater Island. "Where the hell were you two anyway?"

Anne shrugged. "I guess I wasn't watching the time."

"Me either," answered Melody, blowing the question off without even the slightest hint of apology.

Lyle turned around to glare at them. "Well, whatever. We've always watched from the sandbar on Drumbeater, but we'll have to see it from the water this year."

"We'll survive," said Melody under her breath.

Lyle didn't respond. Instead, he said, "Look at that crowd. We haven't got a prayer of finding a space to dock."

In the growing twilight, Jane could see hundreds of people lining the banks of the island as well as many dozens more speedboats, cabin cruisers, rowboats, and canoes all gathered together in the water. On the golf course, hundreds more people were sitting on blankets and lawn chairs waiting for the show to begin. It was a magical sight: kids with sparklers, boats filled with laughing people, the disappearing sunset a luminous peach and pink against an indigo sky. A band had set up near the clubhouse and was playing Sousa marches for the assembled crowd. The distinctly American sound echoed off the boats as it wafted through the sultry night air, creating a sense of festive anticipation.

Cordelia took a long drink of beer then placed a hand over her mouth to stifle a burp. "Did you know that the first time Oscar Wilde ever heard one of Sousa's marches, he threw up?"

"That's ridiculous," said Anne, popping a taco chip into her mouth.

"No, it's absolutely true. It upset his English sensibilities."

"Your mother was English, wasn't she, Jane?" asked Carla.

Jane nodded. "But my sensibilities aren't quite so delicate. I only lived there until I was nine."

"Do you ever think about going back?"

"Sure. Who knows? Maybe I will some day."

"But just for a vacation," added Cordelia, patting Jane's knee. She returned her attention to the boat next to them where a child was holding a particularly large sparkler. "I wonder where I could get one of those," she asked absently, selecting another chip.

Jane tried hard not to roll her eyes. "I think you must have been play-deprived as a child."

"Au contraire, dearheart," she said, examining the chip for imperfections. "I loved it so much, I never wanted to stop. That's why I chose the theatre as a profession." Her cheerfulness fading, she added, "Little did I know what a frustrating puddle I was dipping my playful little toe into."

"Really?" said Anne. "I thought you loved directing."

"She does," said Jane. "She just needs a vacation."

"Some vacation," said Melody from one of the rear seats.

Cordelia gave Jane a look that said she agreed with Melody's assessment but wouldn't pursue it, for *now*. Straightening her turban, the one she'd put together this afternoon out of mosquito netting and fish lures, Cordelia bit down hard on the chip, crunching it a little too loudly for polite society.

Jane got the point. Cordelia wanted to hit the road, wanted to get on with their plans to visit the north shore of Lake Superior. But Jane couldn't leave, not until she'd come to some firm conclusions about what had happened to Belle Dumont. Since there was no real evidence to the contrary, the police had ruled it an accident. But Jane wasn't convinced. Given all the questions she still had, she couldn't just leave to go off and play shuffle-board somewhere. She owed Belle and Helvi much more than that.

Pushing the bean dip closer to Cordelia, she gave her a friendly nudge in the ribs.

"I'm not that easily placated," came the whispered response.

Jane ignored her.

"While you two are here," said Anne, "we should take a midnight swim off the raft."

"What raft?" asked Cordelia.

"We haven't used it in years," said Lyle, his mood growing decidedly more cheerful. "It was pretty beat-up—some of the wood needed replacing. Dad made it for us when we were kids. It's ten feet square. When he moved back here last spring, we spent a couple days repairing it. I'll drag it out some evening. We've got several big inner tubes too. Sometimes we make one of them into a float-ing bar and serve drinks raft-side."

"Sounds fun," said Jane. She couldn't help but notice that Melody had barely spoken since they'd left the dock. Anne seemed concerned as well.

"Want something to drink?" asked Anne, looking over at her sister.

Melody shrugged. "Nah."

"You okay?"

Another shrug. "Why wouldn't I be?"

Anne got up and then sat down next to Melody. "It's okay, Mel. We're all feeling the same way. Death makes normal life seem out of whack. I've spent the last few days thinking everyone's priorities are all screwed up, but really, it's me. I can't judge others just because they want to get on with their lives. I feel guilty that I'm get-ting on with *mine*."

"Helvi and Dad didn't come tonight," said Melody softly. "Maybe I shouldn't have either."

"Everybody deals with loss in their own way," said Carla gently.

Lyle turned around and gave his wife a hard look.

Jane wondered what that was all about. It was almost as if he wanted to cut her off before she could say something he didn't like. Come to think of it, Carla hadn't said much since they left the dock either.

The boat began to slow. Lyle cut the motor as the first of the fireworks began to explode across the night sky. After dropping anchor, he sat back with the rest of the party to enjoy the show.

After a few minutes of annoyingly loud bangs with disappointingly few bursts of color, Jane glanced over her shoulder and saw a lone boat headed their way. It was approaching slowly in the darkness. From this distance, it looked like a bunch of lights bobbing and swaying to the movement of the waves. She watched it for another couple of seconds and then returned her attention to the fireworks.

A few minutes later, feeling the need to stretch, Jane got up. This time she saw that the approaching craft was a houseboat. Colored Christmas lights adorned the top. Realizing she'd seen it before, she grabbed the binoculars from the seat next to her. Sure enough, it belonged to Quinn Fosh. Adjusting the focus, Jane could make out his form sitting in his La-Z-Boy in the front cabin. The screen doors, the ones separating the interior of the boat from the front deck, were open.

"Oh, shit," said Lyle, noticing it too. "We've got company."

Cordelia stood. "Give me those," she said, yanking the binoculars out of Jane's hand.

"What do you suppose he wants?" asked Melody.

"Oh, he's probably drunk as a skunk," said Anne.

Jane tapped Cordelia's shoulder. "Come on. Let me look again."

Cordelia brushed her hand away. "Just wait."

"If he doesn't cut his motor pretty soon, he's going to ram us," said Lyle. "Hey," he shouted, cupping his hands around his mouth. "Move off. You're getting too close."

The boat continued straight for them.

As a new round of fireworks burst over their heads, the eerie light illuminated Quinn's face, making his skin look deathly white.

"He looks spooky," called Tom Dumont. "What's that on his neck?"

Cordelia dropped the binoculars to her side. "I may be way off base, but I don't think he's drunk."

The boat was almost on top of them now. Lyle lunged for the controls and started the pontoon's motor, but it was too late. The houseboat skidded alongside, metal scraping against metal until something under the water locked with a loud crunch and everything came to a dead stop.

The sudden impact propelled Quinn out of his chair. As he rolled forward onto the floor, his captain's hat fell off and an empty bottle of Scotch dropped from his left hand.

Somehow, the two boats had hooked together in the water. They floated together now, almost as one unit.

"Somebody help him," pleaded Carla.

In a flash, Anne jumped over the side onto the front deck. As she bent down to him, her foot slipped on something sticky. She screamed, backing up several steps.

Instantly, Lyle was next to her.

"I think he's dead!" she shrieked, a look of horror crossing her face.

Melody jumped over next. "Try to get a pulse," she ordered. Blood was all over the chair and the floor.

"He must have shot himself," said Lyle, grabbing Melody before she could touch him. A gun dangled off the fingers of his right hand. Lyle held Melody tight, closing his eyes and turning his head away.

Jane caught Cordelia's eye.

"I'll leave the heroics to you," said Cordelia under her breath. "I'm staying put."

Jane leapt over the railing and landed next to Anne. No matter how horrible it was, she had to see it for herself.

Quinn's eyes were open and staring upward as the last of the fireworks exploded across the sky. Part of his head was missing. Jane covered her mouth with her hand, feeling woozy and disoriented as she stared down at him.

"We've got to call the police," declared Anne, her voice rising to a shout. "Somebody, call the police!"

Lyle switched off the motor.

Steadying herself on the rail, Jane stepped around the lifeless body into the small cabin. She wasn't sure yet how her stomach was going to react. As she looked around the cluttered space, her eyes fell to a plastic wineglass on the floor on the other side of the La-Z-Boy. She bent down to take a closer look. It seemed out of place since Quinn had obviously been drinking from the bottle of Scotch before he died. Around the rim she noticed a dry powder. She was about to pick it up when Lyle called, "Nobody touch anything!"

With a guilty look on her face, she straightened up, her eyes taking in the small kitchenette area. It was a mess, yet strangely, her nose picked up a slight whiff of pine cleaner. Quinn obviously did a lot of eating, but very little cooking or washing up. The food he had on board was either canned or boxed. Everything was stuffed together haphazardly in the open shelves, a half-eaten box of crackers resting next to a can of poisonous bug spray. It was a health inspector's nightmare. The counter was covered with cracked and peeling Formica. No wonder most people got food poisoning from eating at home, if home looked like this. Not that Quinn had died of something so outwardly benign.

On the end of the counter near the sink Jane could make out a round, slightly raised white circle. She moved closer to get a better look, but still had no idea what had caused the mark. In the sink she noticed the same whitish powder that was on the rim of the wineglass.

Other boats were pulling alongside now. Voices shouted questions and offered help. Anne, Melody, and Lyle were all moving about the small cabin, wondering out loud if Quinn had any sort of ship-to-shore radio.

A deep male voice called from a distant boat that the police had been notified and would be here in a few minutes. The lake was so glutted with boats, it would take extra time.

As Jane was about to head back outside, she looked down and saw that the wineglass was gone. She stood for a moment, remembering Lyle's admonition not to touch anything. Glancing around the cabin, she saw that it was nowhere in sight. But it couldn't have just disappeared. Other than Jane, the only people on board were Anne, Lyle, and Melody. Catching Anne's eye as she rushed past, Jane lowered her voice and asked, "Did you notice a wineglass over there next to Quinn's chair?"

Anne seemed bewildered by the question. "What wineglass?"

"There was a glass of wine next to his chair. I saw it when I first came in. It had some kind of powder around the rim."

Anne shook her head. "Sorry, but I don't have a clue what you're talking about."

"Me neither," said Melody. She took hold of Anne's arm and together they moved back outside.

Jane touched Lyle's shoulder as he was beating his own hasty retreat. She asked the same question.

"Jesus, Jane. We got a possible suicide here and you're

worried about some stupid wineglass?" He shook his head in disbelief, continuing into the open air.

It wasn't that she was *worried*. She just couldn't imagine what had happened to it. Tucking it away inside her mind for further thought, she stepped out onto the deck herself. The fresh air felt cool and brisk against her flushed face.

As she moved to the railing she saw that in the few minutes she'd been inside, Quinn's houseboat had been encircled by other boats, each packed with eager on-lookers hoping to get a firsthand glimpse of the grisly scene. One of the boats switched on a spotlight, shining it over the deck. Jane held up her hand to shield her eyes from the light.

Once back on board the pontoon, she felt her stomach lurch and then go hollow.

Cordelia was there to ease her down onto a chair. "Are you all right?" she asked, giving Jane her can of beer.

As Jane looked up at the silly Christmas lights on Quinn's boat, hearing hundreds of voices talking all at once, she gave a half nod, feeling Cordelia's arm slip reassuringly around her shoulders. In the distance, a shrill siren was moving slowly toward them. All she could do was close her eyes and shiver.

"He was a vile man," said Carla, her thin, quiet voice strangely potent as it cut through the cacophony of sounds surrounding them.

Jane looked up.

Carla sat on the other side of the deck, her two sons on either side of her. "Do you think it was a suicide?" she asked, her tone a mixture of coldness and calm.

"I don't know."

"I'm not sorry." She waited a moment before continuing. "You probably think I'm terrible to say that, but I don't care."

Others, no doubt, shared her sentiment. Quinn Fosh

was hardly a man whose loss would be mourned. Yet a life had ended. Jane couldn't help but think it had ended for a reason.

As she leaned back against the railing, watching the brightly lit police boat weave its way through the darkness toward them, she had a sinking feeling that the reason had something to do with Belle Dumont.

15

Anne was awakened the next morning by the sound of a ringing phone. She checked the clock on the nightstand next to her and saw that it was seven forty-five. Much too early. No one had gone to bed last night until well after midnight. The phone gave one more jarring ring and then stopped. Either the caller had hung up or someone else had answered it. Perhaps Melody or Helvi had grabbed it downstairs.

Anne knew she'd never get back to sleep. She was too nervous. As soon as her mind switched on, she felt jumpy. Anxious. To be honest, she'd felt this way for months. It was a bad time to decide to quit smoking. Slipping into her robe, she headed for the stairway.

Once downstairs, she followed the smell of bacon into the kitchen. Melody was sitting behind the round oak table, polishing off her last bite of scrambled eggs. She waved her fork in greeting. "Morning," she smiled, emptying her glass of orange juice. "I was starving. Hope I didn't wake you."

"No," said Anne, making no attempt to hide her impatience. "The phone did." She pulled out a cigarette from a pack on the counter, lit up, and then sat down.

"Sorry about that."

"Who was it?" She took a deep drag, feeling herself begin to calm down.

"Who else? Pfeifer."

Anne groaned. "What did he want?"

"I don't know. As soon as I heard his voice, I hung up."

Melody looked positively radiant this morning, Anne noticed. "I thought Jeff Weintz was going to serve him with some sort of restraining order." She drew the ashtray closer.

"Yeah. But I suppose it takes time."

"It can't happen soon enough for me. I'm sick of him calling here at all hours of the day and night."

"No sicker than I am," Melody said.

Anne glanced at the loaf of bread on the counter. She'd just bought groceries yesterday. By the looks of it, Melody had eaten at least four slices. "You sure must have been hungry."

"Famished." She poured herself more milk.

"And you're in an awfully good mood."

"Why shouldn't I be? Quinn's finally out of our hair. And Pfeifer soon will be."

"Don't you feel any sadness about Quinn's death?"

"Oh, please. I never liked him when he was alive; why should I care that he's gone? Besides, who knows what makes someone commit suicide? That was his business. I'm just glad he won't be around to mess up our inheritance." She pushed away from the table. "The idea that he was my uncle made me nauseated."

Anne didn't disagree. "Now we'll never know if he had anything to do with Mom's death."

"Of course he did."

"How can you be so sure?"

"You know what your problem is, Anne?"

"My *problem*? Hey, I thought I was perfect. You're the only one with problems around here." She flicked some ash into the ashtray.

Melody gave her a sickly smile. "Nope. You second-guess yourself way too much. You think or do something and then you're not sure it's right."

"Am I supposed to believe *you* never have second thoughts?"

"Actually, very few. When I make up my mind, that's the end of it."

"And you've made up your mind about Quinn."

"Yup. So has Lyle. He was a horrible man, Annie. He stuck it to Mom and he was about to stick it to us. I say good riddance."

Anne crossed her arms over her chest. "You better say that a little more softly, sis."

"Why?"

"Just . . . try a little discretion for once. It goes a long way."

Melody nodded. "Okay, sure. Say, excuse me a minute. I've got to take care of something. I'll be right back." She raced out of the room.

Anne was a bit startled by her sister's abrupt departure but shrugged it off. As she sat listening to the birds chirping happily out on the lawn, the grandfather clock in the living room chimed the hour.

Eight A.M.

Time for a cup of coffee. Stubbing out her cigarette, she got up and walked over to the cupboards. As she peered out the window over the sink, she noticed that Helvi was outside weeding the garden. That was an odd one. Helvi hated gardening. Anne had never seen her touch a trowel or a spade before. Just like everyone else, Helvi had been up late. Normally, on any given Saturday, she slept in until at least nine. What was so compelling about the garden this morning?

Getting down a mug, Anne poured herself a cup and then stepped out onto the back deck, savoring the soft breeze as it caressed her skin. The air was sweet, perfumed by a grassy fragrance reminiscent of so many summer mornings spent here as a child. Breathing in deeply, she experienced that same mellow, almost bittersweet longing that always touched her when she came home. She wanted to move back, chuck all the stresses and strains of her catering business, and just find something safe and mindless to do for the rest of her life. Now, with the promise of an inheritance, coming home might really be possible.

And yet, even as her senses were seduced by the sight of Pokegama spread out in all its lush beauty before her, that same old pull to succeed, to live life on her own terms, to make her mother proud, and to build a business that reflected *her* thoughts and ideas wouldn't go away. The need for success had always been part of her—probably always would be.

Sure, it was her ambition that had gotten her into her present financial troubles. Because of two new accounts, she'd overextended herself financially. When both went out of business before she could begin servicing them, she was left holding the bag—an expensive bag she had no idea how she'd cover. She was often surprised by the depth of her ambition, occasionally even ashamed of what she'd done to ensure her success. If it weren't for the money she was about to inherit, she would never dig herself out. As much as she was loath to admit it even to herself, her mom's money was going to be her salvation. She needed it and she wasn't going to apologize.

Melody was right. She did second guess herself way too much.

Anne took a sip of coffee and then returned to the kitchen. One more cigarette and she could face the day. As she struck a match, she remembered that Melody had said she'd be right back. So where was she?

Crossing into the hallway, she approached the bathroom door. Inside, she could hear someone throwing up.

"Mel?" she called softly, standing right outside. "Are you all right?"

"Fine. Just go away," came the terse response.

"You're not fine and I'm not going away." She stood her ground.

A few seconds later the door opened. Melody emerged from the dim room wiping her reddened, sweaty face with a washcloth. "I don't know what came over me." Her smile was forced. "I had a couple of funny-tasting hot dogs in town yesterday afternoon. Must be food poisoning."

Anne didn't buy the explanation. "Maybe you should see a doctor."

"No. It'll pass."

"Have you been sick like this before?"

Melody elbowed past her sister into the living room, folding her slender body into a chair. "I'm never sick."

"You were just now."

"Forget it, Anne. See, I'm much better." She opened her arms wide and made a silly face.

Anne shook her head. "Have you been losing weight? You're looking awfully thin."

"You can never be too thin or too rich."

"That's a stupid saying and it's not an answer."

"Oh, come on. Lighten up. You worry too much." She jumped to her feet, balancing on one foot as she took a bow.

The phone gave a sharp ring.

"He's right on time," said Mel, looking over at the grandfather clock. "Every half hour."

"Doesn't that guy have anything better to do with his life?" Anne tossed her half-smoked cigarette into the cold fireplace.

"I think maybe . . . I should talk to him."

"Why?"

"Not talking isn't getting me anywhere. Maybe I can get him to back off."

"I guess you have to do what you think's best," said Anne.

"Give me some privacy, okay?" She sat down on the couch.

The phone continued to ring.

Anne gazed down at her sister, wishing she could do more to help. "You call if you need anything. I'll be right upstairs."

Melody picked up the receiver, mouthing, "Thanks."

"Don't hang up!" Pfeifer sounded angry.

Melody wasn't up for another fight, especially this morning. She took a deep breath and said, "What do you want?"

"First tell me you won't cut me off."

"Just say what you have to say. I'm not making any promises."

His voice almost a whisper, he said, "Did you hear about Quinn Fosh? He's dead."

"I was there, Pfeifer."

Silence. "What do you mean?"

"I was there at the fireworks when he was found."

"Oh. Right." Another pause. "Say, babe." His tone turned conversational. "I hear it was quite a sight."

"Who told you that?"

"A buddy arrived at the scene about the same time as the police."

Melody wasn't aware he *had* any buddies. Pfeifer prided himself on being a loner. He said it meant he didn't need anybody.

"How come you didn't tell me he was your uncle?" he asked, more curious than upset.

"Jeez, how'd you find that out?"

"I have my ways."

She could tell he was smiling. "I just found out myself a couple of days ago."

"I guess it was kind of a blow, huh? Finding out you had an uncle and then losing him right away."

"Yeah. I'm devastated."

He laughed. "Shit, he was *some* nutcase, wasn't he?"

"I guess."

"Hey . . . Mel?"

"What?"

"I miss you."

"Is that why you call every half hour? You're driving me crazy."

"But see, if you'd talk to me once in a while, I wouldn't call so often. The thing is . . . you may not agree with me, but I've decided it's your family that's the problem."

"My family? What's that supposed to mean?"

"They've turned you against me. They never thought I was good enough for you in the first place, remember? It's like . . ." He hesitated. "Well, like they're keeping you a prisoner out there at that lake house."

"Don't be ridiculous." Melody knew how he obsessed over ideas until he blew them way out of proportion.

"I'm ridiculous, huh? I wouldn't call me names if I were you."

There it was again. Always the threat. It's how he'd kept her in line, almost from the beginning. She hadn't understood it at first. And maybe, like he said, she did provoke him. But he had no right to beat her up. She'd spent the last year trying to cover up the bruises so her family wouldn't see. "I'm not going to take that crap anymore, Pfeifer. If you want to know why I left, just think about how many times you hurt me."

Again, silence. Finally, "I know. God, I know." His voice grew low and dejected. "I'm scum. I don't understand what gets into me."

"I don't either, but I'm not living that way anymore."

"But didn't you hear my promise? I'll never do it again, sweetheart. I've learned my lesson. A real man never hurts a woman. I know that now."

A couple years ago, when she still loved him, she bought these pathetic moments of contrition. It was because she wanted to believe him. She needed him in her life. Needed his love. Now she saw his love for what it was. "No more, Pfeifer. You can stuff your apologies. I'm not buying."

"See! It was your mother—especially your mother. And now it's Lyle and Anne. Even Helvi. They're turning you against me."

"*You* turned me against you!"

"Look at the way your brother treated me the day of the funeral. He attacked me!"

"Only after he saw you hit *me*."

"It was just a slap, Mel. I needed to get your attention! Don't you know how much I love you?"

"If this is what love feels like, I don't want any part of it." She heard a loud crack. Then a bang. That was one of his best tricks. Breaking dishes. Tossing furniture across the room. Kicking his foot through the wall. Anything to frighten her, to let her know *she* could be next.

After almost a minute he cleared his throat and said, "I hear you got yourself a lawyer." His voice was remarkably calm.

"You really are spying on me, aren't you?"

"Is it true?"

She hesitated, then said, "Yes."

"You know what? This conversation is getting us nowhere."

"Did you expect that it would?"

"You never even asked me how I am or how the job is going. Don't you care?"

"Pfeifer, get real."

"*You* bailed on this marriage, not me. How can I continue to try to put it back together when you don't show me any respect? The only time you've ever respected me was when I got mean. Maybe I'll have to get mean again."

She felt herself begin to tremble. She hated it when she let him get to her like this. He was crazy. Certifiable. Why hadn't she seen it before?

"It's someone else, isn't it?" he demanded. "You've found another guy. I trusted you and look what you've done!"

"Okay, yes. I've been with other guys. Lots of other guys. The entire Viking offense. But I'm not leaving you for another man. I'm leaving you because our marriage is over!"

More silence.

"Don't count on it, babe," he said finally.

The line clicked.

Melody stared at the phone for a moment and then, woodenly, she hung up. Drawing her knees close to her chest, she curled up on the couch and buried her head under a pillow.

16

Jane propped a note against the sugar bowl, took one last peek at Cordelia, who was snoring away amidst quilts and feather pillows in her bedroom, and then headed outside. Neither of them had gotten to bed until the wee hours of the morning. Even though Jane's sleep had been fitful, she was up early. She wanted to talk to Anne to see if there was any further word about Quinn Fosh's death.

After speaking briefly with the police last night, everyone had sat silently on the pontoon as Lyle piloted it back to the dock. Saying a quick good night, Jane and Cordelia had returned to the cottage, where they spent the next several hours sipping brandy and trying to make sense of the evening. Cordelia had finally dozed off around two, though Jane found sleep far more elusive. She couldn't shake the feeling that something was amiss.

Why would a man who thought he might be on the verge of inheriting a great deal of money take his own life? It didn't add up. And that glass of wine—or whatever it was—on the floor next to the La-Z-Boy? What was that all about? Jane couldn't believe no one else had seen it. But if none of them had, had she hallucinated it? The whole situation made her uneasy. She couldn't quite put her finger on it, but something funny was going on. She was determined to find out what it was.

As Jane climbed the grassy slope up to the main house,

she spotted Helvi on her hands and knees in the garden. The section directly behind her was the picture of gardening perfection.

"Morning," she called as she approached, shading her eyes from the glittering lake.

Helvi's head popped up. "Hello, Jane." She immediately went back to her weeding.

Pausing at the edge of the strawberry patch, Jane said, "Pretty nice day. Perfect for a little yard work." She hadn't been alone with Helvi since Belle's death. Every time they began a private conversation, one of the Dumont kids would appear out of nowhere to join them.

"I despise poking around gardens," said Helvi, blowing a lock of white hair away from her face, "but I've got to keep it the way Belle wants it." Most of her hair was covered by a pink and blue cotton scarf. Jane had seen her wear the same one many times before. She called it her *huevi*, a Finnish word.

"Sure," said Jane, touched by Helvi's devotion to her partner's gardening passion, yet a little perplexed that she'd used the present tense. "I understand."

"Do you? Eddy thinks I'm silly. If I don't like gardening, he says, I should just have it plowed under."

"I think you should do what you need to do."

"Right. Thanks." She yanked at a particularly nasty weed, only getting the top half. "I've hardly had a chance to talk to you since you've come up. How much longer are you and Cordelia staying?"

"Through next Wednesday."

"Good. Why don't you pull one of those lawn chairs over and keep me company?" She pointed.

Jane was delighted by the suggestion. Dragging an Adirondack chair to the edge of the pea patch, she made herself comfortable. "So, how are you doing?" she asked, keeping the question as broad as possible. Helvi could talk, or not talk, about anything she chose.

"About as well as one can expect. Some days I feel like I'm swimming underwater. Everything seems a little off, a little foreign and distorted. If I could just raise my head and breathe in real air, everything would return to normal. But it won't, will it."

It was less a question than a statement of fact. "No," said Jane softly, "it won't."

"I guess we have something in common now. You lost Christine, and I've lost Belle." She looked up, wiping a hand across her eyes.

Jane could see tears. She remembered how close to the surface her tears had been for months after her partner's death.

"Tell me something," asked Helvi, removing a tissue from her pocket and dabbing at her nose. "Does it ever get easier?"

Jane thought about it. "Yes," she said finally. "But the sadness never goes away completely, at least it hasn't for me. I still think about Christine, what she might say or do if she were here. I'll always miss her. But, yes, it does get easier. And you go on."

"That's about what I thought," said Helvi. She sniffed a couple more times and then stuffed the tissue back into her pocket. "Let's talk about something else. This subject is just too . . . hard for me right now."

"Sure," said Jane. Her heart went out to her.

"So how've you been?" she asked, drawing her weed bucket closer. "Dating anyone new?"

Under normal conditions, that was always Helvi's first question. The stab at normality made Jane smile. "Actually, I am. Her name's Julia. I met her last winter and, well—"

"You're in love?"

Jane grinned. "That might be a little too strong a word."

"Does she live in Minneapolis?"

"No, in Bethesda, Maryland. She's a doctor."

"What kind of doctor?"

Jane cocked her head. "You know, I don't recall. I'm not sure she's ever mentioned it."

"But she works in Bethesda?"

"No, Washington, D.C."

"Do you know where? I've got relatives out there. I know the area pretty well."

Jane shrugged. "Not really."

"How about her family? Mother? Father?"

"Her mother died last December. Her dad . . . I don't know that either. She's never talked about him."

Helvi sat down in the dirt, her legs drawn up next to her. "How well do you know this woman, Jane?"

Jane found it an odd question, one that rankled. "Well, as I said, we met last winter. She'd come to Minneapolis to arrange the funeral for her mother. Then, in April, we spent a long weekend together in New York. Took in a bunch of Broadway shows. In May, she came back to Minneapolis for a week. She's thinking of moving her practice back to the Twin Cities. Actually, she got a couple of good offers to join already established practices."

"Is that right?" Helvi knocked some chunks of dirt off her trowel. After a moment she said, "You want some advice?"

Jane was a little surprised by the question. "Sure, I suppose." She shrugged.

Helvi pushed the trowel into the dirt. "I think young people today jump into sexual relationships far too fast. Gay or straight, it doesn't matter."

"I hardly think of myself as young."

Helvi smiled. "To me you are. Once the passion begins, the brain sometimes gets parked in neutral. You find you're sleeping with someone you don't really even know. You may think I'm old-fashioned, Jane, but I'm also right. Friendship is the best basis for lasting love."

"We're friends," Jane said, realizing she sounded a little too defensive.

"I'm glad to hear it."

"You know, Helvi, everybody else in my life is always telling me I'm too cautious."

"Well, just remember, you didn't hear that from me." She winked, then flicked an ant off her pant leg. "May I assume Julia feels the same way about you? Offhand, I'd say you're quite a catch."

Jane looked away. "The jury's still out on that one. But I hope so." She hesitated, then added, "The problem is, I'm the first woman she's ever been with."

"Oh." Helvi's eyebrow arched upward.

"I'm sure you remember what a big deal it was to start thinking of yourself as gay, especially with all the stuff society tries to dump on you."

"She's not comfortable with the label?"

"I think that's a great part of it."

Helvi nodded. "I see. Well, you tell her something from me. We fall in love with a person, not a gender or an ideology, and certainly not a label." She shook her head. "Though, you know, I do have to say that I understand what she's dealing with. As someone who just recently came out herself, I know it's not easy. Bring her up to visit me sometime. Maybe we can compare strategies."

Jane smiled. "Great. I will. She's coming back to Minneapolis in three weeks. Maybe we'll take a drive up here."

"Our door is always open." She resumed her weeding.

"Have you had any repercussions from your announcement at the funeral?" asked Jane.

Helvi pondered the question for a moment. "I really don't know yet. Time will tell. I do know Lyle wasn't happy."

"I'm sorry to hear that."

"Yes, but he'll work it through. It just came at a bad

time for him. He wants to run for political office pretty badly—more than I ever realized."

"Maybe the fact that his mother was a lesbian won't hurt him."

Helvi snorted. "And they think people in small towns are naive."

Since the subject had turned more serious, this seemed a perfect time to ask a couple of questions. "Helvi, I was wondering about something."

"What's that?"

"How well did you know Quinn Fosh?"

She hesitated, tossing Jane a pea pod. "Why do you ask?"

"Well, I thought maybe you already knew that he was Belle's half brother."

"I didn't."

"She never told you?"

Helvi shook her head.

"Why do you suppose she didn't?"

"Well," she began slowly, "I was always aware that there were things about her family she kept secret. I never pried. I assumed it was none of my business. If she wanted to tell me she would have."

"Of course, I understand. But . . . did Quinn visit here much?"

"This past year he stopped by occasionally. Before that, we never saw him."

"What made the last year different?"

Helvi wiped her sleeve across her damp forehead. "Belle invested in his business. At least, that's what she told me."

"What business?"

"His flower growing business." She said the words with distaste.

"I didn't know he raised flowers."

"Not many people did. As far as I could tell, he planted

a few gladioli bulbs in his backyard and then forgot to water them. That was the extent of it."

"But, then, why did Belle invest money?"

"I have no idea." She shoved the trowel angrily into the dirt. "That was last summer. One day he drives up in this rattletrap truck; the next time I see him, he's driving a Cadillac. You tell me what was going on."

Jane shook her head.

"I tried to keep out of it, but that man made my skin crawl. And then, this summer, he's here mowing the grass. We used to have a great lawn service. They'd come once a week, just like clockwork. Quinn could barely get out here every two weeks. Sometimes he'd quit in the middle and leave the grass half mowed. Belle'd finish it. Honestly, Jane, it drove me crazy."

Jane decided to take a chance. "Do you think Belle was paying him off to keep quiet?"

"You mean about him being her half brother? According to what he said at the reading of the will, he didn't know anything about it until the day she died. But then, you can't believe a man like that."

"Would it have been a big deal if people found out he and Belle had the same father?"

Helvi shrugged. "That depends. Belle was a very private person. I doubt she would have wanted her private life to become fodder for public gossip. Sure, she might have paid him for his silence—if he knew. Would that revelation have hurt her real estate business, or her standing in the community? I don't know. Small towns are funny places. It's hard to predict how people might react to something like that."

"Do you think Quinn was blackmailing her?"

"She was giving him money for *some* reason. She wasn't investing in any flower business, that's for sure. But lately, I got the feeling she'd become disgusted with him. I'm not sure why."

"Do you think Quinn had something to do with Belle's death?"

"Of course he did!" Her expression turned cold. "He saw his chance to get his hands on more of her money and he took it. He pushed her down that ravine."

"But he couldn't have known she'd die. She might have just injured herself. Besides, from what I hear, I doubt he would have inherited a penny."

Helvi looked down. "I don't know anything about that. I just know what I know. Belle would be alive today if it weren't for Quinn Fosh."

Jane couldn't argue the point, one way or the other. "Do you know why Belle called that family meeting last weekend?"

She wiped a hand across her eyes, gazing up at the sky. "Yes. I do." She paused a moment and then said, "She was finally going to break her silence and tell the kids and me everything she knew about the Dumont family secret. In a way I think she was relieved."

"But you don't know what it was."

Helvi scowled and shook her head. "I don't. But my instincts tell me it had something to do with Belle's mother, Fanny Adams, something to do with the way she acquired her money back in the early Forties. I've heard various explanations, none of which seem genuine. Quinn had records of child support payments his father had made to her, but that wasn't until Belle was fourteen or fifteen. Fanny had already made her fortune by then and had returned to Earlton to build this house. Quinn thought his father had financed her rather expensive lifestyle with those payments, but that's ridiculous." She sat back in the dirt, a thoughtful expression on her face. "Actually, if you're really interested, there is one woman in town who knew Fanny way back when. She's nearly ninety. If you're curious, you could go talk to her."

"What's her name?" asked Jane.

"Angela McReavey. Belle used to take her daisies on her birthday. I think Angela even babysat Belle's kids when they were small. Last I heard, she was living at Restful Meadows in Earlton. I doubt she knows the full story, but she could fill you in on some of the details of Fanny's early life."

"Is Restful Meadows a nursing home?"

Helvi nodded. "If she's still alive, that's where you'll find her."

"Thanks. I appreciate the tip."

As Jane was about to get up, she saw a dark Lincoln pull into the drive. A woman slid out of the front seat holding a glass baking dish. She looked as if she was in her early forties, with dyed red hair and heavy makeup that stood out, even at a distance, like gaudy neon on a theatre marquee.

Helvi glanced over her shoulder. "Oh, it's Mavis. I wonder what she wants."

"Who's Mavis?" asked Jane, watching the woman stumble toward them. Her spike heals didn't negotiate the grass very well.

"She's a neighbor. Her husband, Hal, is a lawyer. A good friend of Lyle's."

"Good morning, Helvi," called Mavis in a startlingly nasal voice. "I thought I'd bring you by some of my favorite hot dish, the kind with those crispy fried onions on top. I know this must be a hard time for you." She wobbled to a stop directly in front of them.

Helvi stood, brushing dirt off her sweatpants. She took the dish from Mavis's hand. "Thanks, Mavis. I appreciate the thought."

"Oh, Hal and I have been thinking about you *a lot*." She gave a nervous titter then looked over at Jane.

"This is a friend of mine," said Helvi. "Jane Lawless. She's visiting from Minneapolis."

"Really," said Mavis, clearly not interested. "Nice to

meet you." She returned her attention to Helvi. "Well, yes, I was telling Hal just last night that it didn't make one *whit* of sense for you to give that keynote address to the annual Girl Scout luncheon this year. You're *much* too upset by the loss of your . . . of Belle." She cleared her throat.

"Don't give it another thought," said Helvi, handing Jane the casserole. "I've already got it prepared and I'm planning—"

"No, really," insisted Mavis. "We can't have you placing undue pressure on yourself. You've got to take it easy."

"But—"

"Give yourself some psychic *space*, Helvi. I insist. It takes time to get over the death of your . . . of Belle." Again, she cleared her throat.

Jane and Helvi exchanged pained glances.

"In other words," said Helvi, "you'd rather I didn't give the speech. Even if I want to."

"Well . . . yes, I think it would be best."

"Best for who?"

"For you, of course, dear."

Helvi held her eyes. "Who's going to give the speech if I don't?"

"Hal suggested that perhaps I should. I've done public speaking, you know."

"When was that?"

Her eyebrows knit together in thought. "I, ah, did that auction last year out at the Rendahls' farm."

Another car pulled into the drive. It was Lyle's Lexus, followed closely by a squad car. As Lyle and the police chief got out, Mavis saw her chance to make a quick exit.

"I'll call you in a few weeks to see how you're doing. In the meantime, enjoy." Realizing that was the wrong sentiment, she amended her advice to: "I mean, *heal*, Helvi. That's your job now. You must just relax and—"

She looked over her shoulder. "I really have to get going. Hal's expecting me to fix him breakfast. He's just a *bear* in the morning until he has his steak and eggs."

"Poor dear," replied Helvi.

Mavis gave them an uncomfortable wave as she stumbled back up to the driveway. She spoke briefly to Lyle and Dennis Murphy and then got into her car and zoomed off.

"Yuck," said Jane, feeling as if she needed another shower. "That was incredibly icky." She had an almost irresistible urge to drop the casserole into the weed bucket.

"Go ahead," said Helvi, reading her thoughts. "We'll leave it out here for the squirrels."

Jane laughed.

"Well," said Helvi, watching Mavis's Lincoln disappear over the rise, "you wanted to know what the response was to my grand announcement at Belle's funeral. That was it. The first of many such messages, no doubt."

"What are you going to do about the speech?" asked Jane.

"I'm not sure."

"Do you know this Hal?"

"He used to be a student of mine."

From the driveway Lyle shouted, "Helvi, Dennis wants to talk to all of us. It's about Quinn Fosh. I think you should come up to the house."

Helvi reached up and removed her *huevi*. "Come on, Jane. You might as well hear this too."

17

"Morning, Dennis," said Eddy Dumont, walking out of the kitchen eating one of Anne's homemade muffins. "How's that son of yours?"

Dennis's tense expression relaxed a bit. "He's fine, Mr. Dumont." He still sounded like a high school student addressing his English teacher. An English teacher he obviously liked.

"How old is he now?" asked Eddy.

"Nine."

"Great age. I remember when Lyle was nine." He squeezed Lyle's shoulder and then sat down on the couch in the living room.

Melody was examining a magazine as she sat in one of the leather armchairs next to the fireplace.

As Jane and Helvi entered from the porch, Lyle called up the stairs. "Anne? Can you come down for a minute?"

Eddy lifted his feet up on a footstool, making himself a bit more comfortable. "Is this an official visit?" he asked, glancing over at Dennis.

"Afraid so." He placed a hand over his gun.

Helvi sat down next to Eddy while Jane took a chair near the front door. She wanted to be able to listen and watch away from everyone's line of sight.

As Anne came down the stairs, Lyle moved over to the fireplace, resting his arm on the mantel.

Jane assumed he wanted to take up a position of authority, though he didn't look particularly self-confident this morning. His suit was rumpled, and the dark circles under his eyes suggested a man who hadn't slept.

"What's all this about?" asked Anne. She stood near the stairs, not quite coming into the room.

"Dennis has some information he wants to give us about Quinn Fosh's death last night," said Lyle, keeping his voice carefully neutral.

"Sit down, son," said Eddy. "You're making me nervous."

"Yes, sir," said Dennis with a serious nod, lowering himself into the leather armchair next to Melody. He leaned forward. "I'm sorry to be the bearer of bad tidings, but after a thorough examination of the crime scene, we've determined that Quinn Fosh didn't shoot himself, as we'd originally thought."

Everyone was quiet for several moments digesting this new information.

Finally, Eddy asked, "How do you know?"

"Well," replied Dennis, somewhat hesitantly, "the gun was found in his right hand."

"So?"

"Quinn was left-handed."

Eddy leaned back, glancing at Helvi out of the corner of his eye. "Oh."

"It seems apparent that someone wanted it to look like a suicide. Except, they made a small mistake."

"Maybe he used his right hand just that once," offered Melody. "I mean, it's possible, isn't it?"

Dennis shook his head. "We tested both of his hands. There's no evidence that he'd fired a gun recently. The other key point here is the gun itself. We traced the serial number and found that it was stolen recently from a home on Pokegama Lake."

"By the Lake Burglar?" asked Helvi. "The same one who's been doing all the break-ins?"

"We think so," said Dennis, his reddish eyebrows knit

together in concern. "That leaves us with one of two conclusions. Whoever murdered Quinn must have bought the gun from a local fence, or . . . it was the burglar himself."

The Dumonts' faces betrayed nothing other than simple interest.

As Jane sat at the edge of the room watching the scene unfold, she couldn't help but be amazed. Either these people were all completely innocent, or she was witnessing remarkably subtle actors playing their parts brilliantly. Surely they knew the best motive for Quinn's murder belonged to them.

"That brings me to this question," said Dennis, his eyes moving from face to face. "Who might have had a motive to murder Mr. Fosh?"

"I'll bet he made his share of enemies around town," offered Lyle.

"That's for sure," agreed Anne from across the room.

"You may be right," said Dennis. "But I've got to start this investigation somewhere."

"And you've come to start it with us." Eddy Dumont closed his arms over his chest.

"I'm afraid so. I want to ask you all where you were between the hours of seven and nine-thirty yesterday evening. According to one of my men, Quinn bought gas and beer at the Amoco station in Earlton just before seven, so he was alive then. His body was found at approximately ten-thirty. The coroner said he'd been dead a good hour, probably more."

"And you want to know where we all were," said Helvi, her voice stern and disapproving.

"Sorry, Miss Sitala. It's my job."

"Well, job or no job, no one in this family had anything to do with it!"

Eddy placed a reassuring hand over hers. "She's right,

Dennis. Ask whatever questions you want, but you won't find the murderer here."

"Then again, we *are* the most likely suspects," said Anne, moving away from the stairs and walking into the living room.

"Yes," said Dennis. "That's probably true."

"Quinn insisted he had a claim on our inheritance. It was a lot of money. People have killed for much less."

"That's enough," said Lyle.

"Or maybe he murdered our mother. Seems to me revenge is another great motive. What do you think? Greed and revenge? A pretty strong brew."

"Enough!" Lyle's expression had grown hard. "Anne, sit down."

She glared at him. Then realizing everyone was staring at her, she eased into a chair and mumbled, "Sorry. It's not every day I get accused of murder." Her eyes flicked to Lyle and then away.

"You have to understand," said Dennis, folding his hands together in front of him, "I'm not accusing anyone. I'm just here to get a few answers."

Jane felt sorry for the police chief. He obviously didn't want to be here. These were his friends.

"Come on, sis," said Melody. "Let's just answer whatever questions he's got and let him leave. I, for one, refuse to take any of this seriously."

Jane kept her eyes on Anne. She seemed more upset than the others. Was it the first small crack in their nearly perfect act, or was it genuine anger and frustration? No matter what Melody said, Anne seemed to be taking it all *very* seriously.

"All right," said Dennis, lifting a notepad out of his shirt pocket. "This shouldn't take but a few minutes." He clicked the top of his ballpoint pen and then said, "Let's start with you, Mel. Where were you last night between seven and nine-thirty?"

Melody sat back and tried to look casual. "Out near Hill Lake taking pictures. I didn't get back until nearly dark."

"What sort of pictures?"

"I'm interested in nature photography. My husband gave me a camera last year for my birthday. It's become a hobby."

"Did you see anyone, or did anyone see you while you were driving around? Anyone who could verify you were there?"

"Not that I recall."

"Did you stop anywhere?"

She shook her head.

"Not even to buy gas or a snack?"

"No."

He studied her, giving himself a moment to think. "Where are these photographs now?"

"I haven't developed them yet."

"When you do, I'd like to see them."

"Sure. Fine."

"Can you be more specific about when you returned home?"

"It was around nine-thirty. I was supposed to be back earlier so we could take a leisurely pontoon ride over to Drumbeater Island for the fireworks, but I lost track of time. We ended up watching from the water. Lyle bitched about it all the way there." She fluttered her eyes innocently at her brother.

"What about you?" said Dennis, turning this time to Anne.

She cleared her throat, looking uncomfortable. "Well, I took Mom and Helvi's speedboat out around eight."

"Alone?"

She nodded.

"What time did you get back?"

"Oh, probably a few minutes before Mel got home."

"Did anyone see you while you were out on the lake?"

"It was a pretty quiet night. Most everyone was either home barbecuing or had already gathered on the golf course or over on Drumbeater for the fireworks."

"Is that a 'no'?"

"No, I didn't see anyone I knew. A few boats passed at a distance, but I didn't recognize them."

"Can you describe those boats?"

She shook her head. "Sorry. I didn't think I'd need an alibi."

"Where did you go? What part of the lake?"

"I went south out of Queen's Bay, then just drifted for a while. I got as far as Little Nesbitt before turning back. I wanted some time alone to think."

"Would you recognize Quinn's houseboat if you saw it?"

"Sure," said Anne. "Who wouldn't?"

"Did you see it?"

"No."

Next, Dennis turned to Lyle. "How about you?"

"Well, I was home all day with my family. We had a cookout. Around eight-forty-five we all jumped in the car and came out here. As Melody's already told you, I wanted to leave around nine so we could watch the fireworks from Drumbeater. But both she and Anne were late."

"Can your wife verify that you were home all evening? You never left."

"Absolutely."

Dennis made more notes. "Good. Now, can I assume that when you got here, Helvi was home?"

"No," said Eddy, breaking into the conversation. "Actually, Helvi and I had gone for a walk in the woods. We'd decided not to go to the fireworks, so we left the kids a note on the kitchen table."

"What time did you get back?"

"Around nine-fifteen," said Helvi. "I was surprised the kids hadn't already left."

"Did you see anyone on your walk?"

"A few woodpeckers and a squirrel or two," she said. "No humans, if that's what you mean."

"What time did you leave for this walk?" asked Dennis.

"Oh, I suppose around eight," answered Eddy. He gave Dennis a pleasant smile. "We can provide each other with an alibi from five o'clock on, if it comes down to that. Helvi and I were nowhere near Quinn Fosh's boat that night."

"Do you own a boat yourself, Mr. Dumont?" asked Dennis.

"Who'd live on a lake without a boat? Sure, I've got two. A rowboat I use for fishing and a small speedboat."

"Does anyone ever use them besides you?"

"Just my kids."

"But no one used them last night?"

"No."

"You know that for sure?"

"Yes. I do."

"Because if you were gone from your place, you might not have seen one of them take it out."

"They'd never do that without my permission." His voice held no room for doubt.

Again, Dennis nodded. "What about . . . Pfeifer Biersman? Melody's husband."

"What about him?" said Eddy, his voice growing cautious.

"Well, could he have borrowed it?"

"He wouldn't need to," said Melody. "He works for Ringly Marine. He's got access to all their boats."

"Is that right?" said Dennis. He made a note of it. "He's one fellow I'd like to talk to."

"You think he had something to do with Quinn's death?" asked Anne, her tone betraying her surprise.

"I have to cover all my bases." After jotting down a few more notes he said, "Well, I guess that about does it." He looked up and attempted a friendly smile. "I really do appreciate everyone's cooperation."

"No problem," said Melody.

Jane decided it was time to ask a question of her own. She raised her hand to get Dennis's attention and then said, "I was just wondering. When you were examining the boat, did you find a plastic wineglass?"

Dennis shook his head. Returning the notepad to his pocket he said, "I don't remember seeing any mention of anything like that in the report. Why do you ask?"

As Jane was about to answer, she realized Lyle, Melody, and Anne were all staring at her with such venomous intensity, she was nearly bullied into silence. "Well," she continued, focusing her eyes on the police officer and ignoring everyone else, "when the two boats collided, I jumped from the pontoon over to the houseboat to see for myself what was going on. As I was looking around, I was sure I saw a plastic wineglass on the left side of Quinn's chair. It was on the floor, filled about three-quarters full. Oh, and the rim had some sort of powder on it."

"What kind of powder?" asked Dennis.

"I'm not sure. The cabin smelled like someone had just been cleaning with Lysol or some kind of pine cleaner. It didn't make any sense to me because the place was such a pit. Quinn didn't look like the kind of guy who ever cleaned much of anything."

Dennis scratched the back of his neck and thought it over. "Yeah, I remember the smell, now that you mention it. I did find a half-empty can of Ajax powder in the sink. But no wineglass."

"You know," said Lyle, his voice amiable yet faintly

cold, "Jane called our attention to it last night. But I have to tell you, I never saw it. And I was on the boat at the same time she was."

"I never saw it either," said Melody dismissively. "Besides, what possible meaning could a plastic wineglass have?"

It was a good question, thought Jane. One without an answer.

"Sorry I can't be of more help," said Dennis, standing and pushing his hands into his pockets. "Melody does have a point. It doesn't seem like it's of much importance."

Jane might have agreed, except that someone had obviously found it important enough to get rid of—and then lie about.

Lyle moved briskly away from the mantel, clamped a hand on Dennis's shoulder, and walked him toward the front door.

Jane wondered if Dennis realized an end had just been put to any further discussion of the matter.

"Let me know if you hear anything more," said Lyle, holding open the screen.

"I will," said Dennis.

"Nice seeing you again," called Eddy Dumont, waving from the couch. "Hope next time it will be under happier circumstances."

"Me too," said Dennis. He gave them all a quick nod and walked back out to his car.

18

Jane lifted the feather pillow covering Cordelia's face and blew loudly in her ear. "There's a storm coming, Cordelia! Can't you hear the wind? The thunder? You better wake up! Save yourself, Cordelia. Hurry!"

Cordelia opened one eye, looked around the room and then turned over. "Go away."

Undaunted, Jane pulled up a chair, picked up the hot cocoa she'd just made, and sat down next to the bed, blowing the rich aroma toward her friend's nose.

The nose twitched. "What's that?"

"Want some?"

"No. I want to be left alone."

"But what about the storm?"

"There *is* no storm."

"Would I lie to you?"

"Yes."

Jane blew across the cocoa again, this time taking a very noisy sip.

"Didn't you see that sign on the door?" demanded Cordelia.

"You mean the one you stole from the Chicago Hilton?"

"You *did* see it!"

"Cordelia, you had the wrong side faced out. Instead of 'Do Not Disturb,' it said, 'Please Clean the Room.'"

"Well then, why aren't you cleaning it!" She yanked the quilt up over her head.

Jane yanked it back down. "I'm your wake-up call." Another little blow over the cocoa.

In complete frustration, Cordelia sat bolt upright and grabbed the mug. Through clenched teeth she said, "You're ruthless, you know that? Utterly devoid of compassion."

"Because I want you to get up? It's almost ten, Cordelia. Hardly the middle of the night."

She tugged on her black silk pajamas and then took an equally loud slurp. "All right, I'm up. Are you happy now?"

"Extremely."

"Good. I wouldn't want you to be anything less than extremely happy."

"Now, get dressed."

"But I haven't even finished my cocoa yet! I need to *ease* into the day. *Ooze* toward consciousness."

"Ooze all you want, as long as you do it in the car. I want to drive into Earlton."

"Why?"

"I'm hungry. I want to find a cafe that serves gooey caramel rolls and have breakfast."

Cordelia's expression grew wary. "Is this another fairy tale? Like the storm?"

"Actually, there were some pretty big thunderclaps a few minutes ago up at the main house. Even some lightning bolts."

"I didn't hear them."

"You wouldn't have. It all happened inside."

Cordelia gave her a blank look. "I don't know what you're talking about, Janey."

"I'll explain once you're dressed. You can wear those . . . pedal pushers again." Jane gave her a little chuck under the chin.

"They're *not* pedal pushers," said Cordelia indignantly. "And they aren't right for my idiom this morning."

"Really?"

"Yes, *really*. I'm in more of a B-52's, retro-mood today."

"You already know that? You've only been up five minutes."

"I've *oozed* that far."

Jane shook her head. "Just cover your body somehow and I'll meet you at the car."

"You're such a fashion hag. If you didn't look so positively fabulous in those light blue jeans and that snug cotton shirt, I'd be inclined to take you under my wing, show you the haute couture ropes, so to speak."

"Thanks, Cordelia. Just get dressed."

Cordelia flounced into the Coffee Cup cafe half an hour later wearing a floral print cotton housedress, circa the 1950s. Her rather remarkable cleavage didn't go unnoticed by several men sitting at the counter. A woman behind the counter also looked up, catching Cordelia's eye.

As Cordelia jiggled past, she gave the woman a secret wink and then sat down in one of the booths, touching the tip of her little finger to her mouth, smoothing her lipstick.

"Boy, you certainly did get dolled up this morning," said Jane, sliding into the seat across from her. She picked up a menu and began perusing it. "I feel like I'm sitting here with Jane Russell."

"It's my first real chance to mingle with the locals," said Cordelia, flipping her auburn curls behind her back. "By the way, did you notice that women's dress shop across the street?"

"Actually, I didn't."

"Well, it's called Tat's. And it's going out of business. When we're done here, I want to run over and take a look."

"Fine."

Cordelia gazed aimlessly around the room, her eyes

lighting on a series of pies behind the counter. "I wonder if we're too early for lunch. I'm not really in an *egg* mood. Of course, there's always those caramel rolls."

Jane loved cafes. Loved homemade stews, greasy burgers, and fresh-baked pastries. Some of the best food in the world came from cafe kitchens. This place was packed, always a good sign. As she took in the crowded room, she noticed that the woman behind the counter kept stealing glances at Cordelia.

"I think you may have an admirer," said Jane.

"Meaning what?" grunted Cordelia, flipping open the menu.

"The woman behind the counter? She's looking at you."

"Why shouldn't she look at me? I am the quintessence of taste and charm."

"Right."

Cordelia gave the woman a little wave. "She is kind of cute."

"Yes, I suppose she is."

Her eyes dropping to the menu, she asked, "Is she still looking at me?"

"Stop it, will you? I feel like I'm back in high school."

The woman pulled out an order pad and walked over. She eyed Jane briefly and then said, "Morning," to Cordelia.

"Can we order lunch now?" asked Jane.

"Sure. Any*thing*, any*time*."

"Great." Cordelia grinned. "Is your chili any good?"

"It's really hot," said the waitress, grinning back. Her eyes quickly returned to her order pad.

Cordelia seemed to be lost in a private reverie. Then, hesitating, she turned the menu over to the back page.

Jumping into the lull in the conversation, Jane said, "I guess I'd like a cheeseburger. Medium-well. With lettuce, tomato, and lots of fried onions. And I want a m. Chocolate. And *two* straws. Got it?"

The waitress wrote quickly. "Anything else?"

"I'd like some water."

"Okay. And what about you?" She returned her attention to Cordelia.

"I think I'll have the chili. That is, if it really is *hot*." She infused the word with great meaning.

"Oh, it is."

"And some raw onions and sour cream on the side."

She wrote it down.

After she'd scurried away, Cordelia leaned back in the booth and shook her head. "You know what your problem is?"

"No, but I'm sure you're going to tell me."

"You don't know how to flirt."

"I beg your pardon."

"You don't, Janey. You never learned."

"And where does one *learn* how to flirt?"

"You know, you're right. If it's not part of your innermost soul, forget it."

Jane placed her elbow on the table and rested her chin dejectedly on the palm of her hand. "I guess I'm just a failure."

"True."

"I'm doomed to live and die alone."

"Well, I wouldn't go that far."

"No?"

"Well, I mean, you and Christine had a great relationship for ten years. And now you've got Julia."

"True. And you've had a series of short-lived fiascoes."

"Hey!"

"Life's funny, isn't it?"

Cordelia slammed the menu down on the table. "Let's talk about something else, shall we?"

"Sure," said Jane pleasantly. "Whatever you like."

A balding, middle-aged man entered the cafe and took the booth directly behind them. He appeared to be alone as he set his briefcase and an armful of papers down on the Formica tabletop. After a quick perusal of the menu, he pulled out a yellow legal pad and began writing, biting the end of his pen occasionally in thought.

Cordelia drummed her fingers on the table. "So, introduce a new subject. I'm waiting."

"Well," said Jane, "remember what I told you in the car coming over here?"

"About Quinn Fosh? It doesn't surprise me that his death wasn't a suicide. Next topic."

"But what if one of the Dumonts was responsible? They sure seemed jumpy about the wineglass I . . . didn't find."

"Proof of nothing."

"Maybe."

"Besides, what possible meaning could it have?"

That, thought Jane, was the $64,000 question. "I'll know when I find out."

"How wonderfully cryptic. You just love these little puzzles, don't you?"

"Don't be so patronizing. It's not a *little* puzzle. The man suspected of murdering our friend's mother has just been murdered. And one of our friends might be responsible. Doesn't that bother you?"

"Of course it does!"

"Then help me think this through."

"I'm kind of a captive audience, aren't I? Where else am I going to wait for my chili?"

Jane picked up the saltshaker and examined the bottom. "I can't help but wonder about the gun that killed Quinn."

"Why? What about it?"

"The police chief said that it was registered to someone who lived on Pokegama Lake."

The man sitting in the booth behind Cordelia stopped writing and turned his head to the side.

Jane noticed the movement and spoke more softly. "It was stolen."

"By the Lake Burglar?" asked Cordelia. "The one you told me about?"

"That's what the police think. And you know what that means?"

"Enlighten me."

"That means the murderer either bought it from a local fence, or—"

"He and the Lake Burglar are one and the same person." Cordelia's voice had dropped to a whisper.

"Bingo."

"Which is it?"

"I don't know. But wouldn't it be incredible if Quinn somehow found out who the burglar was, and that's why he was murdered?"

"That would mean the Dumonts are off the hook."

"Right. Unless one of them is the Lake Burglar, which I highly doubt."

"But then, why were they all so upset about that stupid wineglass?"

Jane's shoulders sank. "I don't know. That's why we have to do some further snooping."

"I hope you're using the *royal* 'we.' After I peruse that dress shop next door, I intend to spend the rest of the day in the hammock, sipping iced tea and reading Proust."

"Oh, come on. Get real."

"I've read Proust!"

"That's not the book I saw you with two nights ago."

"Well, P. D. James, then. They're almost the same."

As Jane's malt arrived, the man in the booth behind them cleared his throat and stood up. "Excuse me," he said, waiting until the waitress had emptied her tray. "I couldn't help but overhear your conversation."

Cordelia reached for one of the straws, dunked it in the metal malt can, and pulled it toward her. "It's not nice to eavesdrop."

"I realize that," he said apologetically, "but, you see, I'm a reporter for the *Earlton Tribune*. I wasn't actually assigned to cover the Lake Burglar for the paper, but I've been following the case closely."

Jane pulled the malt back to her side of the table, poured half of it into the glass, and then pushed the metal can back toward Cordelia. She might as well give in now. At least she had enough forethought to order two straws.

"Can I join you for just a moment?" he asked, hesitating.

"Sure," said Jane. She was delighted to find someone with direct knowledge of the matter.

"My name's Eli Jensen. I do the gardening column, among other things."

"That sounds pregnant with potential meaning," said Cordelia. She appeared to be deciding whether Jane got more of the malt than she had.

"Oh, no. Really, I'm just a small-town newspaperman."

"Nice to meet you," said Jane, shaking his outstretched hand. "I'm Jane, and this is Cordelia."

Eli adjusted his glasses before pulling up a chair. "I'll get right to the point," he said, folding his hands on the tabletop. "Did I hear you say that the gun used in Quinn Fosh's death last night was stolen by the Lake Burglar?"

"That's my information."

"When was it stolen?"

"Recently. That's all I know."

"That would probably be the Ingram house."

"You really do know your stuff," said Cordelia, dipping her straw into the malt, pulling it out, and then licking the end.

"Well, yes, I guess I do." He gave a self-deprecating little laugh. "Crime is kind of a hobby of mine."

"No kidding," laughed Cordelia. "It's hers too." She pointed at Jane with her dripping straw.

"Really?" said Eli.

"Maybe you could answer a couple of questions for me," said Jane, hoping he was the wealth of information his introduction promised.

"I'd be delighted to help, if I can."

"Great. First of all, how long have these break-ins been going on?"

"A little less than a year. And always on a Friday, Saturday, Sunday, or Monday."

"The *weekend* Lake Burglar," offered Cordelia.

"That's right. And only once a month. Although," he added, "in June, there weren't any."

Fascinating, thought Jane. There must be a reason behind it. "How does he get into the houses?"

"Well, the occupants are invariably gone. It's almost as if he knows when the house is going to be empty. Usually, he just walks in. You may be surprised, but a lot of people around here don't lock their doors. After about the fifth heist, people around the lake started getting smart. That's when he started cutting screens."

"You mean they locked their doors but not their windows," said Cordelia.

He shrugged. "I live on the lake myself and I know I was surprised to find a couple of windows I thought were locked weren't. It's really pretty easy to get into a house if you want to. Some folks have even gone so far as to install high-tech alarm systems. The Lake Burglar wouldn't touch those. He's looking for easy access."

"What does he take?" asked Cordelia.

"Oh, mostly jewelry, cash, cameras, guns. Anything simple to transport or easily fenced. But, interestingly enough, no electronics." He paused, and then asked, "Did I hear you say the police think one of the Dumonts had something to do with these thefts?"

Cordelia was about to respond when Jane said, "If you want to find out what the police think, you'll have to ask them."

"Sure," said Eli. "No problem."

The food arrived.

"Well," said Eli, rising and returning his chair to its former table, "it was nice meeting you both. Do you two live around here?"

"We're just visiting," said Jane.

"The Dumonts?" he asked with thinly disguised interest.

"That's right."

"Well, have a nice stay."

"And you have an absolutely *swell* day," said Cordelia, pulling her bowl of chili closer to her. She smiled up at the waitress, who was already scuttling away.

"Eat up," said Jane, taking a bite of her burger.

"I will."

"No, I mean eat up quickly."

"Why? Are we in some kind of hurry?"

"We have another stop to make."

"We do?"

"That's right, Cordelia. When we're done here, we're going to visit Restful Meadows."

"Heavens," said Cordelia. "Not another graveyard. I refuse to go tramping around any more Civil War sections just because you're fascinated by the stones. You're sick, Janey. Only a friend would tell you that. Besides, I already have an agenda. I want to go look at that dress shop." She chewed her first bit of chili.

"Actually," said Jane, "it is a nursing home."

Suddenly, Cordelia began to wave air into her face. "I'm on fire!" she choked, reaching for her water glass.

"Pretty hot, huh?"

She downed the entire glass. "I'm *dying*," she said, gasping for breath. As she looked up, she saw the waitress smiling at her from behind the counter.

"Poor dear," said Jane, watching Cordelia's face turn bright red. "I think she tried to warn you, but you were too busy . . . flirting." She took another bite of her burger. "Mine's just right. Life's funny, isn't it?"

19

"I'm in the kitchen," called Carla Dumont, hearing her husband enter the house through the front door. The clock on the stove said ten-forty-five. If they hurried, they could still make the eleven o'clock service over at the church. Eight years ago she and Lyle had joined a Seventh-Day Adventist congregation in Grand Rapids. Carla's parents had been Seventh-Day Adventists, and since Lyle didn't have any strong religious opinions one way or the other, it seemed the natural choice for their family. She finished wiping the last of the breakfast dishes and put them away quickly in the cupboard.

As her eyes took in the kitchen, it struck her again how much she loved this house. It was their third since they were married, and the one they'd probably live in until the kids were in college. Lyle loved the white picket fence around the front yard. Carla loved the generously proportioned rooms. She'd decorated it all herself, learning about interior design from the magazines she bought at the local drugstore. Lyle preferred traditional furnishings, while she liked to experiment, mixing the old with the new. More than anything else, she wanted to make the house comfortable for her family. If she did say so herself, she'd succeeded wonderfully.

As she took off her apron, Lyle walked into the kitchen loosening his tie. Without even looking at her, he lowered himself into a chair and dropped his head in his hands.

Carla could tell something was wrong. "What is it? You're upset."

He just sat there, unmoving. Finally, after touching a deep nick on the tabletop, he said, "Quinn didn't commit suicide."

"What do you mean?"

"It was murder, Carla. Someone killed him."

"How . . . how do you know?"

"Dennis told me."

"Is that where you were? With Dennis?"

He nodded.

"But . . . is he positive?"

"Absolutely positive."

She clutched the dishtowel to her stomach, resisting the obvious implications. "Do they know who did it?" She held her breath, waiting for his response.

"No. Not yet."

She sat down at the table, taking his hand in hers. "Tell me what you heard."

He turned his head away.

"Don't shut me out, Lyle, not now."

"I'm not."

"You are. You have been for months."

A subtle change had come over her husband ever since he'd decided to run for public office. Not only was he gone from the house during the day but most evenings as well. And when he was home, he'd begun to put pressure on himself and the rest of the family to be the best they could be. From Carla's standpoint, he'd always been an overachiever, but now he walked around the house giving little pep talks. He called it "taking personal responsibility."

The bottom line was, he was driving everyone crazy.

Lyle pushed away from the table and got up, crossing

to the other side of the room. He seemed to need distance between them before he could continue the conversation. As he leaned against the counter, he said, "What is it you want to know?"

"Everything Dennis told you!"

"Carla, I can't go over all that again, at least not right now. Can't you see how stressed I am?"

And wasn't that just the point? Why should Quinn Fosh's death affect him so deeply? She watched the tight way he held his shoulders, the pinched expression on his face. "I want the truth, Lyle. No more stalling. No more half answers. You saw something on Quinn's houseboat last night, didn't you?"

Instantly defensive, he answered, "What makes you think that?"

"The way you acted when we got home. It was like you were on another planet. None of us were even in the same room with you."

"That's not true."

"It is! The boys wanted to talk about what happened. They were frightened. Confused. But you just went off to your study and closed the door." She paused, lowering her voice. "You know who murdered him, don't you?"

"That's ridiculous."

"Is it? Lyle, listen to me. For the last month, we've almost stopped talking. You come home at night, dead tired. You have a drink, take a shower, and then go to bed."

"I'm sorry if I'm not being a good enough husband."

"Oh, cut it out. You're a wonderful husband. I wouldn't have stayed with you for fifteen years if you weren't. You're exactly the kind of person everyone wants to see win a political office. But you're putting too much pressure on yourself."

"Don't you think I should be the judge of that?"

"No! That's just the point. You don't see what's hap-

pening to you—to us, and the boys. You want us to be
flawless, to be the perfect family. The problem is, Lyle,
this isn't the *Donna Reed Show!*"

"I never wanted it to be."

"No? You even get upset if I go to the grocery store
wearing jeans because it presents the wrong image.
Heaven forbid someone might think I'm sloppy."

"Wear your jeans at home, Carla. When you go out,
just try to look your best. That's what I do."

"Great. What's next? Should I water the grass in a
cocktail dress? Wear an evening gown to clean the
garage? People can't live in a glass house, Lyle. We're a
happy family, a great family for the most part, but we still
have problems. Our sons are teenagers. That's a hard age.
You can't ask them to be something they're not."

"I know that. I'm not insensitive. All I'm asking is
that we just *try* to be on our best behavior. Is that so
unreasonable?"

He wasn't listening. "But . . . but—"

"But what, Carla? Just say what you think."

In exasperation, she shouted, "You want our lives to be
one eternal glass of milk!"

Angrily, he pushed away from the counter. "Oh, just
forget it. Do what you want. Everyone else around here
does."

By the acid in his tone, she knew he was referring to
Helvi. He'd been so upset by what she'd done at his
mother's funeral he still hadn't gotten over it. "You know
what, Lyle? You can't control other people. Helvi had
every right to tell this town about her relationship with
your mother."

"Great. But why did she have to pick now?"

To be honest, Carla did understand. A cousin of hers
was also gay. She remembered her aunt saying that when
Tony had come out of the closet, it had sent the entire
family into it. Over the years, Tony had learned how to

deal with his homosexuality, learned how to be strong and stand up for what he knew was right. Yet his family hadn't had the same kind of chance to learn how to cope with *their* feelings, or with other people's attitudes and opinions. Perhaps she and Lyle should have known the truth would come out one day and prepared themselves for it. Unfortunately, both of them had behaved as if they hoped it would all go away. In the end, maybe they weren't quite as open-minded as they'd always thought.

Lyle stomped into the living room and flipped off the TV set. "No matter what I do, no matter how hard I try to be the kind of man people would want for a state representative, everything around me just continues to cave in." He sat down on the couch, leaning his head back and closing his eyes.

Carla followed him. She sat down and slipped her arm across his shoulders. "I know it must feel like that."

"And now this mess with Quinn Fosh. I'm afraid everyone is going to think I had something to do with his death."

So that was it. "But that's ridiculous, right?"

He grabbed her suddenly and and held her close. "I love you, Carla."

The fierceness with which he said the words startled her. "I love you too."

The back screen door slammed and a moment later, Brad and Tom entered the room. Both were wearing suits and ties.

"Are we going to church?" asked Tom, tugging uncomfortably on his shirtsleeves.

Lyle shook his head, disengaging himself from his wife. "Not today."

"Great," said Brad, charging up the stairs.

Tom hung back. "Something wrong?" he asked, staring at his father.

Lyle smiled. "No, I'm just a little tired. Why don't you

take off your good clothes and put on something more comfortable. It's a nice day. Maybe we should try to get in a couple hours of fishing before dinner. Mom wouldn't mind cooking some fresh fish, would she?"

Carla smiled. "As long as somebody cleans them first."

"Do you really mean it?" said Tom eagerly. "We haven't gone fishing once this summer."

"We haven't?"

Tom shoved a hand into his pocket. "Dad?"

"What?"

"Well, I mean, can you and me go even if Brad doesn't want to?"

"Why wouldn't he want to?"

"Oh, you know. He's kind of busy with other stuff lately. I can't even get him to go swimming at the beach."

"That's silly. What could be that important?"

"Oh, you know. Just stuff."

Lyle looked at Carla, then back to Tom. "Go change your clothes, son. We'll discuss it over lunch."

"Deal." He bolted up the stairs with such energy, one of the carpet pads came loose and landed on the piano bench in the living room.

Lyle and Carla both laughed.

Squeezing Carla's hand, Lyle kissed her tenderly and then held her close again in his arms. "Just be patient, honey. We're all going to be fine. Everything's going to work out just the way we planned."

"And, well . . . I guess I can try a little harder," said Carla, looking up into his warm, dark eyes. Sometimes he reminded her so much of his mother. So intense. And so stubborn.

"Good. Me too." He drew away from her, his expression growing serious. "Listen, before the kids come back down, I have to ask you a big favor."

"What's that?"

"Well, see, Dennis is probably going to ask you if I

was home last night before we left for the fireworks.
You've got to tell him I was."

"But—"

"I know. I was gone for a while. But like I told you, I
needed some time to clear my head. I had a lot on my
mind, so I just drove around. That's all. You believe me,
don't you?"

"Of course I do, but—"

"The thing is, it looks bad if I don't have an alibi.
You've got to provide me with one, honey. I've already
told Dennis I was here all evening with you and the
kids."

He was pushing too hard. Sure, he may not have
wanted to get caught in a lie, but why hadn't he just told
the truth in the first place? "Does everyone else in your
family have an alibi?"

He pulled a couch cushion in front of him. "Dad and
Helvi were out for a walk in the woods. But Anne and
Mel were both off by themselves."

"Aren't they worried?"

"I'm not sure. Mel didn't seem to be."

"Then why are you?"

"It was just a reflex, Carla. Can't you understand? The
words came out of my mouth before I realized what I'd
done. I had nothing to do with Quinn Fosh's death, and I
didn't want there to be even the slightest hint that I might
have gone off alone last night."

But he had. And now he was forcing her to lie about it.
"Lyle, I—"

"Come on, Carla. Please. You have to back me up. You
trust me, don't you? I'm telling you the truth."

She smoothed a lock of black hair away from his forehead. "All right. I'll tell Dennis you were here."

"Thanks," he said, pressing her hand gently to his lips.
"I knew you'd come through for me. I'm going to come
through for you too, Carla. Just wait and see."

20

Pfeifer sat at the workbench in his basement, soldering. He'd been constructing the device since the wee hours of the morning. Now, nearly noon, the lamp next to him was beginning to bother his eyes. He leaned back in his chair and snapped it off, taking a sip from his can of Mountain Dew and relishing the cool semidarkness. A diffused, gauzy light seeped in from around the partially closed door at the top of the stairs. It allowed him a faint view of what he'd just completed.

The sight of it made him smile.

"Mess with Pfeifer Biersman at your own peril," he whispered, picking it up and examining the final connection. It was perfect. Just the message he wanted to send. Maybe the only kind of message the Dumonts could understand.

What the hell was Melody thinking? A restraining order? It was Lyle's doing, Pfeifer was positive of that. Not that every last one of them didn't want to break up his marriage. Especially Belle. But then, she wasn't a problem anymore. Neither was Quinn. And you never know. Maybe another member of the clan would be meeting his or her maker soon. He glanced again at the device, running a caressing finger across the top.

Pfeifer was sick of feeling like one of the Dumonts' poor relations. Assholes. He'd worked his butt off to make a good life for Melody. Could he help it if the job base in this area was getting worse by the minute?

Melody liked the finer things in life. So did he. But it was hard. Too hard, sometimes. Hadn't any of the Dumonts ever made a mistake? Sure, he wasn't proud of everything he'd done in his life. And, to be honest, maybe it was easier around here this last month with Melody gone. He didn't feel that constant pressure to bring home the bread for his woman. Like any other guy, there was stuff he regretted—especially what he'd done to get his ass put in prison. He should never have agreed to help that idiot buddy of his fence all those stolen electronics. But what was the harm? He was paid good money just so they could be stored in an empty bedroom in his apartment. He even fixed a few of them—for a good price too.

Okay, it was stupid. But what was really stupid was getting caught. Even so, he'd done his time. Melody didn't seem to mind. She wasn't like the rest of the family. So what if he read *Playboy* and smoked a few cigars every now and then? It was no one's business but his. Except that the Dumonts were probably having him followed. Yeah, that was it. That's how they found out he wasn't pure enough for their daughter.

Right. Pure. Tell me another.

What was pure about a couple of dykes? He wailed with laughter. Were these people morons or what? Dykes with family values? Morally upright lezzies? Come on.

Not that it mattered. He and Melody loved each other the way normal, healthy people did. They were committed. Sure, he knew she'd married him just so she could have someone to feel superior to. But he understood. Her family had always made her feel lower than shit. She wouldn't even admit it to herself until he pointed it out to her.

When they first met, she was a bartender. A crappy job

for a woman. He remembered asking her why someone so beautiful and bright was working in such a dive. She put him off by saying she was hiding, making it sound like she was in some sort of spy movie. At first, he thought it was just a joke—her way of being mysterious. It was only later that he put it together. She was hiding all right, but from her family, not the police. They were the cause of all her problems. Just like his fucking grandparents. Nothing he ever did was good enough. Mel needed someone to love her unconditionally, and that's what he'd given her. Total acceptance. Well, except for the few times she'd pissed him off real bad. Otherwise he'd been a loving, attentive husband. She had no reason to sleep around.

"Damn her!" he muttered. The thought of another man touching her propelled him out of his chair. He crushed the pop can angrily and then chucked it against the far wall. Damn her to hell! If he ever found the guy, he'd kill him. Maybe he'd kill her too.

He pushed his palms hard against his eyes to get rid of the sickening image and then ran a hand through his hair until he calmed down. Returning to the workbench, he flipped the light back on and then stroked the side of the metal device with his fingertips. The cold smoothness soothed him. This was going to be Melody's wake-up call. No more messing around.

It was time to come home.

21

Jane and Cordelia arrived at Restful Meadows just as Saturday lunch was being served to the residents in the main dining room. A dapper, elderly man sat at a piano in the front, entertaining the diners with old standards and show tunes. With a twinkle in his eye, he welcomed Cordelia as she joined him for the second and third verses of "A Fine Romance," dancing her best Fred Astaire moves across the floor until the final bars when she snuggled down next to him, mussing the crease in his blue serge pants and crooning into his delighted ear, "This is a fine romance."

After all the laughter, clapping and even a few whistles had died down, they collaborated on two more numbers, "Ain't Misbehavin'" and "On the Sunny Side of the Street." Jane watched from the back of the room, an amused smile on her face, as they mugged for the crowd, their two voices blending beautifully, almost as if they'd rehearsed together for years.

Finally, blowing kisses all around, Cordelia gave the man a hug and a peck on the cheek and then glided gracefully over to where Jane was standing. With one final wave, she shoved Jane into the hallway leading to the patient rooms.

"Very entertaining," said Jane, moving quickly down the wide corridor.

"Aren't I always?" Cordelia smirked.

"Well, sometimes you're more entertaining than others. That was top-notch."

"I *am* a professional after all."

"Director," said Jane. "Not entertainer."

Cordelia looked down her nose. "Dearheart, one has to know *all* the territory before one can *command*." She fluffed her hair. "And hey, he was pretty cute, wasn't he? I mean, he wasn't exactly Michael Feinstein, but he had great timing."

"You were Fred and Ginger incarnate."

"You're too kind."

"Don't mention it."

After talking to a nurse and finding out where Angela McReavy's room was located, Jane and Cordelia found her sitting in a wheelchair looking out the window at a group of robins pecking their way across the grass.

Jane cleared her throat and then knocked firmly on the open door.

The woman turned to them, her eyes curious and intelligent behind delicate, rimless glasses. Her hair was white and her skin a faint pink.

"Who are you looking for?" asked the elderly woman, her voice tenuous, almost a whisper.

"Angela McReavy," said Jane, moving farther into the room.

Angela examined them both for several seconds before nodding. "I'm sorry, but my memory isn't what it used to be. If we've met—"

"We haven't," said Jane, holding her backpack somewhat awkwardly in front of her. "I'm a friend of Anne Dumont."

"Annie," she said, her face brightening into a smile. "How is she? I haven't seen any of Belle's children since last winter. They often stop by on my birthday."

Jane wondered if she'd heard about Belle's death. She

hated to be the bearer of bad news. "Would you mind if my friend and I stayed for a few minutes?"

"That would be wonderful," said Angela, pointing a shaky finger at a single orange chair next to the bed. "I'd enjoy the company."

Cordelia ducked back out into the hall and returned a moment later carrying another orange chair.

"My name's Jane. And this is Cordelia."

Angela nodded pleasantly to them both. Then, with some difficulty, she turned her wheelchair around so that she was facing them. After adjusting her skirt over her knees, she reached for a small dish of peppermint candies on the nightstand next to her. "Would you like one?" she asked, holding the dish as steady as she could.

"Thanks," said Cordelia, taking several and popping them into her mouth. "I love hard candy."

"Me too," said Angela, pushing out her lower dentures and then letting them snap back into place. "I used to eat a candy bar every day."

Cordelia did a double take. She waited until Angela wasn't looking and then removed the mints from her mouth, dropping them into a wastebasket.

The loud thunks caused Angela to start. "Excuse me?" she said, her attention returning to Cordelia. "Did you say something?"

"Me? No."

"Would you like some more?" Again, she held out the dish.

Cordelia swallowed hard. "Ah, no thanks. You know, I wonder if I could get in to see a dentist today. My teeth feel kind of . . . well they sort of . . . itch."

"Your teeth *itch*," repeated Angela, a confused look on her face.

Cordelia gave a short nod.

"Well, I'll just put these away until you're feeling better," said the elderly woman, setting the dish back down. Her eyes shifting to Jane, she said, "If you came to tell me about Belle, I already know."

Jane heaved an inward sigh of relief.

"Terrible accident. I was so saddened to hear about it. I wanted to go to the funeral, but—" Angela glanced down at her wheelchair. "It just wasn't possible."

"You knew each other well then?"

"She was a good friend. Did you know I baby-sat her when she was a child? And then when Belle's children were small, I baby-sat them as well. Her mother and I go way back."

"Really?" said Jane. This was great luck. It was just the subject she'd come to talk to her about. "How did you know Fanny Adams?"

"Oh, we worked together back when we were just snips of girls. Fanny was a couple years older than me. Poor dear. She died when she was in her fifties and I just kept on going. Not that you can call my present condition *living*. I think my time's about up."

Jane never knew how to respond when people said things like that. She tried to give an understanding nod but knew it was pretty pathetic.

Angela didn't seem to notice. "Fanny and I worked for the phone company in the early Thirties. It was just the two of us then, sitting in a tiny room. We played a lot of cards. Actually, we handled the entire Earlton area, though it wasn't very large. Fanny was the main operator. I was just part-time."

"Could you listen in on other people's conversations?" asked Cordelia, warming to the topic. At Jane's disapproving stare, she added, "Well, I mean, I'm just curious."

"We weren't supposed to."

"But did you?"

Angela gave a slow smile. "I can't answer for Fanny, but yes, I occasionally overheard a few words. You have to understand," she added quickly, "it wasn't like it is today. If you wanted to talk to someone across town, you picked up the phone and asked Fanny or me to connect you."

Cordelia gave Angela her best this-is-just-between-you-and-me wink. "I'll bet you knew better than anyone else what was happening around here."

"Well," she said, looking very pleased with herself, "I suppose you could say Fanny and I both had our fingers on the pulse of the town. That's how Fanny used to put it."

"You knew *all* the gossip," smirked Cordelia, encouraging her.

She gave a confidential nod.

"Ever hear any gossip about Herbert Fosh?" asked Jane. She realized Cordelia might be on to something here. Not that it was Cordelia's intention to be "on" to anything. She just loved good dish.

"Oh my, no. He was a pillar of the community." She leaned back in her chair and sighed. "You know, I always thought being an operator was kind of a fun job myself. Fanny, on the other hand, hated it. She had some rather grand ideas about what she wanted to do with her life. When I first met her, Belle was just a tyke—probably two or three. We worked together until she left town."

"What year was that?" asked Jane.

"Let me think." Her thin hands drew together in her lap. "Oh, probably around '38, I suppose. It was before we got into the war, I remember that much."

"Why did she leave?" asked Cordelia.

Angela shook her head. "I don't know. I suppose she just felt she could make a better living somewhere else. Somehow or other, she got herself a car. I never understood how she came up with the money for that."

Jane could take a pretty good guess. "Did you know Herbert Fosh was the father of her child?"

"Gracious me, no! Not then. I saw it all in the paper

the other day—all about Quinn Fosh's claim. But there was never any inkling of it back then. If it's even true."

"You don't believe it?" asked Jane.

She shrugged. "I've lived long enough to learn not to believe everything I read. Especially in the *Earlton Tribune*. And as I said, Herbert Fosh was a revered name around this area. His father was an eminent physician, and so was Herbert. Actually, I did see Fanny talking to him now and then, but I never thought anything of it. I guess I figured he was her doctor."

"I'll buy that," said Cordelia under her breath. "I'll bet he just *loved* to play doctor."

"Excuse me?" said Angela. "I didn't hear you. Did you want another mint?" She snapped her dentures again.

Cordelia's eyes grew large. Barely moving her lips, she said, "No thanks."

"Just help yourself when you want one."

Cordelia bared her teeth in an imitation of a smile.

Angela continued. "Quinn isn't a bit like his dad. He has no morals, if you ask me. If he says he has proof Belle was his half sister, then I suppose he does. But if I were Anne, Lyle, or Melody, I'd look at that proof awfully carefully. Who knows what he's up to."

Jane glanced at the folded newspaper next to the dish of mints on Angela's bedside table. "Have you read the paper today?" she asked.

Angela shook her head. "I usually save it until late afternoon, after my nap. Why do you ask?"

"Well," said Jane, shifting uncomfortably in her chair, "I'm sorry to be the one to tell you, but Quinn died last night."

The elderly woman's mouth dropped open. "Land's sakes," she muttered, her eyes darting away and then back to Jane. "How?"

"The police think it was a murder. Someone shot him while he was on his houseboat. Actually, the Dumonts invited Cordelia and me to watch the fireworks with them last night. We took their pontoon out around nine-thirty. About ten-fifteen, I noticed Quinn's houseboat moving in our direction. A few minutes later it hit us."

"How terrible!"

Or ironic, thought Jane. "Yes, it was, although it wasn't moving very fast. Quinn was already dead. Several of us jumped on to see if there was anything we could do. It's funny," she said, hesitating. She picked up the paper and handed it to Angela. Quinn's death was the front-page headline.

"What's funny?" asked Angela, adjusting her bifocals and reading down the column.

"Well, when I was looking around, I saw this plastic wineglass filled with liquid. I don't think it was wine. It was a funny greenish color. Maybe a pine cleaner of some kind. Oh, and the top was covered with powder. Some Ajax was found in the sink, so maybe that was it. But, you know, when I asked the Dumont kids about it a few minutes later, no one had seen it."

Angela seemed to be absorbed by what she was reading. After almost a minute she replied somewhat absently, "Yes, that is funny. It kind of reminds me of something the kids used to do when they were small." She flipped to the next page.

"What do you mean?" asked Cordelia, pushing the dish of mints to the other side of the nightstand, as far away from her as they could get.

"Oh, just that when they were small, they used to make what they called 'Robber's Wine.' Sometimes I'd come into the kitchen after they'd gone to bed and there it would sit—one of their mother's best wineglasses, full of whatever concoction they'd put together. Sometimes it was shampoo and furniture polish. Other times calamine lotion and Bactine. But it always had cleaning powder on the top. God knows why."

Jane was fascinated. "Kids sure do some strange things. But why did they make it before they went to bed?"

"You know, I asked Belle about that once. She said she didn't entirely understand it herself. She'd talked to them about it and they said it was to protect the house from robbers. If a bad man entered the house to steal things he'd see the wine and drink it. Since it wasn't really wine, but poison, he'd die and the house and everyone in it would be safe."

Cordelia began to laugh. "I absolutely love it! What a great idea. I may have to try it myself."

"They didn't do it all the time," added Angela. "But once in a great while I'd see it sitting there on the counter. I always thought it was kind of cute. So did Belle. That's why she never made them stop."

"I wonder what gave them the idea in the first place," said Jane.

Angela snapped her teeth, thinking it over. "Well, I think it started shortly after their father moved out. Belle mentioned once that perhaps it was in response to his leaving. The kids didn't feel as safe when he wasn't there. And then Fanny died right around that same time. Maybe they were frightened by all the loss."

"That makes sense," said Jane, nodding.

"Belle was in a pretty bad state herself back then, nervous and out of sorts. Of course, who wouldn't be? Her mother was dying of cancer and her marriage was coming apart. Lucky for her she had such good friends. And a good lawyer. If life's taught me anything, it's to always make friends with the best lawyer you can find. And Bobby Weintz was the best. He and his wife, Eileen, Fanny, and then me and my husband were pretty close back in the late Forties, early Fifties. Our families used to get together for picnics. The kids all liked each other. If you're interested in finding out more out about Fanny, go talk to Bobby. But don't call him that. He'll know you've been talking to me. I'm the only one who ever dared call him anything other than Robert. He was always kind of a stuffed shirt, if you know what I mean."

Jane smiled. "Where does he live?"

"With his son, Jeff," replied Angela. "Jeff's a lawyer too, just like his dad. I think Jeff inherited the Dumonts as clients. Seems logical. Robert must be in his nineties now, just like me, so you better talk fast. Say—" She stopped, her gaze moving from Jane to Cordelia, and then back again to Jane. "Here I am, talking away. I'm not even sure why you're here, or why you're so interested in the Dumonts?"

"Like I said," answered Jane, "Anne's a good friend of mine. The police aren't exactly sure yet who was responsible for Quinn Fosh's death, but they're taking a hard look at everyone who knew him and had any kind of motive."

"I see," she said, digesting Jane's words. "And that means anyone in the Dumont family?"

"I'm afraid so."

"And since you think they're all innocent, you're trying to help."

Jane felt a pang of guilt. At this point, she wasn't sure what she thought. "Something like that."

"Well, good for you. If I were a little younger, I'd help you myself. Sorry I can't be of more use."

"Oh, I think you've given me another lead," said Jane, rising from her chair.

Cordelia rose as well.

"I appreciate you taking the time to talk to us."

Angela took hold of the wheels on her chair. She snapped her lower dentures loudly several times as she accompanied them to the door. "Where are you off to next?"

"To the drugstore," said Cordelia, giving a silent shudder.

"We are?" replied Jane.

Cordelia gave Angela a parting wave. "I have to go buy a toothbrush."

"You already have a toothbrush," said Jane.

"I need *another*," she snarled. Her face resumed its pleasant smile as she lifted Jane by her sweater and dragged her down the hall.

22

Melody wished now that she hadn't packed the picnic basket quite so full of food. For one thing, it was too heavy to carry comfortably. For another, she had no business eating so much. She sighed, remembering her leisurely stroll down the aisle at the supermarket less than an hour ago. Absolutely everything had looked so good it was hard to decide. Even before she'd left the parking lot she'd eaten an entire package of brownies. God, but she hated herself when she acted like that. At all costs she had to maintain her figure. Her looks were one of the few things she still had going for her.

The plastic handles on the picnic basket dug into the palm of her hand as she trudged through the woods to her father's cabin. It was a good half mile away. If she was lucky, he wouldn't be home. She could just leave him a note and then borrow the speedboat without being subjected to any third degree. She loved his new boat, loved how fast it could go. It was just the tonic she needed after Dennis Murphy's announcement this morning. After Dennis had gone, her father had simply left, taken off without a word. Mel could tell by the look in his eyes that he was angry. She just wasn't sure who he was angry *at*.

Over the years, Melody had witnessed very little of her father's anger. He always tried to deal evenly and fairly with his children. By nature, he was a friendly, laid-back kind of guy, and that's how most everyone saw him. But once, when she was about eleven, she and her brother and sister were staying at his house in town for the weekend. She could still remember the evening. It was hot and sticky, and for some reason, her dad wasn't talking much.

As they were sitting in front of the TV set watching a movie, he'd gotten up and grabbed a baseball bat from the front closet. During a commercial, he'd ducked out the back door. Later, she found out that he'd smashed a neighbor's garage windows. Completely demolished every one of them.

It was never entirely clear to her exactly why he'd done it. No one would discuss it. After he'd paid the neighbor damages and agreed to donate time at the local hospital, it all seemed to blow over. But Melody had never forgotten. Even though no one wanted to admit it had happened—everyone in the family seemed to be ashamed of such a reckless outburst—Melody had formed a new-found respect for her dad. In all the commotion surrounding the incident, somehow, he seemed to sense not only her understanding, but her outlaw approval, and it formed an even stronger bond between them. She and Eddy Dumont were a lot alike. In a family of Dudley Do-Rights, she'd finally found a kindred spirit.

That's why she knew her father wouldn't mind if she borrowed the boat. Even though she didn't always think before she acted, her father loved her. His understanding and acceptance was one of the only parts of her life she could truly count on.

As she got to the edge of the woods, she saw his cabin about thirty yards away, nestled comfortably beneath several large pine trees. If he was home, his car had to be inside the small garage. Hopefully though, he wasn't. She had a key to the front door, and knew where he kept the key to the boat. But first, she'd better make sure the boat was where it should be.

Switching the picnic basket to her other hand, she

made straight for the dock. The day was hot and humid, a repeat performance of the last week and a half. A thin haze clung to the trees along the far shore, making them seem delicate, indistinct, much like an impressionist painting. It was a perfect day to spend on the water. She couldn't wait to feel the wind against her face, her worries set aside for even a few hours.

At the top of the hill leading down to the beach, Melody stopped. Damn. Her father was sitting at the end of the dock, his bare legs stuck like two white sticks into the water. He was reading a book. The boat, in all its inviting sleekness, was just to his left. She could hardly leap into it, start the motor, and zoom off without him noticing. Well, tough. If he had plans to take it out himself, she could still use her mother's boat. This was just more fun.

Slipping on the sand as she made her way down the hill, she shouted, "Hey, Dad. That better be a classic you're reading!" She laughed as she saw him turn around, a guilty smile on his face.

"What a nice surprise," he called.

As she trotted out to the end of the dock, she heard him say, "It warms my heart to see how much you care about literature."

Easing herself down next to him, she said, "So, what's happening?"

"Nothing much." He eyed the picnic basket. "How about you?"

"Well, I was wondering . . . I mean, just on the off chance that you weren't going to use the speedboat this afternoon, I thought maybe I could borrow it."

"You going out alone?"

"Just for a couple of hours. I need to get away. Take a 'time out,' like you always used to say."

He nodded, adjusting his sunglasses. "Sure. That's fine with me. 'Course, you could have used one of your mother's boats."

"Yeah, I know. But I like yours better."

He gave her a knowing smile. "She's great, isn't she? Just like a rocket. I had her up to fifty yesterday with no problems."

"I had her close to sixty once while you were on vacation." Oops, wrong thing to say.

He cocked his head. "You took her out while I was gone?"

She shrugged. "You weren't around to ask and I . . . well, I didn't think you'd mind."

He shook his head. "Melody, what have I always said? You don't use my things without my permission."

She tried on a sheepish smile. "I'm sorry, Dad. Really. I won't do it again."

"See that you don't." Even when he tried to sound gruff, it didn't work. His affection still came through loud and clear. And yet, something seemed to have upset him.

"What's wrong?" she asked, noticing his eyes shift to the rope tying the boat to the dock.

"Nothing."

"Hey, don't kid a kidder."

He hesitated, then said, "You didn't use the boat yesterday, did you?"

"Me? No. Why?"

He reached over and squeezed her knee. "Forget it, hon. I'm probably just getting so old I don't know what I'm doing anymore."

"That's ridiculous."

"Is it?"

"What's going on, Dad? You think someone took it out without asking?"

"Well—"

"Because I didn't. Honestly."

"I believe you. It's like I said, I'm probably just mixed up."

"About what?"

He glanced over at the rope again. "When I tie the boat off, I usually use a knot I learned in the navy. It's kind of unusual. You don't see it much. But when I went to take the boat out about an hour ago, I noticed the knot was a simple hitch."

She shrugged.

"Like I said, don't worry about it. I'm not."

For the next few minutes they sat watching a sailboat round the bend of the island.

Finally, Melody said, "Dad, I've been meaning to ask you something."

"Ask away."

"Well, how come you came back so early from your vacation?"

After positioning his back against one of the dock posts, he said, "Your mother called me."

"Really?" She felt her stomach tighten. "Why didn't you mention it to anyone?"

He shrugged. "Nobody asked."

Not a good answer. "Why'd she call?"

"I don't know exactly. She just said she was worried about one of you kids and thought I should come home."

"I can't believe you'd cut your trip short on the basis of *that*."

"No," he said, his cool blue eyes taking in the far shore, "normally I wouldn't have. But it was the way she said it. I knew it was important."

"Did she, ah . . . say which kid?"

"Afraid not."

"Or anything that might have given you an indication what it was about?"

"Nope." His eyes flicked to her and then away.

Pressing her lips together tightly, Melody continued, "But I suppose you've got a theory."

"Yes, I suppose I do."

"You think she wanted you to come home because of me."

He waited a second before answering. "Yes."

"Because of the divorce?"

"Of course the divorce. What else could it be?"

Her relief was so great, she almost fell backward. Thinking that it was perhaps best to match his serious expression, she said, "I'm sorry, Dad. I failed again."

"It takes two to break up a marriage, honey. And as far as I can see, you tried your darnedest."

"I did."

"I know that. So did your mother."

But her mother had also known something else. From the moment Melody had allowed her secret to slip, she'd regretted it. No matter how badly she wanted a confidant— and her father could easily become that person now—she had to keep it to herself. Still, just as she suspected, her mother was about to spill the beans. That was all she needed. A microscope held directly over her crumbling life. Shuddering, she felt her father's arm slip around her shoulders.

"Everything's going to be all right, sweetheart," he said, holding her tight. "Whatever you need, I'll be there for you. We all will. Pfeifer's no match for this family."

For a brief, contented second, she snuggled into his arms, trying to think positively. It was all such a mess. Even so, she had to keep her emotions under wraps. To her horror, she saw with each passing hour how hard that was becoming. She wanted to tell her family everything, make them understand. Especially her dad. If anyone could comprehend why she'd done what she'd done, he would. But she couldn't. There was too much at stake.

"You take that boat and have a relaxing afternoon," he said, standing and lifting the picnic basket in after her.

"Thanks. I really appreciate it."

"Bring it back whenever you like." He tossed her the key.

Melody started the motor. It purred just as it always did. "I love you, Dad," she called, feeling a sudden need to tell him that.

"I know." He smiled back. "I kind of like you too."

As she sped far out into the lake, watching his form disappear into the hazy summer sunlight, she felt her body quake and her eyes fill with tears, stinging as they drained down her cheeks. Even now, all alone, away from Pfeifer, she couldn't turn off the fear.

All her life, Melody had been force-fed on the importance of family, of sticking together, protecting one another. Strange, but she'd never really understood her mother, never understood why she valued strength so highly. If only she could talk to her now, what a conversation they would have. Melody finally understood. But with that understanding came an overwhelming sadness. Like a woman struggling through a drenching rainstorm, one that wouldn't stop but instead filled up the puddles, then the grass, and finally the roads, if she didn't find higher ground soon, she'd drown.

23

Even though Anne had arranged to take two weeks off after her mother's death, she still had some work that needed her attention. Late Saturday afternoon, she decided to take out the pontoon and float around on the lake while she did a little paperwork. It was the coolest spot she could think of on such a hot day. Also, she had a lot of thinking to do, and to do it she needed to get away from the concerned, otherwise known as *prying*, eyes of her family.

Helvi was still digging in the garden as Anne passed by. She stopped briefly, explaining where she was headed. Since it was now nearly four and she might not get back until sundown, she didn't want Helvi to wait dinner for her. She'd just grab a bite when she got home.

Anne was somewhat perplexed that Helvi seemed so stressed by the weeds in her mother's garden. She appeared determined to make it perfect, almost like a picture, not like a real garden at all. In the past few days, they hadn't said very much to each other. Perhaps, when she got home tonight, she'd suggest they have a glass of wine together. Maybe sit on the screened porch. Listen to the crickets. Thank God Helvi was the one person she didn't have to worry about. She seemed to be dealing with her loss like the good soldier she was. And anyway, Anne had plenty of time to make sure Helvi was all right before she had to leave for the Cities .

Once she was out on the lake, her mind seemed to

wander. No matter how hard she tried, she couldn't make herself get down to business. Finally, after spending a good hour staring blankly at a page of numbers, she shut her briefcase and rose, leaning against the pontoon's railing.

Across from the Dumont house on Queen's Bay were several densely wooded islands. On the west shore of one of them, the smallest, was her favorite swimming beach as a kid. She and her brother and sister would row over in the morning with a picnic basket packed by their mother and spend a good part of the day just lying around on the beach, eating apples and peanut butter sandwiches and playing in the sand. It seemed so ridiculously idyllic as she thought about it now. And so long ago.

Heading the boat into the wind, she set a course straight for Pumpkin Seed Island. Why hadn't she thought of this spot before? If there was any place on earth that represented peace and safety to her, it was there.

As she rounded the north point, she spotted another boat pulled up and beached on the sandbar. It was the exact place where they used to build their sand castles. From the shoreline out to the tip of the sandbar was a good fifty yards. Unfortunately, what was worse than having unwanted company was that Anne recognized the boat. It was her father's.

For just a moment, she considered abandoning her plan. Maybe it was best if she just turned around and went home. She slowed the motor, drifting in toward shore. Hearing someone whistling, she saw a flash of color and then her sister emerge from the woods. She was carrying a picnic basket. She stopped briefly to retrieve a towel from inside, flapped it several times, and then placed it down on the sand, smoothing out the wrinkles.

Anne was instantly annoyed. This was the one day she wanted to be alone, to spend time on the island, and Melody had beaten her to it. "Nuts," she said under her breath.

At that same moment, Mel looked up and saw the pontoon. She whipped off her sunglasses, her expression even more annoyed than her sister's.

Anne waved.

Melody waved back.

Anne plastered on a fake smile.

Melody's smile was equally phony.

"What a surprise," called Anne.

"Yeah. Small world." Melody got up and crossed to the edge of the water. "You coming ashore?"

"That was my plan."

"Well." She seemed to be searching for something to say. "I guess you better drop anchor then."

After making sure the boat was secure, Anne took off her sandals and waded in. The wet sand felt great as it squished between her toes. "You look like you're about to get in some serious sunbathing," she said, nodding to Melody's rather scanty attire.

"Yeah, I changed into my swimsuit—"

"—in the woods," said Anne, finishing her sister's sentence.

They both laughed.

"Just like old times, huh?" said Melody, raising a sarcastic eyebrow. "You showing up to ruin my fun."

"That's how I felt ever since you were born."

"Really. Tell me you didn't just *love* being in charge."

While they continued their verbal jousts, another boat, this time a small rowboat, rounded the south end of the island. In the past hour, the clear blue sky had been replaced by a cloudy one. As Anne looked up, she saw an even thicker bank of clouds moving in. A crack of thunder echoed just over the tops of the trees. She probably should have checked the weather report before she left. It was just the kind of sweltering summer day that easily spawned a storm.

Melody squinted. "Is that Lyle?"

"I think so," said Anne. "That looks just like the blue T-shirt and white shorts I gave him for his last birthday."

"What the hell is he doing here? I feel like I'm in the middle of a freaking Dumont family reunion."

Anne gave her a sideways glance.

Seeing the two boats and then his two sisters, Lyle stopped rowing.

"He's swearing," said Melody, giggling under her breath. "I can just hear him."

Lyle resumed his slow progress toward shore. A few yards out he called, "I hope someone brought the peanut butter sandwiches and apples."

Anne helped him pull the boat up onto the beach.

"What are you two doing here?" he asked, securing the oars.

"We could ask you the same question." Melody smirked.

"I just wanted to spend a few peaceful hours alone."

"Me too," said Anne.

"Me three," said Melody. "Gee, I haven't said that in years."

"Like you miss it," said Anne with a groan.

Mel shrugged. "Well, actually, sometimes I do."

Lyle dragged his boat farther up on the land. "Sorry I interrupted your solitude, but you should see the clouds moving in from the southwest. Forgive me for being a pragmatist, but we better find some shelter fast."

"Where?" asked Melody. She plunked herself down, pulling her legs up underneath her. "Should we go stand under a tree? Come on, Lyle. Even Mr. Corporate Corporate knows better than that. Besides, I'll bet it blows over without a drop."

Anne felt a large splat on her arm. "How much do you want to bet?"

"I have six different deli salads and half a chocolate cheesecake in the picnic basket over there. If it rains, you can have it all."

"How on earth were you going to eat all that by your-self?" said Lyle, his face full of mock astonishment.

Melody gave him a sickly smile. "I consulted my crystal ball before breakfast and saw that you two were going to join me this afternoon. So, being a good hostess, I planned ahead."

Since Mel's eating habits were already a source of some concern for Anne, she didn't respond.

"And what do I get if *I* win?" asked Melody, playfully burying her sister's feet under several inches of sand.

"You won't," said Anne, feeling another raindrop hit her nose. A huge clap of thunder reverberated overhead.

"The wind's dying down," said Lyle, his face growing serious. "Not a good sign."

For the next few minutes, they stood close together near the water and watched the sky turn an ominous yellow-gray. Suddenly, the wind picked up again. A heavy rain began to fall.

"I've never seen a storm come up this fast," said Anne.

"I have," said Lyle, his expression grim.

"What are we going to do?" shouted Mel. She raced back into the woods with the picnic basket, pushing it under a low-hanging bush.

Anne's eyes grew large and frightened as a brilliant bolt of lightning struck a tall, wispy birch at the edge of the woods. It fell just a few feet from her, its branches scraping against her bare legs as she tried to jump away.

Lyle seemed almost frantic. "Here," he shouted, turn-ing the rowboat over. "Crawl under!"

Another flash drew Anne's attention to the pontoon. It was bobbing and dipping in the water, straining hard against its mooring rope. She turned to look for her dad's boat, but it had disappeared completely.

"I'm scared!" cried Melody.

Late afternoon became night as lightning illuminated the far shore.

"Just get under," shouted Lyle. He held the boat up as both his sisters slid under. Squeezing under himself, he said, "We've got to hold on to the seats. If the wind picks this up, we're in real trouble." As he squirmed around, finding a more comfortable position, a brown paper sack fell out of the corner of the boat and landed in the sand, mere inches from Anne's face.

"What's that?" asked Melody.

"It's nothing," said Lyle. With one quick movement, he reached down and pushed it deep into the sand.

Melody huddled close to her sister, eyeing it suspiciously. "It's a bottle, right? What is it? Johnny Walker Red?"

Lyle spit sand out of his mouth. "Jeez, we're not in tenth grade anymore. Just stuff it."

"At least we can die with a buzz," she offered.

"You're such a comic," sneered Lyle.

Anne would have pursued it, but the lightning and thunder were so constant now, she thought Melody might be right. They were all going to die.

Lyle was straining with all his might to hold the boat down. "Keep holding on," he ordered.

"I am!" shrieked Melody.

Anne's heart pounded wildly in her chest. She saw another flash of lightning, followed by a crack of thunder.

"What's that noise?" said Melody through chattering teeth. "It sounds like an airplane. No plane would be flying in this weather!"

Lyle shook his head. "I don't want to know."

Suddenly, an incredibly strong burst of wind slammed the rowboat hard against the ground. Lyle's head was pinned under one of the front seats. Seconds later, the wind picked the boat up, shaking them all like rag dolls and tossing Melody and Anne to the ground. Lyle was the only one who held on.

"God, somebody help him!" yelled Melody. She grabbed his legs, her hands slipping as she fumbled for a grip.

The boat acted like a kite. Before Anne realized what was happening, both Lyle and the boat were swept into the air, Melody hanging on to one of his legs.

"Let go!" cried Anne, trying to wipe the rain out of her eyes. It was a losing battle. "Please!" The roar of the waves was so loud, she could barely hear herself shout.

Another bolt of lightning zigzagged across the storm-darkened sky. About twenty feet away Melody dropped with a loud scream into the water. Lyle waited a few more seconds and then dropped himself. In that short space of time, he was so far out Anne couldn't even see him anymore.

"God," cried Anne. "Lyle! Melody?" She was seized by panic. Her sister wasn't a good swimmer. Even an Olympic gold medalist would've had trouble with those waves. Lyle was stronger, but he was so much farther out.

Anne scrambled to the edge of the sand. The waves were heavy and high. They knocked her down and sucked her under. Struggling with all her might, she tried to lift herself up and out of the water so that she could see what was happening, but the waves slapped her back down, frightening and disorienting her. As she burst into the open air for the third time, she felt someone grab hold of her arm. She reached down and drew up her sister. Feeling incredibly elated, Anne dragged her to shore. Together, they pushed and clawed their way up the sandy beach until they reached the edge of the woods.

"Are you all right?" asked Anne, smoothing back her sister's hair and finding a cut just under her scalp line. They collapsed into each other's arms.

Melody coughed over and over, the sound deep and guttural as she tried to rid her lungs of water. "I think so. But what about Lyle?"

Anne had no answer.

For the next few minutes they sat in dazed silence, watching the tempest blow itself out. Finally, as the sky grew lighter, Anne stood. A steady, gusty drizzle was all that was left of the storm. Even though her legs felt wobbly and weak, she surveyed the choppy water. "I better swim out and look for him."

"No!" cried Melody. "It's still too rough."

"I'm a better swimmer than you are. Just stay here. Don't go anywhere, promise?"

"But Annie!"

"I want to know where I can find you when I get back."

Melody hung on to her sister's hand for dear life. "Lyle's the strongest swimmer of any of us. He'll be fine."

Anne felt sapped and deeply shaken, but she couldn't just wait around and do nothing. "We don't know that. I won't go out far. I just want to look."

"I can't lose you both!" wailed Melody. "Not now!"

"You won't lose either of us. Just do as I say and stay here. If you see a passing boat, try to wave it down."

Melody sniffed, wiping a hand over her nose. "Okay," she said, trying to be brave.

"I love you," said Anne, squeezing her sister's shoulder. "You know that, don't you?"

Melody's face looked raw and scared, but she smiled. "I love you too."

As Anne dashed to the edge of the water, her eyes searching the horizon for her lost brother, she came to an important conclusion. Perhaps it was odd timing, but there it was. She'd been agonizing all day over whether or not she'd done the right thing last night. But now, standing here in the aftermath of a terrible storm, feeling such an intense need for her family to be whole and safe, she knew she had had no other choice.

24

"My uncle Angus would have called that storm a 'gully washer,'" said Cordelia. She was sprawled on the living room couch, examining her fingernails for imperfections.

"I've never heard you talk about your uncle Angus before," said Jane, wiping the last dinner dish. The thunderstorm had come through just as they were finishing their salmon and leek frittata. Since Jane had some free time on her hands, she was experimenting with new recipes.

"Sure. Angus Thorn. My father's brother. He was the black sheep of the family—or as he liked to call himself, for obvious reasons, the black *cow*."

Jane didn't groan, but it was a struggle. "I see where you get your unusual sense of humor."

"I beg your pardon? My humor is entirely of my own creation."

"What did this Angus do for a living?"

"He sponged."

"Can you be more specific?"

"Well," she said, leaping up and straightening the dishtowel over the moose head. "He moved from one relative's house to the next. Since the Thorns are a large and lively family, as you already know, he was on vacation all of his adult life. He said he was a true psychic, long before they became fashionable. He always knew when someone in the family needed him."

"You use the past tense. Is he dead?"

"Oh," sighed Cordelia, "that's just wishful thinking on my part." She pulled the sunglasses out of her hair, stuck them over where the eyes of the moose should be, and then stood back to view her handiwork. "Actually, he wrote a very schmaltzy romance novel in the early Seventies. It was kind of a fluke. Made him a ton of money."

"That's fascinating."

"It was sort of an early *Bridges of Madison County*—without the bridges. He used several lusty poultry barns."

"You're kidding."

Cordelia wiggled her eyebrows. "Read the book."

After wiping off the kitchen counter and shutting the cupboard doors, Jane joined her in the living room with a cup of after-dinner coffee.

"But," continued Cordelia, uncovering the tip of the moose's nose for a more interesting effect, "he spent everything he earned. And since he never felt like writing another lurid masterpiece, he returned to his earlier profession."

"Psychic sponging."

"Exactly. Last I heard, he was staying in Scottsdale with my cousin Ralph and his wife, Darla. I think one of them tried to drown him in the kiddy pool, but he survived."

"Has he ever come to stay with you?"

Cordelia's eyes flicked to Jane with a you've-got-to-be-kidding flutter. "He may be lazy, but he's not stupid."

Jane gave Cordelia a sympathetic nod. "Say, if you want dessert, there's that chocolate raspberry torte I made yesterday. It's in the refrigerator. "

"Don't mind if I do." Her attention returned to the moose. After a moment of intense scrutiny, she removed the sunglasses, whipped off the towel, and then placed the glasses back over the eyes for maximum effect.

Jane nearly choked on her coffee.

"Well, I mean, *really*. The poor thing *is* dead. *We* can't do anything about it now. And it seems cruel to me to keep him in the dark."

"You're such a sensitive soul."

"I know."

Sitting down on the couch, Jane asked, "So, what do you think about all we learned today?"

"You mean our little visit to Angela McReavy?"

"Yes, for starters."

"Well. I suppose you're right. We did learn something very significant."

"And that would be?"

"Never eat hard candy." She said it with a completely straight face.

"Be serious."

"I am!"

"Then just listen for a second. I've been thinking."

"Do tell."

"You're going to think I'm jumping to a rather risky conclusion, but"—she sat down on the couch—"what if that wineglass I saw on the boat last night was Robber's Wine?"

"You mean the stuff the Dumont kids used to make before they went to bed?"

She nodded.

Cordelia thought it over. "Kind of far-fetched, don't you think?"

"Maybe."

"But it's also kind of neat." She began to pace. "I can see it all now. It was a symbol, a way of saying they'd taken care of a bad man. Maybe even a robber."

Exactly Jane's thought.

"Too bad it got lost in the shuffle," said Cordelia.

"It wasn't lost," said Jane. "One of the Dumont kids took it."

"You're sure of that?"

"Positive." She sipped her coffee. "I'm also interested in what that guy we met at the cafe had to say."

"About the Lake Burglar?"

"Right. I think that could be the key here."

"Why?"

"Well," said Jane, walking back into the kitchen to get some cream, "I have a hunch Quinn's murderer and the Lake Burglar are one and the same person."

"Unless Quinn was the Lake Burglar."

"No, I don't think so. The reason he had that new Cadillac was because Belle was giving him money."

"For his flower business?"

"That was just a cover story."

"Then, why? Because she wanted to keep him quiet about their personal connection?"

Jane shook her head. "I don't know. But if what he said at the reading of the will was accurate, he didn't know she was his sister until the day she died."

"But what did they talk about that morning?" asked Cordelia, sitting back down on the sofa and fluffing her hair absently. "In the note Quinn sent Belle, he said he wanted to talk to her about one of her kids. What if one of them was the Lake Burglar and he knew about it? Maybe that's what he was blackmailing her about all along."

"But if that's true," said Jane, opening the refrigerator door to find the carton of cream, "Belle would have put a stop to the burglaries right away. She wouldn't have let them continue for nearly a year."

"True," said Cordelia, her body slumping against a pillow.

A ringing phone interrupted their conversation.

"I better answer that," said Jane, picking up the receiver. "Hello?"

"Jane, is that you?"

At first she didn't recognize the voice. Then, "Julia! What a great surprise." She pulled one of the kitchen chairs away from the table with her foot.

"I called your aunt and she said you'd changed your plans. You weren't staying at Blue Fin Bay after all."

"Yeah, it's kind of a long story." She sat down, unable to keep from smiling. "It's so wonderful to hear your voice."

"Yours too."

"What's up?"

"Does something have to be 'up' before I can call you?"

"No, but it usually is. You haven't changed your plans, have you? We're still on for the last week in July."

"Well, actually—"

Jane could feel the muscles in her neck tighten.

"I do have kind of a problem with that date now."

"Why? You said you had to be back in Minneapolis then to finalize the deal with the practice you're joining. The Millburn Group, wasn't that the name?"

"I know that's what I said."

Jane could see Cordelia creep into her bedroom. She was attempting to give Jane some privacy, though she was probably standing just inside the door. "Has something changed?"

"Actually . . . it has."

"Like what?" She got up and moved to the kitchen window overlooking the lake. A beautiful peach and gold sunset had replaced the threatening sky of a few hours ago.

Julia didn't say anything for several seconds. Finally, she asked, "Why are you making this so hard?"

"Making *what* hard?"

"I, ah . . . haven't even asked you how you are."

"I *was* fine."

"Your aunt sounded all caught up in her wedding plans. I even talked to Edgar for a few minutes."

"Did you? How nice. You're changing the subject, Julia. I don't mean to be pushy, but I wonder if you could tell me what we're talking about."

More hesitation. "Cordelia was right."

"About what?"

"She said that sometimes you reminded her of the Spanish Inquisition."

"What!"

"And it's true, Jane. You do."

"How flattering. You called all the way from Maryland just to tell me that?"

"Oh, don't get upset."

"Why would I get upset? By the way, just for future reference, *when* did Cordelia share this perceptive little nugget with you?" Jane turned around and saw the tip of Cordelia's nose emerge from the bedroom doorway.

"When I was staying with you in May. We were having dinner at your restaurant, and—"

"Never mind." She tapped her fingernails impatiently on the countertop. "Just tell me why you're not coming, and when I can expect to see you."

Another silence. When Julia spoke again, her voice had lost some of its warmth. "I've decided not to accept the offer from the Millburn Group."

Now it was Jane's turn to be silent.

"It just wasn't right for me."

"But you're still moving back to Minnesota, right?"

"I . . . I'm not sure."

Jane felt all the blood drain from her face. "But . . . what about—you know. You and me?"

"We can still see each other. We've got vacations. And Christmas and lots of other holidays."

"We can't build a relationship only seeing each other a few times a year. I thought you wanted—"

"I do," Julia said, with enough urgency and firmness to assuage Jane's fears—at least temporarily. "I don't know where this relationship is going, but I want to keep seeing you."

"Seeing me?" she repeated, giving herself a moment to

regroup. "Then I hope they develop TV-phones pretty fast or I'd say we're sunk."

"You're such a pessimist sometimes, Jane."

"I get it. I'm a *pessimistic* member of the Spanish Inquisition. This gets better all the time."

"Oh, come on."

"Just think for a minute, Julia. You live in Bethesda. I live in Minneapolis. Forgive me, but I see that as a problem." She had to control her frustration. It was beginning to sound less like disappointment and more like anger. Neither emotion was going to take her anywhere she wanted to go. "Just answer one question."

"If I can."

"What's so wrong with the Millburn Group? When you were here in May you were completely sold on them."

Another pause. After several long seconds, Julia said, "Well, I've reevaluated what I want out of my work life. And that's not it."

"Okay. But if you want to be in a group practice, there must be thousands of doctors in the Twin Cities. Why not find another one?"

"It's not that simple."

"Why not?"

"Look, this isn't a conversation we can have right now. I'm expecting an important phone call."

"I thought we were *having* an important phone call." Jane sat back down at the table, resting her head in her hands. Ever since she and Julia had met, she'd had the vague sense Julia wasn't being completely forthcoming about her reasons for wanting to leave Bethesda. There seemed to be holes in her life that she never talked about. As Jane watched her coffee grow cold, she remembered the words Helvi had spoken to her just this morning: *How well do you know this woman, Jane?* Right now, it seemed like a pertinent question.

"Just be patient with me, okay?" said Julia. "You know how I feel about you."

And wasn't that the crux of the matter? Jane wasn't sure. It would be so easy if she could just turn off her emotions. Not care. But when it came to Julia, for whatever reason, her normal reticence and caution simply didn't exist. Helvi was right. She had jumped in way too fast, and now she was paying the price. "When will I see you again?"

"I'm not sure."

She heard a short beep on the line.

"That's my call," said Julia. "I've got to take it."

"Sure. Well. I guess I'll see you around."

"I care about you, Jane. You believe that, don't you?"

She could tell Julia was rushing to get off. She also felt like a dog being tossed a scrap.

"I hate this," said Julia.

"Bye," said Jane.

She hung up.

With one, stupid, five-minute conversation, all Jane's plans for the future had just been torpedoed. She'd probably been crazy to make those plans in the first place. "Cordelia, you can come out now."

Cordelia waited approximately thirty seconds and then emerged from her room, her hair mussed as if she'd been lying in bed.

"Cut the act," said Jane. "You heard everything."

"Moi? I do *not* eavesdrop."

"Sure you do. It's your mission in life."

Cordelia sauntered over and sat down opposite her. "I'm sorry, Janey. That sounded pretty rough."

"It certainly wasn't what I expected. Do you think I'm silly, trying to build a relationship with a woman I barely know?"

"You're asking me?"

Jane sat back and laughed. "True. For a minute there, I forgot who I was talking to."

"Go for it, Janey. Don't hold back. Julia could be the best thing that ever happened to you."

"Or the death of me."

Cordelia took hold of Jane's hand. "Maybe. But if you don't live your life, you're going to die with a lot of regrets."

So, who was the voice of reason? Jane wondered. Helvi or Cordelia?

Again, the phone rang.

Cordelia's expression brightened. "Maybe it's Julia calling to apologize."

Jane had no such illusions. She reached over and picked it up. After listening for a few seconds she said, "Sure. We'll meet you right away."

"What is it?" asked Cordelia, her eyes fixed on Jane's.

Jane replaced the receiver. "It was Helvi. Seems Anne took the pontoon out several hours ago. She's not back yet and Helvi's worried something might have happened to her in the storm. She called Eddy, but he's not answering his phone. And just as she was about to call us, Carla Dumont phoned. She said Lyle hooked their rowboat up to their trailer earlier in the day and she hasn't seen him since."

"Heavens!"

"Helvi wants to take the speedboat and go look for them, but she doesn't want to do it alone."

"What are we waiting for? Time is of the essence!"

"I suppose you're right."

Cordelia gave Jane's arm a small squeeze. "Maybe when we get home, Julia will call back."

"Right." And maybe, thought Jane, the sun will turn purple and fish will fly. This wasn't exactly her idiom, as Cordelia liked to say, but all she really wanted to do for the rest of the evening was wallow in self-pity.

25

Lyle was exhausted. Every muscle in his body ached. As he lay facedown on the end of the sandbar, his breath coming in gulps, he couldn't believe he'd been so stupid. Before he let go of the boat, the storm had carried him a good hundred yards off the beach. Swimming back to shore in the choppy, churning water had felt hopeless at times, the waves like hard fingers grasping at him and pulling him under. But he'd made it. He was alive, and that's all that mattered.

Sitting up, he saw his sisters rushing toward him. He wondered idly if he looked as scared as they did. "I'm all right," he shouted, waving a weary hand.

Both women descended on him, hugging his shoulders and smothering him with tears and cries of relief.

"Are you sure you're all right?" asked Anne, leaning back and examining him visually.

"Fine. Just a little tired."

Melody plunked herself on the sand next to him, wiping the tears away from her eyes. "God I'm glad you're safe. We were just frantic. Anne tried to swim out to find you, but it was no use. We're trapped here. All the boats are gone."

"I can see that." He could also see a lot of tree damage. All the way out to the tip of the point the beach was littered with deadwood. "I guess we'll just have to wait until someone comes to rescue us." The rain had stopped, but the wind was still gusty. Nobody should be out on the lake right now. It would be many hours, perhaps even tomorrow, before it was calm enough for safe boating.

"We may have a long wait," said Anne, her eyes scanning the distant horizon.

"Well," said Melody with a resigned shrug, "at least we have food."

"What food?" asked Lyle.

"I brought that picnic basket. Remember? Believe it or not, it made it through the storm in one piece."

"Hey, all that food belongs to me," said Anne with mock indignation. "You bet it wouldn't rain, Mel. I bet it would. I won."

"But you're going to share, right?" grinned Lyle, tickling Anne in the ribs the way he used to when they were kids.

They all broke into silly giggles, their tension released as they rolled around in the sand, pointing at each other's disheveled appearances and making rude comments.

Finally, Melody leapt to her feet and ran back to the woods where she'd hidden the basket.

"You know," said Lyle, stretching his arms high above his head. It seemed they all felt a little giddy from their near-death experience. "This is kind of like being stranded on a desert island." He pulled his wet shirt away from his body. The wind would dry them all soon enough. "Wouldn't it be nice if we could just stay here for a while? Forget all our problems and just eat and swim and doze on the sand."

"That sounds great," agreed Anne. "And since nobody knows where we are, we may just get our wish."

Melody returned with the picnic basket. "First, before we dig in," she said, settling down next to her brother, "we need to clear up a small mystery."

"No way," said Lyle. He grabbed for the basket. "Food first. Nearly drowning always makes me hungry."

Melody slapped his hand.

"Hey."

"Just wait a sec, will you?" She opened the other end of the basket, reached in, and drew out the paper sack. It was the same one that had fallen out of the rowboat—the one Lyle had buried in the sand.

"What the hell?" He tried to yank it away, but she held it out of reach.

"What do we have here, brother dear?" She smiled coyly as she dangled it enticingly off the end of her index finger. "It can't be a bottle of booze, it's too light."

"Just cut the crap," said Lyle, lunging for it and nearly falling over sideways.

"Give it to him," snapped Anne. "You're both acting like two-year-olds." For some reason, the comment made her giggle.

Melody continued to smirk as she ripped open the top and removed the contents. Her smile faded as she saw what it was. "My God," she whispered.

Anne's eyes opened wide. "Where'd you get *that*?"

"Give it to me," demanded Lyle. He snatched it away, all traces of his good humor gone. "It's none of your damn business." He quickly stuffed the plastic wineglass back into the sack.

"Why'd you bring that thing out here?" asked Melody.

"To get rid of it, why do you think?"

"But . . . why here?"

He squeezed the back of his neck, not sure how much he should say. This was incredibly rotten luck. He'd intended to bury the evidence, alone and without witnesses, and that would be the end of it. Jane Lawless and her prying eyes and her big mouth could go to hell.

"Because," said Anne, answering for him, "this was our favorite place when we were kids. We spent more happy times together on this island than anywhere else. And, unfortunately, Lyle's a sentimental old fool."

"Meaning what?" said Melody.

"Forgive me for being blunt," Anne continued, "but we all know one of us murdered Quinn Fosh."

"What!"

"Oh, cut the act. It's just the three of us here now. We don't need to pretend anymore. How do we all know? Because each of us saw that plastic wineglass on the boat last night. The murderer left a calling card only we would recognize."

After several seconds of uncomfortable silence, Melody said, "Actually, I have to say I thought it was kind of a nice touch. And yeah, I agree with you, Lyle. This is the perfect spot to bury the evidence."

"I'm so glad you approve." His tone dripped sarcasm. Not that he was surprised his sisters knew. "So, now what?"

"It kind of takes your breath away, doesn't it?" said Melody. "To think one of us is a murderer."

"Quinn killed our mother," said Anne, her expression betraying nothing other than coldness.

"We don't know that for sure," said Lyle.

"Sure we do," replied Melody. "And he was about to mess with our inheritance."

"But did he deserve to die?" asked Anne.

"There you go again," said Mel. "Second-guessing yourself."

"Hey! You think *I* did it?"

"Didn't you?"

"She couldn't have," said Lyle. "Because I did."

The two woman gave him appraising looks.

"You admit it?" said Anne.

"Sure."

Melody broke into a slow grin. "That's impossible, bro, because I'm the one who did the deed. Besides, you've got an airtight alibi. Your lovely wife."

"And since I don't have a lovely wife," said Anne,

"you were right the first time, Mel. I admit it—but only to you two. I'm the guilty party."

Melody shook her head. "You know what we're doing, don't you? We're all trying to protect each other, just like we did when we were kids."

"So what if we are?" answered Lyle.

"But I'd like to know who *really* did it," said Melody. "No recriminations. No blaming. I'd just like to know. So, here's the deal. Since we all seem to be having difficulty telling the truth, let's all close our eyes. Whoever is guilty will make an X in the sand in front of them. The other two will make O's."

"Sort of like ticktacktoe," offered Anne.

"Are we agreed?" Melody's eyes moved from face to face.

Anne and Lyle nodded.

"Great. Now, close your eyes and write."

Lyle could sense his sisters' nervousness as they each made their mark. When Melody called time, he opened his eyes.

They all stared at the ground.

"Three X's," said Anne, shaking her head in disbelief. "What's that supposed to mean?"

"We got a couple of liars around here," said Melody, starting to laugh. "I'm sorry," she said, covering her mouth. "I can't help myself."

Lyle removed the wineglass from the package. Part of the cleaning powder was still stuck to the rim. "Okay, even though I appreciate both of you trying to protect me, I'm the one with the glass. I took it because I was afraid one of you would implicate me. I never thought either of you would be on board when the body was discovered."

"No kidding," said Anne absently. She held the glass up to the fading light, studying it with great interest. "I wondered what happened to it."

"But," said Mel, hesitating for just a second, "how do we know for sure one of us did it?"

"Who else knows about Robber's Wine?" replied Anne.

"Nobody," said Lyle. "It kind of narrows the field."

"Actually, as I think about it, that's not true." Anne sat forward, passing the glass to Melody. "Helvi knows. So does Dad."

"I thought of that too," said Lyle, "and I'm absolutely positive neither one would murder Quinn Fosh. It's impossible."

Melody raised a finger. "I agree."

"So I guess we're back to us," said Anne.

"Well, there is one other person I can think of." Melody dropped the glass into the sand. "Pfeifer. I told him about Robber's Wine a couple of years ago. He thought it was a cool idea. We even tried it one night when we were both pretty plastered."

"Without us?" said Anne, her tone aghast and amused at the same time.

"All right, let's say he planted it," said Lyle. "Why? What's his motive?"

"To implicate one of us in Quinn's murder?" offered Melody.

"Does he really hate our family that much?"

"More."

"But why did he murder Quinn in the first place? It's not reasonable to think he'd do it just so that he could blame one of us. After all, that wineglass is a pretty vague clue. He couldn't be sure the police would pick up on it."

"True," said Anne. "And what reason could he have for wanting to murder Quinn?"

"So, we're back to us," said Lyle. "We all wanted to see him dead."

"Well, actually," said Anne, "that's not the same as saying we all wanted to *murder* him."

"True," said Melody, twirling the rim of the glass around in the sand.

After crumpling up the paper sack, Lyle leaned back and said, "You know, I suppose under the circumstances this sounds callous, but I'm starving. Why don't we break out some of that food?"

Melody pushed the picnic basket across to him. She waited until he'd opened one of the salads and then said, "But I'm still confused on one point."

"What?"

"What about the gun?"

"What about it?"

"Well, Dennis said it was stolen by the Lake Burglar. If one of us *did* murder Quinn Fosh, how'd we get it?"

Lyle chewed thoughtfully. "Simple. I bought it from a local fence."

"Right, like you know a lot of local fences." Anne snorted.

"I know one, and that's all I needed."

"Not me," said Melody, shaking her head soberly. "It was Quinn's gun. In a moment of passion I picked it up and killed him with it. End of story. *He* must have been the Lake Burglar."

Anne pulled the picnic basket in front of her and peered inside. "You're all wrong. If you want to know the truth, I'm the Lake Burglar."

"Right." Melody laughed.

"I'm not kidding," she said soberly.

Lyle stared at her. She was a good actress. If he didn't know better, he'd swear she was telling the truth. "You're also not very smart, Annie. How come you left the gun on the boat? Why didn't you try to get rid of it?"

"Do you want the truth, or the lie I was going to tell the police?"

"The truth," said Lyle, "since we're all so good at it."

"Okay. I brought the gun with me that night. I didn't

think anyone would notice the sound of a gunshot because it was the Fourth of July. Firecrackers were going off all over the place. Quinn and I argued. When it was all over, I put it in his right hand—to make it look like a suicide—and then climbed back down to my boat and left. How the hell did I know the guy was left-handed?"

"Fascinating," said Melody under her breath. "You have a vivid imagination."

She shrugged. "So, what are we going to do? We all seem to be the murderer."

"Funny, I didn't see any of you there." Melody grabbed a large chunk of cheesecake and nibbled the edge.

"Well, for starters," said Anne, "we all better keep our mouths shut." She sniffed Lyle's cole slaw but rejected his offer of a bite. "You know what? I think it's disgusting that you two can sit there and eat at a time like this."

Lyle shrugged. "Sorry, but I'm hungry. What about your friend, Jane Lawless? We made a bad mistake with her. We should never have denied seeing the wineglass."

"What's the difference?" said Melody. "She doesn't know shit. Besides, the Robber's Wine is the only physical evidence tying us to the murder. What could she know about that?"

"True," said Anne. "But Lyle's right. Denying that we ever saw the glass looks fishy. Jane's a bright woman. She knows we're lying."

"But she's leaving midweek," said Melody. "And she's got nothing concrete. Besides, who goes around spending their free time solving crimes?"

Anne bit her lip, her eyes dropping to the sand.

"Don't worry about her," said Lyle. "Worry about Dennis. He's the one we've got to convince of our innocence."

They sat silently for a few minutes, watching the sun

set over the west end of the island. The light was growing faint.

Feeling a refreshing breeze ruffle his damp hair, Lyle realized the weather had turned cooler, calmer, much less humid. The storm was over and they were all alive and safe. Watching his sisters now, even after everything that had happened, he felt a curious sense of peace. It was something he hadn't experienced in a long time.

"We need to decide what to do with the wineglass." He held it up.

"What were you going to do with it before Melody and I ruined your plans?" asked Anne.

"Bury it in the sand. Maybe say a short prayer."

She nodded. "Good idea. Let's do it."

Huddling together, they dug a hole. After a moment of silence, Anne pushed it deep into the ground. When it was all done and the wineglass lay buried under the cool, wet earth, Anne looked up at the darkening sky and said, "We're all in this together now. Whoever did it, whatever happened, we need to be strong and take care of each other, just like Mom always said we should."

"Amen," whispered Melody.

Lyle put his arm around his two sisters and drew them close. "You're shivering," he said, looking down at Anne. "Are you cold?"

"Just scared."

"Me too," said Lyle.

"Me three," said Melody.

Glancing back at the water, Lyle felt his body tense. He let go and stood up, squinting to get a better view. "Look out there. Isn't that Mom's speedboat?"

Anne scrambled to her feet and stood next to him. "I think so."

They both began to wave.

Melody continued to nibble on her cheesecake. "I wish we were still kids," she said softly.

"What?" said Lyle. It looked like Helvi on the boat. And Jane and Cordelia.

"When we were kids, the Robber's Wine worked. It protected us from bad men. At least no one ever hurt us."

"God, I wish we had a flare." He began to jump up and down and shout at the top of his lungs.

Anne knelt down next to her. "Maybe it still has some magic left in it."

"I don't believe in magic anymore, Annie."

"Why not?"

Drawing her arms tightly around her stomach she said, "Oh, I don't know. I guess . . . I grew up."

26

It was after one A.M. Pfeifer crept along the grassy hill overlooking the Dumonts' dock, the words to Springsteen's "Thunder Road" pounding in his brain. Melody had worn him down. Blocked him at every turn. If only she could understand him—understand his need for her. But that's what tonight was all about.

The lights in the main house had been turned off now for over an hour. He'd waited in the woods, seeing Melody return with her brother and sister. Helvi and the two guests staying with them were also on board the boat. Pokegama was so choppy they'd had a hard time docking. But the water was quieter now. He'd wondered where the pontoon was, but it didn't matter. It was the speedboat he was after. And there it sat, waiting for him in the cool moonlight.

Pfeifer didn't move until a cloud passed over the moon. Then, erupting out of the brush, he tore across the open yard and down the steps to the dock. Revenge, he thought to himself, was an energizing emotion. This family was a sitting duck, just waiting for an enterprising young man to come along and show them who was boss. *The Boss,* he thought, laughing to himself.

Reaching into his back pocket, Pfeifer removed a headlamp. He slapped it on, adjusting the strap tight around his forehead, knowing he was going to need both hands free to do what needed to be done.

Easing himself down into the rear deck of the boat, he took off his backpack and set it on one of the seats. Switching on the light, he removed the device from the backpack and sank to his knees in front of the motor. This was going to be a piece of cake.

He smiled to himself as he worked, wondering what tomorrow would bring. When Anne or Helvi—or whoever—came down to take the speedboat out, they were going to get one hell of a nasty surprise.

Compliments of Pfeifer Biersman.

27

With a beach towel tucked firmly under his arm, Brad Dumont led the way down to the dock. It was a cloudless Sunday morning. Small whitecaps dotted the windy lake as waves lapped roughly against the shore.

"I told you," said Tom, bringing up the reluctant rear, "I don't think this is such a good idea." He was carrying a small cooler.

"If you want to bail, *bail*," said Brad. "But I'm going." He trotted out to the end of the dock and hopped into the speedboat.

"But what if we get caught?" persisted Tom. He hadn't brought a towel since he knew his brother had no intention of swimming.

"We won't."

"But Dad got really mad at us the last time you hotwired the boat." Tom stayed on the dock and watched his brother take off his shirt.

"Look," said Brad, turning around, "Mom's upstairs going through some of Grandma's stuff. That's why we drove out here this morning. She said she'd be busy for hours. Helvi's in the garden messing with the strawberry plants. Aunt Anne's gone into town, and Aunt Melody's sick."

"Yeah," said Tom, his expression growing serious. "She sounded awful, didn't she?"

They'd both stood outside the bathroom door and listened to her throwing up.

"Exactly. So who's going to see us?" asked Brad.

He had a point.

"If you don't want to stay, just go back and stick your nose in the book you brought."

"I . . . don't know. Maybe . . . maybe I should go tell Mom what you're doing."

"Hey, asshole. Don't mess with me."

"Maybe I will and maybe I won't," said Tom.

Brad jumped out of the seat. "You think you can take *me* on?" He seemed amused by the idea.

Tom wiped a hand across his mouth. "Okay, okay. Just chill, will ya? But . . . I mean, why don't we grab a couple of fishing poles? We could have a great time."

"A great time's what I'm planning, asshole. Besides, fishing's for jerkoffs like you."

"And Dad?"

"You said it, I didn't." He walked over and removed the clips from around the top of the motor. "Hey, what the hell's *that*?" He leaned over and stared at a rectangular object sitting right on top of the carburetor.

"What's what?" asked Tom.

"*That,* asshole," he said, pointing. "I've never seen anything like it before." He touched one of the attaching wires.

"Just start the thing," said Tom, stuffing his hands anxiously into the pockets of his shorts.

Brad glanced over his shoulder. As his gaze moved to the towel he'd brought with him, he said, "Wanna see what I got with me today?"

"No." Tom's eyes bounced away.

"Sure you do. You're just shy. I was too, at first." He sat down casually on one of the rear benches, flipping open the towel to reveal a small metal canister and several balloons.

"Where'd you get it?"

"None of your business. It's just laughing gas, Tommy. Nothing to worry about." He gave an innocent shrug.

"You make it sound like it's cotton candy."

"It is. It can't hurt you."

"Then why are you always hiding it from Mom and Dad?"

Brad narrowed his eyes. "Because it's my business. Nobody else's. Got it?"

Tom nodded.

"You say one word to them and you're dead meat."

"You think you're so tough."

A smile crept around the corners of Brad's mouth. "That's right, asshole. You wanna try me?"

One day, Tom was going to show his brother he wasn't afraid of him. Even though he was. "You're the asshole."

"Just get in the boat. Unless you're too chicken."

How could Tom possibly make his brother understand that he was worried about him? No, it was easier just to stick close. Just in case he got into trouble. "All right. You win."

"I knew you'd see it my way." Brad grinned.

"But I want to drive."

"Fine. See, I can be reasonable."

Before jumping on board, Tom handed the cooler to his brother. As he climbed into the driver's seat, he turned, watching Brad open up a can of Mountain Dew.

"Just wait," said Brad, smirking. "We're gonna have a blast."

Even though Tom hated to admit it, he was curious. He turned back to the wheel, impatient for his brother to start the motor.

Brad sat down on the edge of the boat, quickly finding the two wires he needed. "Blast off!" he called.

"Hey! What are you two doing down there?" Carla

Dumont stood at the top of the hill, hands on her hips, an angry expression on her face.

Tom closed his eyes and cringed.

Brad dropped the wires. "Hi, Mom," he called, waving and smiling as if they'd done nothing wrong. "We thought we'd take the boat out for a little ride." With one quick movement, he moved over and covered up the canister. Then, remaining completely casual, he rolled up the towel.

"You two are in big trouble. Get up here right now."

"But Mom," whined Brad.

"Now. I've already fixed your lunch. When you're done eating it, I want you both to help me carry some things out to the car. We'll decide later whether I tell your father about this or not."

"Shit," whispered Brad without moving his lips. He continued to smile. "Sure thing, Mom. We'll be right up." He turned to his brother. "If you hadn't given me such a hard time, we'd be out on the lake by now."

Tom shook his head. "We probably would have been grounded for the rest of our lives."

"You're such a pathetic little shit, you know that?"

"I thought I was an asshole."

Brad gave him a dirty look as he leapt out of the boat and headed back up the dock.

28

"What's she *doing*, spending every waking moment in that garden?" muttered Cordelia, keeping her voice down. She bobbed along next to Jane, sipping from a can of cream soda.

After a leisurely lunch, Jane and Cordelia decided to take out the speedboat As they reached the dock, Cordelia put her hand on Jane's arm and whispered in her ear, "Just look up there." Her eyes flicked to the top of the hill. "It's like she's standing guard, daring some poor schmuck of a weed to stick its head out of the dirt. It's not normal."

"It's apparently how she's chosen to grieve," said Jane, continuing on to the end of the dock. "The garden was important to Belle. Helvi wants to care for it. Keep it alive. Maybe, in a way, she thinks it will keep Belle alive."

"But she hates gardening. She's always hated gardening."

"I know, but people change."

In frustration, Cordelia crushed the empty pop can. Easing herself down into the back of the boat, she said, "I don't think so. She worries me."

"A lot of things worry me," said Jane. After stowing their gear underneath one of the seats, she hopped into the captain's seat.

"You mean like Robber's Wine," said Cordelia. She

pulled a small bottle of sunscreen out of her back pocket and began applying it liberally to her arms and face. "Are you going to ask Anne about it?"

"First chance I get. If it really was Robber's Wine on Quinn's boat two nights ago, I don't much care for the implications."

As Jane was about to start the motor, Cordelia gave a loud whoop, and then cried, "Is this a vision I see before me? Or some kind of weird time warp?"

Jane had no idea what she was talking about. Turning to look, she saw a woman making her way down the grassy hill toward them. For a moment, Jane wasn't sure she believed her own eyes or Cordelia's. "Is that who I think it is?"

"Unless we're both having the same hallucination." Cordelia removed her sunglasses for a better look. "Yup. Blonde hair. Great body. Expensive threads. And see, she's even smiling, always a good sign. I'll bet you could spot that delicious smile of hers a mile away."

Jane was so stunned, she could hardly speak. "What's going on?"

"I don't know, dearheart, but we're about to find out."

Julia waved as she approached.

Jane waved back, sliding out of the driver's seat and jumping back up on the dock. "I can't believe you're here."

"I didn't know if you'd want to see me." She stopped a few feet away, easing her hands into the pockets of her gray linen slacks.

"Don't be ridiculous," said Jane.

They moved toward each other a bit stiffly and embraced.

Holding Julia at arm's length, Jane asked, "How did you get here? Why?"

This time, Julia's smile was less tentative. As she brushed Jane's cheek with the tips of her fingers she said,

"I couldn't leave it the way we did last night. After our first phone call, I tried again for several hours, but when you didn't answer, I thought maybe I'd really blown it."

"No, of course not."

"Then, why didn't you answer?"

"We had a bad storm here last night. Some friends were stranded on an island, so Cordelia and I helped find them and bring them home. I don't think we got back to the cabin until after midnight."

"Oh," said Julia, looking greatly relieved.

"You could have called to find that out."

"I didn't think you were answering." She took hold of Jane's hand. "We have to talk. In person, not on the phone."

Jane wasn't sure she liked the sound of that. She glanced back up the hill. "Where are your bags?"

"I didn't bring any. I'm only going to be here for four hours."

"Four hours!"

"I got a flight out of D.C. this morning. My travel agent booked a connecting flight to Grand Rapids. When I was on the plane I struck up a conversation with the woman sitting next to me. Seems she knew where the Dumonts lived and offered to give me a lift after we landed. So, here I am. But I've got to be back to the airport by five-thirty. If the planes are on time, I should be home by midnight. I have to work tomorrow."

"But four hours?"

Cordelia cleared her throat. "Hi there. Remember me? Your new tenant?"

"Oh, hi, Cordelia. It's great to see you again."

"I can see that."

"No, really. But . . . what's this about you being my tenant?"

"Have you forgotten Linden Lofts?" she said, fluttering her eyelashes.

Jane cringed at the mention of the name. It wasn't a pleasant memory. Last winter, Julia had inherited an old building in the warehouse district of downtown Minneapolis. The top three floors had been turned into lofts. Jane had stayed there for several weeks, attempting to help an old friend with a problem.

"I've rented 5A," said Cordelia triumphantly.

"Is that right?" said Julia, glancing at Jane and then back to Cordelia. "That's . . . great."

"Yup. I'm moving in at the beginning of August. When Jane and I get home from our little vacation, she's going to help me pack."

"I am?" said Jane. This was news to her.

"Now, both of you, listen up to your auntie Cordelia. Go find yourselves a quiet corner and have that talk."

Jane's smile turned apologetic. "I'm sorry about our boat ride."

"No problem," Cordelia assured her. "I may still take it out myself, or just veg in the hammock. Don't give me another thought."

"Oh, don't worry," said Jane, returning her attention to Julia, "I won't."

"Make yourself comfortable," said Jane, tossing her keys on the kitchen table in the cottage.

"I will." Julia put her hand on Jane's shoulder and turned her around. After a lingering kiss she said, "I missed you."

"I missed you too," said Jane, trying to get her bearings as Julia's fingers caressed the back of her neck. It was hard to concentrate on anything else.

"I wish I had more time here. This place is great."

"It is," said Jane. She felt Julia's hand move lazily down her back, slip under her shirt, and then move slowly back up. "I don't think this qualifies as talking," she said, closing her eyes and giving in to the sensations. Before she could say any more, Julia's mouth covered hers again, forcing everything out of her mind except the moment.

"So, can I assume you didn't fly all the way from D.C. just for *that*?" Jane lay in bed, holding Julia in her arms. The afternoon sun streamed in through a crack in the curtains, striking the dresser mirror and creating tiny prisms of light on the walls of the bedroom.

"Don't sell yourself so short."

"Oh, I'm not. I just think there's more on the agenda here than an afternoon romp."

"Is that all I am to you?"

"What if I said yes?"

Julia looked up into Jane's eyes. "I wouldn't believe you. You're too much of a straight arrow to dally with a girl's affections and then toss her out."

Jane couldn't help but laugh. "A straight arrow, huh?"

"No pun intended."

"This is *so* frustrating. Why can't you move back to Minneapolis in the fall like you originally planned?"

Very gently, Julia stroked Jane's arm. "I can't have this conversation right now. Not here. Not like this."

"Why not?" Jane was more confused than ever.

"Because when I'm with you . . . I don't ever want to leave."

"Is that so bad?"

She sat up. "No. It's just not possible right now."

"Why not?"

She cupped Jane's chin in her hand and gave her another slow, sensuous kiss.

As Jane felt her body respond, Julia said, "Let's get dressed."

"What?"

"I'm starving. I haven't eaten since last night. Let's drive somewhere and have lunch. What do you say?"

"I . . . well, sure. If that's what you want."

"Let's go somewhere nice. Quiet. Where we can talk with a little distance between us."

"That's just our problem, Julia. Too much distance."

"Well then," she said, getting up and beginning the search for her clothes, "we'll work on it over lunch."

Jane decided to drive into Earlton. It was the closest town, and Melody had mentioned that the restaurant at the Fosh Lake Country Club was pretty good. Driving down Main Street, she made a short detour so that Julia could see the hospital complex. One of the new wings was still under construction.

"There it is," said Jane, pointing. "St. Gervais."

"Hey, I've heard of that."

"No kidding." She was a bit surprised. "Well, it's not exactly the Mayo Clinic, but it's got an excellent reputation."

"You bet it has. Pull into the parking lot. I'd like to take a closer look."

Even though Jane wasn't all that enthusiastic about spending time in and around a hospital, she was glad to oblige. "You're here, you might as well see what interests you."

After parking in a lot across the street, they both hopped out of Jane's Trooper and stood looking at the two main buildings.

"This might just be what I'm looking for," said Julia. Her face took on a look of intense concentration.

"Meaning what?"

"Come on." She led the way into the lobby, glancing quickly at her watch. "Listen, give me half an hour. Forty-five minutes max. We've still got plenty of time to have a nice lunch."

"Okay. But what about our talk?"

"Just meet me back here by four."

As Jane watched her walk away, she couldn't help but wonder what was going on. Sitting down in the waiting room, she picked up a magazine but was unable to concentrate. Her head was still spinning from Julia's unexpected appearance. Her eyes bounced restlessly around the reception area. As she was about to get up and go find a drinking fountain, she saw Anne Dumont emerge from one of the elevators. Her gaze fixed directly in front of her, she made straight for the front lobby doors.

"Anne," called Jane. She was the last person Jane expected to see at St. Gervais. "Wait up."

At first Anne seemed surprised to see her. Then, her eyes darting away, Jane noticed that she looked nervous. She fidgeted with her car keys, her expression something less than friendly. "Hi. What are you doing here?"

"A friend of mine from out east stopped by to visit this afternoon. I thought I'd show her the sights."

"Really. And you brought her to a hospital?"

"She's a doctor."

"Oh."

"Hey, are you feeling all right after your ordeal last night?"

Anne's face grew stony. "Ordeal?"

"Getting stranded in the storm."

"Oh, of course. Yeah, I'm fine."

"Good, because there's something I wanted to ask you."

"What's that?"

"I'd like you to tell me everything you know about Robber's Wine."

Her face lost all its color. "What?"

"I see you know the term."

"I . . . I, ah—"

"I've got a few free minutes. I thought you might too."

"Well, I—"

"Because I have a theory. I thought maybe you'd like to hear it."

Anne just stared at her.

"Come on. There's a nice garden area between the two buildings. Let's go check it out."

Jane held the door open as Anne moved stiffly outside.

29

Jane sat down on a wooden bench next to a thick row of pink petunias. She could almost see Anne's mind working, trying to come up with a plausible excuse to extricate herself from this conversation.

"You know," said Anne, sitting down next to her, "I promised Lyle and my dad that I'd help them tow the pontoon back to our dock. Pete Hammond called earlier today and said it had beached itself on his property after the storm."

"Really. I'm glad you found it."

"Yeah, so if this can wait—"

"It can't," said Jane.

Anne's mouth drew into a thin line.

"I need you to tell me about Robber's Wine."

Anne's face often had a rather stern quality to it, but today she looked positively brittle. "I don't know what you're talking about."

"Sure you do. It was something you, Lyle, and Melody invented when you were kids. A wineglass filled with shampoo, cleansers, Bactine, whatever was at hand that you thought might be poison. I understand it was even topped off with cleaning powder."

"Who told you that!"

"Angela McReavy."

"Angela?" she repeated. She seemed to be putting it together in her mind. "You went to see her?"

222

Jane nodded.

"But why?"

"Look, I'm sorry if it seems like I'm prying, but I cared about your mother too. I know the police think it was an accident, but I'm not so sure."

Anne looked away, her eyes rising to the top of the far building.

"You know a whole lot more than you're telling me, don't you?" said Jane.

"But why Robber's Wine?" asked Anne. "It has absolutely nothing to do with my mother's death."

"All right. I can't argue that. But it does have something to do with Quinn's. It was Robber's Wine I saw on the boat the night Quinn died, wasn't it? It fits the description perfectly. My guess is that it was some sort of gesture. A symbol. Whoever put it there did so with complete confidence it would have no meaning to anyone other than the Dumont family. If you hadn't lied about it, Anne, I might never have realized its importance. But you did lie. You all lied."

Anne's eyes dropped to the ground in front of her. "I told them. It was just like waving a red flag under a bull's nose."

Jane was a bit taken aback by the analogy, not that it didn't have a certain ring of truth. "It *was* Robber's Wine then?"

Anne gave a grudging nod. "I suppose there's no point in denying it any longer. But that doesn't mean someone in my family murdered him."

"Then who put it there?" asked Jane. "Who else even knew about it?"

"Well, Pfeifer, for one."

"Melody's husband?"

"Exactly. He hates our family. He'd do anything to smear us."

"But—" Jane's mind raced as she thought it through.

"Since the police had no way of knowing what the plastic wineglass meant, it wouldn't incriminate anyone. It just looked like the rest of the junk on Quinn's boat. A little hard to explain, perhaps, but of no particular significance to the murder. And even if the police did think it looked suspicious, how could they hope to make sense of it? Only your family recognized it for what it was, and certainly none of you would talk."

"Pfeifer was going to tell them."

"But how could he without incriminating himself? After all, he wasn't on the boat that night, unless he *was* the murderer. He couldn't exactly walk in and say, 'Oh, by the way, did you notice a wineglass filled with strange stuff on the floor next to Quinn's dead body? One of the Dumonts left it after they shot him.' "

Anne put her head in her hands. "He did it, I know he did."

"But why? He must have had an independent reason for wanting to hurt Quinn. What was it?"

"I don't know!" She ran a hand over her eyes. "This is such a mess. All I know for sure is that no one in my family is capable of murder."

It was such a naive statement, but Jane let it pass. "Look, Anne, I know this is hard. It's been hard for me too. I've tried to put it all out of my mind and just have a normal, relaxing vacation, but it won't go away. It keeps eating at me. The thing is, if what you say is true, then it's all the more reason the evidence should be examined carefully."

Anne leaned back in the seat. She seemed to be thinking. After a moment she said, "What do you want to know about Robber's Wine?"

Jane felt sure Anne's response was going to be not just careful, but calculated. There would be no emotional outpouring. No shared confidences. She'd hoped to be able to break through some of Anne's resistance and get her to talk more openly, to trust her, but it wasn't happening. It hurt her to realize that her need to find the truth had become, in a very real sense, a threat to her friends. At this moment, deep down, she didn't like herself very much.

She sat forward, resting her arms on her knees. "Tell me how you came up with the name Robber's Wine."

"Well," began Anne, haltingly at first, "it was right around the time Grandma Fanny was diagnosed with cancer. After she came home from the hospital, Mom insisted she move from the cottage into the main house. I was about six. That would make Lyle five and Melody three and a half. I remember standing outside Grandma's door late one night and listening to the two of them talk. Something Grandma said scared me. Then she said the only thing protecting the family was Robber's Wine."

"Are you sure that's what you heard?" asked Jane. It didn't make much sense.

"I was six years old, for crying out loud. How the hell should I remember? It *sounded* like Robber's Wine to me."

"Fascinating," said Jane, more to herself than to Anne. She decided to try another question, knowing Anne was unlikely to give a truthful response. "Who do you think placed the Robber's Wine next to Quinn the night he died?"

"You're asking me who I think the murderer was?"

She nodded.

"I told you. Pfeifer! And if our friendship means anything to you, I hope you'll stop pressing the issue." When Jane didn't respond quickly enough, she added, "If not for me, then for Mom."

Jane closed her eyes. This was the worst thing Anne could have said. If she didn't believe someone in her family was responsible, she'd never resort to this kind of emotional blackmail. Straightening her back, Jane said,

"You can't imagine how sorry I am about all this, Anne. You're right. It's a mess."

"Then you'll stop asking questions? Stop trying to find Quinn's murderer?"

"What about your mother's death? Don't you want some closure there? Don't you *need* to know what happened?"

"Not at the expense of my family."

She couldn't make it any clearer. She'd drawn a line in the sand and asked Jane not to cross over it.

"You have no right to invade our privacy," she continued. "No one does."

Jane thought of something she'd recently seen in the local newspaper. The quote went something like, "Nothing causes a spotlight to shine on a man's life—and those around him—like being the victim of a homicide, or winning an election." At the time she'd read it, she'd laughed. She wasn't laughing now.

"So?" asked Anne pointedly. "Are you going to back off?"

Jane shook her head. "I don't know."

It wasn't the answer she wanted. Her face hardened into a mask of coldness as she stood up. "All right. Then I'm going to have to ask you to leave. Today. I want you and Cordelia out of the cottage before dark."

"Anne, don't do this."

"You leave me no other choice."

"Of course you have other choices. Maybe you should have a little more faith in this family you're so quick to defend. I should think you'd want to see the real murderer caught, if for nothing else than to show the world your innocence."

"You think you're so smart."

This was the last straw. Jane stood, coming eye to eye with her friend. "Murder is wrong, Anne. It's never a solution to a problem. And now, since I've got informa-

tion the police don't have, if one of you really is guilty,
I'll feel like an accomplice."

"You and your precious conscience." She spit the
words at her.

"Look," said Jane, feeling her own anger rise in her
chest, "I'm going to say it one more time and I hope
you'll listen. If you've got a murderer in your family, it's
a wound that's going to fester and bleed. It could take
you all down."

Anne glared at her for several uncomfortable seconds
and then spun around and walked away.

30

The restaurant at the Fosh Lake Country Club was crowded, much busier than Jane had expected late on a Sunday afternoon. As she and Julia entered the main doors, she noticed Lyle at a table near the front of the bar. It was a dark room designed to look like a library, with lots of old hardcover books, Tiffany-style lamps, and dark paneled walls. He was sitting with a group of men in business suits, most of them drinking, smoking, and laughing as if they'd just heard a dirty joke they particularly liked.

As she waited for the hostess to return from the far end of the dining room to seat them, Lyle spotted her, waved, and then got up, leaning over and speaking briefly to the man next to him. Then, walking quickly in their direction, drink in hand, he gave Jane a broad smile.

"Business meeting?" she asked, nodding to the group he'd just left.

"I guess you could say that." He looked pleased with himself. "I thought I should get together with some of my backers and see if I'm completely dead in the water after everything that's happened." Realizing he didn't know the woman Jane was with, he introduced himself.

Julia's smile was friendly. "Nice to meet you. I'm Julia Martinsen. A friend of Jane's."

"She's just here for a few hours," added Jane, hoping he'd get the hint and leave them alone.

"Really?" he asked. "Where are you from?"

"I work in Washington and live in Bethesda."

"No kidding." He seemed to warm to the conversation. "You work for the government?"

"No, I'm a doctor."

"Oh." He nodded, his curiosity dissolving to polite interest.

"What did your friends tell you about your political future?" asked Jane, catching the hostess's eye.

His broad smile returned. "That the public has a very short memory. It was exactly what I wanted to hear. If I can just stay clean from here on out, my chances are excellent."

"That's great," said Jane, realizing the tone of her voice carried little enthusiasm.

"Yeah. Well." He swirled the ice in his glass and then downed the last of the liquid. "I guess I better get back to my meeting. It was nice meeting you." He extended his hand to Julia.

"Good luck," she said, shaking it firmly.

"Thanks. See you later, Jane."

Jane wasn't so sure they would ever see each other again now that Anne had kicked her out of the cottage, and probably out of the Dumonts' lives forever. Cordelia was going to be more than upset, not only with Anne, but with Jane for pushing so hard to get at the truth behind Belle Dumont's death that she'd alienated a good friend.

The hostess seated them at a table next to a window overlooking the marina. In the distance, the lake spread out before them like a glimmering blue jewel, the sun still high in the late afternoon sky.

"So," said Julia, after ordering a spinach salad and a margarita, "what's wrong?"

"Wrong?" repeated Jane, taking a sip of her water. Since she wasn't hungry, she'd just ordered iced tea.

"Ever since we left the hospital, you've seemed worried. Is it me? Something I've done?"

Jane shook her head. "It's a long story. Too long for the time we've got left. But it hasn't got anything to do with us."

"Promise?"

"Scout's honor. Now, let's talk about you and me."

A smile crept around the corners of Julia's mouth. "I don't mind if I do."

Jane matched her smile. "So, you flew all the way from Maryland just to talk to little old me. What did you want to say?"

Julia pulled her own glass of water in front of her. "Actually, that's history now."

"Pardon me?"

"I think I may have found a new home." Her hand swept to the window.

"The Fosh Lake Marina? I think you can do much better than that, Julia. Trust me."

"I'm not so sure. This town seems perfect. The hospital here is just what I want."

"And what *do* you want?"

"Well, for starters, a small town. A slow pace. Privacy. And a hospital with terrific facilities. I'm going to have to do some more checking, but I think Earlton is exactly what I've been looking for." She slipped her hand over Jane's. "I agree, there was too much distance between us. How would you feel about a three-hour drive."

"I'd prefer a five-minute walk."

Another smile, this one far more tender than amused. "I think it's just about right. For now."

"Okay," said Jane, leaning back as the waiter set the margarita in front of Julia. "I suppose it's better than Bethesda. For now."

Julia took a sip from the large balloon glass. "I know you've been letting me take this relationship at my own pace, and I appreciate it. You've let me lead so that I'm always comfortable with what's happening between us."

"Is that what I'm doing?"

"Yes." She smiled. "It is. I don't think you're the kind of woman who lets people take over all that easily. At least not when you see something you want."

"And you think I want you?"

"Oh, I don't think, I know."

Jane was surprisingly annoyed by the statement. "Maybe I'm being too obvious—too easy. I'm not presenting you with enough of a challenge."

Julia shook her head. "I don't want to play games. You don't either, Jane. We're both too old for that. Besides, in the short time I've known you, I've learned you don't play games. You're not an actor in your own life."

"Sounds like you've known a few."

"More than a few." She drew back, taking another long sip of her margarita. "Not that you're all that easy to get to know."

"I'm not?"

She picked up the glass and held it in both hands, staring at Jane over the rim. "Sometimes when I look at you, I see such sadness. I don't know where it comes from, but I'd like to. Usually, you hide it pretty well, but then it pops up again, often when I least expect to see it. Like when we're laughing, or just sitting together, having a glass of wine. It makes me want to take you in my arms and tell you everything's going to be all right, but that's always seemed like such a male conceit to me. I can't make everything all right for you any more than you can for me. Still," she said, putting her glass down, "I'd like to try."

"Is that how you see me?" said Jane. "Sad?" It was a revelation to her.

"Oh, much more than that," said Julia. She sat forward, leaning her arms on the table. "You're intense, but private. You have friends, but you don't let anybody—with the exception of Cordelia—get very close. You're funny and fun to be with. And you're very bright, but sometimes people confuse you and it drives you crazy. You process the world slowly, much more slowly than Cordelia. If you ask me, she's too quick to judge sometimes, too quick to form opinions based solely on her intuition. You try to understand the world more logically, though you're smart enough to know it's not always a logical place. But you don't give up until you do understand, at least as much as you can. In other words, you're stubborn."

"Gee, thanks."

"Oh, and one more thing. This is just my personal opinion, you understand, but I think you're very beautiful. I'm sure I'm not the only person who's ever told you that."

"No, I hear it all the time," said Jane, feeling a little overwhelmed. "It gets kind of boring. You understand."

Julia laughed. "Am I making you uncomfortable?"

"Yes, I think you are."

"Then, bear with me one more second." She reached into her purse and removed a lump of black tissue paper. She handed it to Jane. "This is for you."

"What is it?"

"Open it."

Jane drew back the paper. When she saw what it was, she was almost too surprised to speak. "It's a ring. A scarab, right?"

Julia nodded. "It's genuine. Egyptian. Set in gold. I saw it in a shop window several weeks ago and bought it that same afternoon. Will you . . . wear it?"

"Of course I'll wear it." Jane could hear the hesitation in Julia's voice and it confused her. "Why wouldn't I?"

Julia nodded to Jane's left hand. "That ruby you always wear. I assume it has some meaning to you?"

Jane looked down at the ring, centering the square-cut stone on her finger. "It was Christine's."

"Your first partner."

"She wore it for years before she died. I guess, after she was gone, I needed that physical link to her."

"I understand," said Julia, her voice growing soft. "But would you consider wearing my gift to you too? It might not have as much meaning, at least not yet, but I'd like to think we have our own special connection now."

Jane tried the ring on several of her fingers until she found the best fit—the middle finger of her right hand. "There. It's incredibly beautiful. I don't know what to say." She was so touched. It had been such a long time since she'd felt like this—excited, frightened, even a little out of control.

"Just promise you'll give me some time. There are a lot of things you don't know about me yet."

"You keep saying that, but you never clarify what you mean." Jane didn't want to show her frustration right now, but it was hard to hide.

"Just promise me you'll give me that time."

"Julia, we have all the time in the world, especially if you really are moving back to Minnesota."

She held on tight to Jane's hand. "I wish we could go back to your cottage."

Not that they had a cottage to go back to. Jane decided to omit that bit of information. "You'd miss your plane."

"I . . . I can't do that."

"I know." She smiled. "Now who's the one who looks sad?" As her eyes dropped to Julia's drink, her attention was drawn to the rim of the glass. "Salt," she said under her breath, her mind flashing to the night Quinn Fosh died. The interior of his boat. Even as she saw the image float in front of her eyes, she rejected its intrusion into her thoughts.

"What about it?" asked Julia.

"What?"

"You said 'salt.' "

"Did I?"

Julia's salad arrived.

"Yes, you did." She picked up her fork and started eating. "This is great dressing. Want a taste?"

"Sure." Jane's eyes strayed briefly to a table halfway across the room where a young man sat alone, making no effort to hide the fact that he was staring at them. He looked familiar, but she couldn't place his face. She didn't want to upset Julia, but thought perhaps they should stop gazing quite so intently into each other's eyes. Before she had a chance to broach the subject, the man got up and walked over to them. Jane could feel her body tense. She had no idea what he wanted, but didn't much like the brooding look in his eyes.

"You don't recognize me?" he asked, standing rigidly next to the table.

"No, I'm sorry—"

"Pfeifer Biersman."

"Oh, of course." This private conversation with Julia was turning into a public event. Jane had gone for days without seeing anyone she knew. Today, however, her life was turning into old home week. Pfeifer had grown a goatee since she'd seen him last, which was probably why she didn't recognize him, though he still looked every bit as oily and tough. "What can I do for you?" she asked, wishing he'd go away.

"You can give Melody a message from me next time you see her."

"I don't know when that will be."

"Well, it'll be sooner than me. Did you know she had that lawyer friend of the family slap a restraining order on me?"

"No, I didn't know."

"Well, she did." He hooked a thumb over his belt, glancing disinterestedly at Julia, and then back to Jane. "Tell her I love her. No strings. No more arguments. And that I miss her, not just her mother's money. God, I hate when she starts on that. I mean, I liked having the extra money just as much as the next guy, but it's Melody I want to come home to. She can keep her inheritance."

"I'm sure she'll be glad to hear that."

"Hey, I'm the only guy in the world for her. You got that? Be sure to tell her I'm waiting."

"I will." Now just go away quietly and leave me alone, she tried to say with her eyes.

" 'Cause she's going to see it my way. I made sure of that. She's going to come crawling back."

"Really."

"You bet."

Julia put down her fork, her eyes rising to his with undisguised impatience. "Look, if you don't mind, we're having kind of a personal conversation here. We'd like to get back to it."

He glared at her. "Well rudy-toot-toot. Who the hell do you think you are, lady?"

The waiter strolled up. "Is there a problem?" He was an athletic-looking young man, a football player type, a good fifty pounds heavier than Pfeifer.

"Yeah, I got a problem," he drawled. "That bitch has a big mouth. And I don't like it."

The waiter grabbed his arm. "I'm going to have to ask you to leave, sir."

"*Sir,* my ass." He pulled away.

"Listen, you can leave under your own steam, or I'll carry you out. What's it gonna be?"

Pfeifer seemed startled by the hard edge in the man's voice.

"Hell," he said, hooking both thumbs over his belt. "That's right. Protect these two faggot ladies' privacy. Didn't you see them cuddling up to each other? It's disgusting."

The waiter bent down next to Pfeifer's ear and said,

"You mean *dykes*, asshole. Faggots are men. Like me. What do you say we go outside and discuss it?" He grabbed him by the scruff of the neck.

Pfeifer pushed him away. After straightening his shirt, he took one last look at Jane and Julia, uttered the word "Fuck" with as much dignity as he could muster, and then stomped out the front door without a backward glance.

"Thanks," said Jane, taking a deep breath.

"No problem," said the waiter. "Can I get you anything else? Another drink?" He looked at Julia.

"No thanks."

After he was gone, Jane whispered, "Are you sure you want to try a relationship with a woman?" She held both hands under the table, covering the scarab protectively with her other hand. The expression on Julia's face was almost unreadable. For a moment, Jane had the sinking feeling she was going to say she wasn't sure.

After a long pause Julia said, "That happens everywhere, doesn't it." It was more a statement than a question.

"I'm afraid so."

"It's so unfair."

"I know."

She picked up her fork. "I think I told you once that I had a lot of gay male friends in D.C. It's funny, I never knew what it felt like to be on the other side. Maybe it's just what I needed."

"Meaning what?"

She held Jane's eyes. "Meaning drink your iced tea. I'm fine. Better than fine. We've got so little time left, let's not waste it on a bigot."

Jane held on tight to the ring under the table, breathing a silent sigh of relief.

31

Melody sat at the kitchen table with a carton of milk, a bowl of chicken salad, and a hefty wedge of cinnamon coffee cake spread out before her. Her right arm rested on the tabletop, her head drooping against the palm of her hand as she picked through the salad bowl for bits of green olive. She knew she looked like hell.

She'd fallen asleep right after lunch and stayed asleep all afternoon, something she'd never done before. Her hair was a snarl on top of her head, and her skin, normally smooth and blemish free, was beginning to show signs of acne. It was all the sugar and fat she'd been eating. She couldn't seem to stop herself. Or maybe it was just the stress of the last few weeks. She missed her mother terribly, thought about her almost all the time. Depression had settled into every muscle, every bone of her body.

Taking a gulp of milk, she heard the front screen door slam. A second later Anne stalked into the room, tossed her purse down angrily on the kitchen counter, and then whirled around, glaring at the table of food. "What are you doing?" she demanded.

Melody's eyes rose to the ceiling in frustration, then came to rest on her sister. "Good afternoon to you too," she said, keeping her voice even and pleasant. "Yes, I'm just dandy. Thanks for asking. And how are you?"

"Cut the crap. I want to know what's going on."

"What do you think's going on? I'm having a snack."

"Right. You eat and then you throw up. I'm not going to sweep it under the rug any longer. I refuse to ignore your destructive behavior!"

"Jeez, you're really loaded for bear."

"What am I supposed to think?"

This was the last straw. Melody erupted out of her chair. "You're supposed to stay the hell out of my life!" she shouted. This was all she needed. The third degree from Ms. Sisterly Compassion.

"That's not good enough," said Anne, catching Melody by her arm. "I spent most of the afternoon talking to a doctor."

"You what?" She broke free and pushed her sister away. "You have no right to meddle in my life! Who the hell do you think you are?"

"I have every right," said Anne, her eyes dropping to the chicken salad. She looked back pointedly at her sister. "I love you, Melody. You need help. You're sick."

"What are you talking about? I'm tired. Stressed. That's all."

"I went to the hospital in Earlton today."

"On a Sunday?"

"That's when the doctor was free and could see me."

"What doctor?"

"I talked to a specialist in eating disorders." Anne's voice grew softer as she said, "You're bulimic, Melody. If you don't get help, you could die."

"I'm *what*?"

"The doctor told me you'd resist the diagnosis. That's part of the illness. You're a classic case, Mel. Your marriage is on the rocks. You've always had trouble with self-esteem. I know you think one of the only things you've got going for you is your looks. It's completely understandable that you'd try to control your weight.

You're stressed to the max so you're eating to comfort yourself. I'm not blaming you. I'm trying to help you!"

Melody sank down, dazed, into a chair, shaking her head in disbelief. After a moment she began to laugh, louder and louder until she was nearly hysterical.

Anne rushed to her side. "You've got to get a grip. We all have to stay strong, stick together. You can't go to pieces now, Melody, you just can't!"

Staring at her sister's concerned face, her laughter changed to giggles. "You're such a turkey, Anne. You even look like one. A pathetic, pop-eyed turkey."

Anne sat down opposite her, her lips tightening at the corners. "That's right. Insult one of the only people left who cares about you."

Holding her sides, Melody leapt up and raced to the living room couch, falling headfirst onto a bunch of bed pillows.

Anne followed, waiting next to the mantel for her sister to pull herself together.

After a few seconds, Melody flopped over onto her back, tears rolling down her cheeks. She batted them away, realizing she wasn't laughing any longer, but crying. The pain she'd kept inside had finally burst free. Even though she tried to stop the flow of emotion, she was almost past caring. Almost, but not quite. She sat up, using the pillowcase to wipe away the tears streaming down her cheeks.

Anne waited a few moments longer, her disgust all too apparent. Finally, she said, "If you don't help yourself, Mel, nobody else can."

"Oh, shut up," sniffed Melody, wiping a hand across her nose.

"I've got the phone number of that doctor. It's in my purse. I want you to call him first thing in the morning."

"You're way off base." She just wanted her sister to leave.

"I'm not wrong. And I'm not going to sit here and see you destroy your life."

"I'm not destroying my life!"

"Then what do you call that table filled with food in the kitchen?"

"I was hungry!"

"Fine. But what were you going to do after you ate?"

"Sit outside and burp."

"Be serious."

"I am! I'm not bulimic, Anne. I'm *not*."

"You're sick."

She stood up, flinging the pillow across the room. "You're wrong!"

"Am I? If you're not bulimic, then what are you?"

"I'm pregnant!" she screamed, realizing the moment she said the words she'd made a big mistake.

Anne's mouth dropped open. "You're what?" she said, her voice barely a whisper.

"There, are you happy now? The entire family can gloat. Poor little Melody. She could never figure out her own life and now she's going to bring an innocent baby into the mess."

"I . . . I—" She swallowed back her surprise. "I didn't know."

"No, you *didn't* know. None of you know what I've been going through. Only Mom. She was the one person I confided in and I was terrified she'd hate me for the rest of my life."

Anne steadied herself by taking hold of the edge of the mantel. "Why didn't you say anything?"

"Because Pfeifer *doesn't* know, you idiot!" Her voice dropped to a whisper. "Do you think he'd ever let go of me if he thought I was carrying his child?" She waited, allowing the importance of her words to sink in. "The more people who know, the more chance he has of finding out. I can't take that risk."

Anne seemed paralyzed by the revelation.

"You're useless," said Melody, grabbing her car keys. "You were right the first time. Nobody can help me but *me*." She stuffed them into the pocket of her sweatpants and headed into the kitchen. Bursting out the back door, she knew she had to get away.

The outside air felt cool against her hot skin. As she stomped past the wood beams supporting the deck, a hand gripped her shoulder and spun her around.

"Don't make a sound," said Pfeifer, dragging her into a rocky section behind one of the tall shrubs, one hand at her throat, the other held tightly over her mouth.

Melody could hear Anne's voice shouting, "Come back and talk to me, Mel. I'm so sorry. I didn't know." She was silent for a moment. Then, "I'll be inside, waiting. Please," she pleaded. "I'm sorry. I'm *really* sorry."

Melody struggled to get away, but it was no use. Pfeifer had her pinned to the ground under the full weight of his body. She felt a moment of panic, but then calmed herself by remembering she'd been beaten up many times before. She'd survive this as well.

Pfeifer smelled of garlic and sweat and some sort of sweet aftershave he always wore when he wanted to have sex. For a minute, she had the feeling she was going to vomit right through his fingers.

After the back door slammed shut, Pfeifer brought his mouth close to her ear and said, "So you're pregnant, huh?" He pushed his groin into hers.

Melody felt her heart sink. Since she couldn't speak with his hand over her mouth, she just looked at him, silently wishing he'd crawl away somewhere and die.

"Very interesting. You know," he said, sitting up a bit, "you're a mess."

She rolled her eyes.

"So, when were you going to tell me?" He lifted his hand.

"I wasn't," she said, turning her face and spitting out the taste of his skin.

"No? That wasn't very nice. I mean, I'm going to be the proud daddy. It takes a little getting used to." He smoothed back his hair.

"Not necessarily," she grunted, squirming out from under him.

He held on to her arm. "What do you mean?"

"None of your business."

"No," he said, wiping a dirty hand across his mouth. "You meant something. I want to know what!"

"Why are you here? Don't you know you're breaking the law?"

He laughed. "What do I care about a damned piece of paper? I came to bring you home." He glanced over his shoulder at the Dumonts' speedboat. "It's not safe around here anymore."

"You got that right."

"Hey!" He slammed her to the ground again. "I don't want any more of your lip. I've had about as much as I can take today from mouthy women."

"Lighten up, will you?"

He slapped her hard across the face. "Now tell me what you meant."

She clenched her teeth and closed her eyes, steeling herself for another blow.

"Tell me!"

"All right!" She cracked one eye. "You're . . . not the father."

"Huh?" His eyes narrowed.

"You heard me."

"How do you know that?"

"I *know*."

His eyes grew large and angry as he reached behind him and pulled a gun from his belt, cocked the trigger and pointed it right at her stomach. "You're lying. Tell me you're lying!"

Stammering out the first words that came into her head she said, "All right. Yes. I'm lying. I'm just trying to hurt you." With her right hand she grabbed a rock.

"No you're not," he said, his face turning red with fury. "You bitch! I could kill you!"

In one sudden, swift movement she slammed the jagged edge into his forehead. He fell backward, dropping the gun and moaning as blood began to ooze from the open wound.

In an instant she was up and running. She could see the boat he came in. It was beached about a hundred yards up the shore. Feeling in her pocket for her keys, she made straight for the dock.

Her luck was holding. The speedboat was sitting right where she'd hoped it would be. The water was her best chance to get away. On land, he could outrun her. Out on the lake, she had the edge. She knew Pokegama better than he did.

Rushing to the end of the dock, she untied the mooring ropes. Then, leaping into the back of the boat, she jumped into the driver's seat and stuck the key into the ignition.

"Is it time to get up?" came a sleepy voice.

She looked around and saw Cordelia pull a light plastic tarp off her body and sit up, rubbing her eyes and yawning. She must have been sleeping on one of the seats.

Melody had no time to explain. She glanced back to the top of the hill and saw Pfeifer standing next to the deck, shielding his eyes from the sun. She could have sworn he had a smile on his face. Why the hell wasn't he chasing her?

"Are we going for a ride, dearheart?" asked Cordelia, standing and stretching like a big, elegant cat. "Say, you know what? I'm feeling a little seasick. Sleeping on the bounding main always does that to me. I think I'll just get off and go find a couple Dramamine for dinner." She placed a hand over her stomach and inched gingerly toward the other side of the boat.

"Sorry, no time," called Melody.

With her eyes fixed firmly on the island in the distance, she twisted the key and started the motor.

32

Lyle made a right on Fenton Avenue and then pushed the button on the CD player in his car to select another song. He was in a great mood after his meeting. Nothing was going to stand in his way now. If the family could just get past this murder inquiry and stay clean, his political future would be made in the shade. Since the only evidence linking him or any other family member to Quinn Fosh's untimely demise was buried deep in the sand on Pumpkin Seed Island, his high spirits weren't dampened at all by the thought of a lengthy police investigation. Maybe he'd even encourage Dennis, offer his help and support.

As he rounded the next corner and sped down Sixth heading for home, he saw an ambulance and a squad car parked in his drive. Feeling the hair on the back of his neck prickle in a kind of cold dread, he pulled up in front of the house, grabbed his briefcase, and slid out of the front seat. Now what? he thought to himself as he raced up the front walk.

He stopped briefly in the living room, looking around for signs of life.

"Lyle, is that you?" called his wife. "We're back in Brad's bedroom."

He rushed down the hall. As he entered the room, Carla seemed relieved to see him, though her face was tense with worry.

Two paramedics were on their hands and knees, working on his son Brad. He'd been placed on a low stretcher, his youthful features pale and drawn. A policeman was on the phone in the kitchen.

Lyle felt his pulse quicken. "What's wrong?" he demanded, kneeling down next to him. His own movements were jerky. Frightened.

His other son sat on the bed, an anxious look on his face.

One of the paramedics was taking Brad's blood pressure. The other pointed to a rag on the floor. "He was inhaling Freon."

"What on earth! Why would he do that?"

"To get high," said the first paramedic.

Lyle gazed down at Brad, his mind sluggish and confused. "But where would he get it?" he protested. Surely they must be wrong.

"Tell him," said Carla, nodding to the boy on the bed.

Tom kept his eyes averted. "He . . . he said he was going to drain some Freon out of the air conditioner in your study, Dad. He wanted me to do it with him, but I said I was scared."

It took a minute for it all to sink in. The officer in the kitchen was still talking on the phone, though he looked as if he was just about to hang up. A toothpaste commercial blared from the TV in the living room.

"Is he going to be all right?" asked Lyle, his voice unsure and thick with an emotion he couldn't even identify.

"Yeah, he should be okay," said the paramedic who was checking Brad's blood pressure. "But we have to take him in. Get him looked at by a doctor. Don't be surprised if they want to keep him overnight. You won't be able to ride in the ambulance, but you and your wife will need to be there to admit him. We'll take him over to St. Gervais."

Lyle gave a guarded nod.

"Your son over there's a hero," said the policeman, entering the room, a notepad clasped in his left hand. "He found Brad facedown on the floor, his nose buried in that rag. If he hadn't had the presence of mind to pull him away and then call 911, we might have had a very different outcome."

Lyle caught his wife's eye. "Where were you?" he asked. He didn't mean it to sound accusatory, but it came out that way.

"At the grocery store," she replied coldly. "In my mink coat and pearls so I wouldn't embarrass you."

He closed his eyes.

As they wheeled the boy out, Brad took hold of his dad's hand. His grip was weak, his skin cold. "I'm sorry," he whispered, his eyes filled with tears.

Lyle bent down close to him and gave him a kiss on his forehead. "I know you are, son. You've got to get well now, that's your only job." He tousled the boy's hair and cupped his cheek tenderly in his hand.

Carla shot her husband a withering look as she left with the policeman.

Feeling sapped and completely alone, Lyle walked to the window overlooking the back of the garden and placed his right hand on the cool glass. After a few moments he heard Tom say, "Are you mad at me?"

Lyle spun around. "No! Where would you get an idea like that? You saved your brother's life!" He was so absorbed by his own thoughts he'd completely forgotten the boy was in the room.

Tom kept his eyes on his hands. "He's been doing different stuff for months. Freon. Glue. Spray cans. Balloons filled with junk he calls laughing gas."

Lyle walked over and sat down on the bed next to him. "Where does he get it?"

Tom shrugged. "Friends mostly. And stuff around the

house. I tried to tell him it was stupid, but he wouldn't listen. So I kept an eye on him. You know. Just in case."

Lyle put his arm around his youngest son and hugged him close. Tom was always the quiet kid, the good kid, the one who wanted to build model airplanes together or throw the ball around in the backyard. How many times had he disappointed him in the past year?

"Do you forgive me, Dad? I mean for not telling you?"

Lyle felt himself begin to shake. "I think it's the other way around. I'm the one who needs to be forgiven."

Tom slipped his arm around his dad's back. "You wouldn't have caught him. He's real sneaky. Even I didn't know what he was doing half the time and I'm almost as sneaky as he is."

Carla returned to the room. "I'm going to the hospital. I'll take my car so you can keep on doing what you need to do to make yourself a great success." Her voice was heavy with a kind of repressed fury. "Tom, you come with me."

Lyle let go of his son. "Give your mother and me a couple of minutes by ourselves, okay, Tom? Then we'll all go to the hospital together."

"Sure, Dad," said Tom, scrambling to his feet. "Should I go wait in the car?"

"Good idea." Lyle gave him an encouraging smile and a pat on the back.

After he was gone, Carla just stared at the floor where Brad's nearly unconscious body had been found. "He could have died," she said, her chin trembling as she pressed her lips together tightly to hold back her emotion.

"I know," said Lyle.

"Do you? Do you care?"

"How can you ask me that?"

"Don't you think I saw the look on your face when you walked in here? All you could think about was the possibility that one of us had screwed up your life again."

"That's not true! My only concern was for my son."
Even though he protested loudly, he knew she was right.

Carla put a hand over her eyes. "I can't take this anymore. I can't take your ambition, your need to prove
yourself. You're just like your mother."

"What's that supposed to mean?"

"Oh, please. You lived with her. You should know. She
always had to be better than anyone else. Wiser. Kinder.
Smarter. More successful. Her kids had to be the best and
the brightest. She pressured you constantly. I understood
her reasons, even sympathized. Since she was gay, she
wanted to show the world—and prove to herself—that she
wasn't less because of it. So she created two monsters—
you and Anne—and one poor soul who refused to play the
game."

"Is that how you see me?" asked Lyle, his voice
incredulous. "A monster?"

"Yes!" she roared. Then, her head falling back against
the door frame, "No. I mean, I don't know anymore. You
and Anne try too hard. You want too much, from yourselves and from others. Especially from your family.
We're not automatons, Lyle. Not your perfect little Step-
ford family. The kids and I, we're flesh and blood. We
make mistakes. We're not always motivated, or good or
moral."

"I'm not either," he whispered.

"I know that. Funny, but I wasn't sure you did."

His head snapped up. "What's that supposed to mean?"

"It means, Lyle, that I want you to make a choice. You
can have your career in politics, or you can have me.
Before someone planted all those political aspirations in
your head, we had a good marriage. Oh, I know you'll
always be ambitious, but I can deal with that as long as
it's just us and not the entire state of Minnesota running
our lives in the cause of some ridiculously contrived
image. I love you, Lyle. That's not at issue. But I'm not

going to live like this any longer, and I won't allow the kids to live with this pressure either."

Lyle knew there was no choice. His family came first. Carla might not believe it, but his mother had taught him that too.

"I'll be out in the car with Tom," said Carla. "If we don't see you in a few minutes, I'm going to leave without you."

"I'll be out," he said, glad that she'd given him a moment to collect himself. He had a lot of thinking to do. If it was the last thing he ever did, he needed to put matters right with his wife and kids. It might take some time to get used to the idea that he was never going to hold political office, but if anything had shown him the light, tonight had. Besides, after the news got out about what his son had done, his political career would be dead in the water anyway.

An ironic image, he thought to himself as he stood and walked through the empty house, switching off the TV set. He wasn't the only person to find himself dead in the water recently. Perhaps he wouldn't be the last.

33

Melody maneuvered the speedboat carefully away from the dock and then opened the throttle up full and shot out of Queen's Bay. She set a course straight for the island. Looking back over her shoulder, she could see Pfeifer hurry down the hill. After pushing his own boat out into the water, he jumped aboard somewhat awkwardly and started the motor.

Cordelia had fallen over one of the rear seats, holding on for dear life. As the bow hit the wake of a large cabin cruiser, covering her with spray, she shouted, "Slow down, Melody! Are you crazy?"

Melody wasn't sure she had an answer to the question, so she just kept driving. The cruiser was already too far away and moving too fast to flag it down. No other boats were in the immediate area.

"I'm being kidnapped," shrieked Cordelia, making her way slowly toward the front seat. "Or didn't you notice I was here?"

Even at full throttle, Pfeifer was beginning to gain on them. "I noticed," said Melody. "But I was kind of pressed for time." She found the lever to reset the trim of the boat, hoping they might pick up some extra speed.

"What's the hurry?" asked Cordelia, cupping her hand around her mouth so she could be heard more clearly above the roar of the motor.

Melody nodded over her shoulder at the boat following them.

"Who's that?" asked Cordelia.

"Pfeifer."

"What's he want?"

"To kill me."

Cordelia blinked. "You're joking."

"I wish I were."

A shot came crashing through the front windshield.

"What the hell!" cried Cordelia, ducking her head. "That idiot's shooting at us!"

"You better stay down," called Melody, banking the speedboat hard to the right and then back to the left. She had to present Pfeifer with a more difficult target. She knew he wasn't all that great of a shot, but he could get lucky.

"I'm not having any fun," shrieked Cordelia as they continued to zigzag across the lake. She'd sunk to the floor of the boat, holding a seat cushion over her head. "I think I'm going to throw up."

Pumpkin Seed Island was directly in front of them. Banking again to the left, Melody aimed the boat straight for the narrow shallows between the main island and the smaller one. She had a plan. If it worked, they might be able to lose him. If not, she didn't have a clue what she'd do next.

Another shot came whizzing past her ear. "Get up!" she called to Cordelia.

"Are you nuts? I happen to be a rather large target, in case you never noticed."

"You have to stand up," shouted Melody. "We need to jump."

"Have you lost your mind? I'm not jumping into the water at this speed."

"No no! We need to jump *up*. Both at the same time. There's a shallow, rocky section about two minutes ahead of us. Right at the last moment I'm going to hit the tilt and trim and pull the motor and the lower part of the boat out of the water. The lighter we are, the better chance we have of making it through in one piece."

"This is ludicrous," yelled Cordelia. "I want to go home."

Another shot whizzed past Melody's shoulder. "As far as I can see, it's our only chance to get away from him. He'll be alongside us soon. What do we do then?"

"How do you know this will even work?"

"I did it once before."

"Really."

"I was with a bunch of high school buddies. We were pretty drunk."

At that inspiring bit of news, Cordelia tried to crawl *under* the seat.

"Get up!" ordered Melody.

"No!"

She reached down and shook her arm. "Do you want to survive this or not?"

"I want to live a long, peaceful life. I want to sit by a roaring fire and sip cocoa with my cats. I want to be *anywhere* but here!"

"Fine. But first you have to get up and jump with me." She glanced over her shoulder again. Pfeifer was grinning at her.

"What if the lake was higher that summer?" yelled Cordelia.

"That's possible."

"We could die!"

"No, I don't think so. But we could get hurt."

"Oh, great!"

"Or Pfeifer could shoot us both. Take your pick."

Inching her nose ever so slowly upward, Cordelia climbed to a crouching position. "I have a bad feeling about this."

"Just close your eyes and think positive."

"Oh, fabulous," she said, making a sour face. "I'm going to die with Norman Vincent Peale at the helm."

Melody looked behind her one last time and saw Pfeifer closing in on them. He was driving like a madman, standing upright, steering the boat with one hand, holding the gun with the other. She held her breath as she saw him take aim. An instant later, she felt a hot, stinging sensation near her right elbow. When she looked down, she saw blood and knew she'd been shot.

There was no time to dwell on it now. Returning her attention to the shallow passage between the two islands, she shouted, "Do you see the rocks?"

Cordelia gulped, then nodded.

There they were, glistening like jewels under the water. The lake was becoming more shallow with each passing second.

"Are you ready?"

"No!" shouted Cordelia.

"On the count of three." As they neared the rocky corridor, Melody called, "One." She eased the motor out of the water. "Two. Jump!"

They both leapt into the air as the boat skittered along the top of the rocks. When they landed, Melody heard the bow scrape dangerously hard, but as the seconds passed and they still seemed to be afloat and in one piece, she heaved a sigh of relief. Readjusting the pitch of the motor, they sped off toward open water.

"You're bleeding," cried Cordelia, touching her arm.

"I know."

"Do you have a first-aid kit?"

"Look!" shouted Melody, pointing behind her. Pfeifer's boat was hurtling toward the rocks at full speed.

Realizing he was in trouble, Pfeifer cut the throttle, but it was too late. The boat smashed into the rocks with such force that it flipped upward and then slammed back down into the water, breaking apart. At almost the same moment a ball of fire burst into the air. Orange and yellow flames shot skyward.

"Oh my God!" shrieked Melody, a hand rising to cover her mouth. She was too stunned to do anything but gawk. As debris rained down all around them, she felt the sound of the explosion hit her body, almost like a blow. "His gas tank must have struck just right." Realizing they had to go back and help, she slowed the boat and banked hard.

"Do you see him?" asked Cordelia, stepping over to the side and squinting into the distance for signs of movement.

"No."

"I wonder if he could survive something like that?"

I hope not, thought Melody, cutting the motor. As they floated in toward the passage, she knew she should feel intensely guilty for thinking such a terrible thought. But she was way past all that now.

"I don't see anyone moving," said Cordelia, her voice tentative, unsure.

"Me either." Melody scanned the area carefully. Pieces of the shattered boat bobbed and dipped in the waves. One of the larger rocks, its tip jutting out of the water, had snagged an empty orange life vest. Water lapped lazily against the wreckage, putting out all traces of fire. In just a few minutes, the lake had swallowed up the explosion and returned to tranquility.

Boats sped toward them now from every direction.

Shaking her head in dazed disbelief, Cordelia sat down on one of the backseats, continuing to gaze at the debris. "Horrible," she said under her breath.

"Yeah," said Melody. "Horrible."

And so simple. With one crazy twist of fate, all of her worst problems had vanished into thin air.

34

Jane raced down the hill toward the dock where Cordelia sat talking to a police officer, a frayed plaid blanket wrapped tightly around her shoulders. Even at a distance, she could see Cordelia's hair was wet.

As she got nearer, she could see two other officers standing in the rear of the Dumonts' speedboat. They appeared to be examining the motor. The side clips had been removed and the top taken off.

"What's going on?" she called, slowing her pace as she approached. "What are all the squad cars doing up in the drive?" She leaned against one of the dock posts trying to catch her breath.

Cordelia's eyes rose to hers as she tugged the edges of the blanket even tighter around her body. "Welcome back. It's about time." She sniffed, then sneezed.

"Bless you. Why are you all wet?"

Cordelia sighed, sniffed again, and then said, "Melody and I took a little unscheduled spin in the speedboat."

"Why?"

"Pfeifer was trying to kill her."

"What!"

"He's dead, Janey." She took the handkerchief the policeman offered her and wiped her nose.

"How? Why?"

The sergeant eased himself to a standing position and

flipped shut his notepad. "Thanks for your statement, Ms. Thorn. We may need to talk to you again."

Cordelia nodded. "I shall look forward to it, Bob."

"Oh, and just keep the handkerchief."

"You're a real *mensch*."

As he crossed to the men in the boat, Jane simply stood and watched, too bewildered to speak.

"What'd you find?" he asked, pushing the pen behind his ear.

"It's some sort of bomb," said the shorter of the two officers. After snipping one last wire he lifted the device free, holding it by a gloved hand. "Pretty slick. It's small, but it could have easily blown the back of the boat off. Probably more."

"So why didn't it work?" asked the sergeant, scratching his head.

"One of the wires was loose."

Cordelia closed her eyes and shivered. "I think I'm going to be sick."

"Bag it," ordered the sergeant.

"I beg your pardon." She whipped her head around.

"He meant bag the *bomb*," said Jane, leaning over to massage her friend's shoulders.

"Well I should hope so."

"Think we'll get any decent prints off the thing?" asked the sergeant, holding the device carefully while the other two officers climbed back up on the dock.

"I think this is one of those Maalox Moments," groaned Cordelia, waving air into her face. "I'd like mine straight up. No ice."

Jane waited until the policeman had reached the end of the dock before sitting down next to her. "What happened?" she asked, giving Cordelia's shoulders another reassuring squeeze.

"I told you, it was awful!"

"All right, that's a good place to start. What was awful? What happened?"

She took a deep breath and then related the entire story, stopping occasionally to punctuate her disconnected narrative with small shrieks and shudders. When she was done, she pulled the blanket up over her head and said, "I'm going to hide now."

Jane took a few moments to digest the information. This was incredible. While she was seeing Julia off at the airport, Cordelia and Melody were being chased around the lake by a madman. Not that she was completely surprised. She'd always suspected Pfeifer was unstable. As she sat and listened to the waves lap against the sandy beach, she still had questions. "Cordelia?"

A tiny voice said, "Cordelia's hiding. Go away."

Jane tugged on the blanket. "Can't she talk to me for just another second?"

"Why?"

"I need to know what happened after the police boat arrived on the scene."

One eye peeked out through a crack. "Oh," she said in her normal voice. "I suppose I didn't quite finish the story. Well, all right. First they took care of Melody's arm. I guess it wasn't serious, though it bled a lot. Then they fished Pfeifer's body out of the lake. I assume they're going to do an autopsy."

"He was dead then?"

"Nobody survives an explosion like that, Janey." She retreated once again under the blanket.

Good point. Jane sat for another minute, staring at her new ring. Finally, she said, "Cordelia, I'm sorry to have to tell you this, but we have to go back to the cottage now and pack."

Again, an eye peeked out through a crack. "Why?"

"Well, Anne and I got into kind of a heated discussion in town a couple hours ago and—"

"About what?"

"Robber's Wine."

"Oh, no," groaned Cordelia, throwing her hands in the air. The blanket fell limply to the deck behind her. "If I never hear those two inane words uttered again in this lifetime, it will be too soon. This has been some holiday, Janey. A shitty, depressing vacation if you ask me."

"I wasn't asking."

"Well, too bad. Why don't you just stop all this snooping and apologize to her."

"I'm afraid it's too late." As she looked up, she saw Helvi steaming down the hill toward them. "We've got company."

Cordelia's eyebrow arched upward. "Hey, she's taking a rather cavalier risk, don't you think?"

"Meaning what?"

"She's left the garden unattended. What if some nasty weed mounts a frontal attack while she's gone? She could lose a strawberry. Maybe even a pea."

"Zip it," whispered Jane out of the corner of her mouth as Helvi stepped onto far end of the dock. She waved. "How's Melody doing?" she called.

"As well as can be expected," said Helvi. "She's pretty shaken up. Her father's taken her to the hospital so that a real doctor can look at her arm. I'm headed there too as soon as I'm done here." She walked up to them and leaned on one of the posts. "But I think she'll be fine. And how are you, Cordelia? You look . . . wet."

Another sneeze. "I guess I'll live."

"That's good to hear."

"Yeah." She gave a serious nod. "But I'm sorry we have to leave."

Helvi seemed confused. "Leave? I thought you were staying a couple more days."

"It's kind of a long story," said Jane, not really wanting to get into it right then. She tried to catch Cordelia's eye to warn her off the subject, but it was no use. Cordelia was getting too much mileage out of playing the injured victim.

"Anne's tossing us out," she said, a pout forming.

"I don't understand," said Helvi.

Jane elbowed her in the ribs.

"Ouch!"

"I'm sorry, Helvi," said Jane, proceeding somewhat more cautiously. "You see, Anne and I had a disagreement a couple of hours ago. She asked Cordelia and me to leave."

Helvi's brow creased with concern. "She has no right to do that. This is my home, not hers. She's welcome here anytime she wants, but she can't issue orders. As far as I'm concerned, you two can stay as long as you like."

"Thanks, but—"

"No, I won't hear of it, Jane. Absolutely not. You stay put. I'll talk to Anne myself."

"I don't want to cause any problems between you two."

"Don't worry about it. Besides, I was planning to have everyone over for dinner on Tuesday night so we could all say good-bye to you properly. What do you say? Is it a date?"

"Are you sure you're up to it?" asked Jane. As far as she could tell, Helvi still looked a bit frayed around the edges. Certainly not ready to entertain.

Helvi's eyes darted up to the garden before she spoke again. "You know," she said after a moment, "I'll tell you truthfully, these last few days have been the worst of my entire life. I've tried to carry on, but it's been a nightmare. Everything I do, everywhere I go, everything I look at reminds me of Belle—and of what I've lost." Her voice began to quaver so she stopped for a moment and cleared her throat. "Even though I feel that I've been coping pretty well, I still feel like I'm in a dream. But . . . it's not, is it?"

Jane thrashed around in her mind for some words of comfort but came up empty. "No," she said softly. "It's not."

"Anyway, I can't just sit and mope any longer. I've got a family to take care of." She brushed a tear away from under her glasses. "Oh, I know I've got some fences to mend with Lyle, and some hard times ahead with Melody, but we'll work it all out. I know now that it's going to take me the rest of my days to come to terms with Belle's loss, if I ever really do, but I've got to get on with my life. I think it's what she'd want."

"No more weed patrol?" asked Cordelia, her expression both amused and understanding.

Helvi matched her look. "No. No more."

"Glad to hear it."

She smiled, then hesitated.

Jane could tell she was struggling with something, a thought or a feeling she wasn't sure she wanted to express. In the end, her reticence got the better of her and she said, "So? Are we on for Tuesday night?"

"Absolutely," said Cordelia eagerly. "We accept."

Jane hoped Anne wouldn't boycott the event. She also hoped that before she and Cordelia left on Wednesday morning, she'd know the whole truth behind both Quinn's and Belle's deaths. The problem was, the family had closed ranks so tightly she wasn't any closer now than she had been eight days ago. And what was even more depressing was that since she had so little to go on, she had no confidence that she'd ever have the means to arrive at the truth, no matter how hard she tried to find it.

35

Helvi walked up the winding path leading to Mavis and Hal's front door. After ringing the bell, she waited outside, taking note that the handle on the brass knocker was badly encrusted with grime.

Mavis answered the door wearing pink striped lounging pajamas, her hair done up in a tangle on top of her head and held together by chopsticks. Helvi assumed it was some sort of attempt at fashion, but like most of Mavis's attempts, it fell flat.

"Why, Helvi," exclaimed Mavis with a fake lightness. "What a nice . . . surprise." She smiled through clenched teeth as she poked her head surreptitiously outside to see if any of her neighbors were about, witnessing Helvi's arrival.

"I'd like to talk to Hal," said Helvi. She handed the now clean and empty casserole dish to Mavis, remembering the delight she'd felt when she'd dumped it—crispy fried onion topping and all—into the garbage.

"Hal?" said Mavis, the look on her face suggesting she wasn't quite sure who Helvi was talking about.

"Unless you've had a stroke, you know who I mean. Now, go fetch him." She stood with her hand on her hip, waiting to be invited in.

Mavis closed the door partway and lurched off to find her husband.

A good two minutes later, Hal came to the door, a golf club slung over one shoulder.

Helvi wondered if he was planning to shoo her off the property with it.

"Miss Sitala," he said formally, using the name he'd always called her in school. "Won't you come in?"

"How kind of you to ask," said Helvi, her sarcasm lost on such a buffoon. She entered the large front room, seeing that Mavis had taken up a perch on one of the recliner rockers. A long strand of dyed red hair drooped over her right eye.

"What can I do for you?" asked Hal, sweeping the golf club grandly to the fireplace, indicating that she should take a chair.

Helvi remained near the door. This was going to be short and sweet and right to the point. She had no interest in staying one second longer than necessary. "I've come to tell you both that I've talked with the Girl Scout committee chair and have reinstated myself as the guest speaker at the mother-daughter luncheon next week."

"But *I'm* doing that," protested Mavis. She looked at her husband for support. "You said—"

"What was it you said, Halden?" asked Helvi. "I, for one, would like to know."

Hal seemed to grow uncomfortable under her scrutinizing gaze. It was a gaze Helvi had perfected long ago, the one she often used on recalcitrant students. Hal had been one of the worst.

"Well, I, ah . . . just that I thought it would be best if you didn't put any undue pressure on yourself. I mean . . . Belle's death must have come as a big shock. You need to rest. Take care of yourself."

"That's just what I'm doing," said Helvi. "And I'm doing it by not hiding from the community I've loved and served for over forty years. I won't stay in the closet any longer just to make people like you comfortable with your prejudice."

"But, Helvi, you misunderstand. I'm only thinking of you."

"Halden, I'm not even going to dignify that load of crap with a response."

On that rather crude note, she turned on her heel and marched back out the front door.

36

"Look at this," said Dennis Murphy, pausing next to the dresser in the bedroom of Pfeifer and Melody's house. After Pfeifer's death the day before, Dennis had obtained a search warrant. He didn't expect the evidence he was looking for to be lying around in such plain sight. Yet here it was, almost as if it had been waiting for him.

The young sergeant accompanying him stared down at the open jewelry box. "Hey, some of this stuff fits the description of property stolen by the Lake Burglar."

"I know. And look at this." He bent down and removed a bedsheet covering the back part of a handgun. "That's old man Zinnsmaster's piece. I'd recognize that pearl handle anywhere. And I found two more in the basement—a Smith & Wesson Model thirty-one, and a five-shot snubby. We better check the serial numbers on those, but I'll bet he lifted that stuff too."

"Roger, chief." The sergeant moved energetically around the room, looking under the bed and flipping back the pillows.

"He's got a workshop set up in the basement," continued Dennis, crouching down to examine the contents of a wastebasket. "I'd say that's where he built the explosive device he attached to the Dumonts' boat."

"Did we get positive I.D. back on that yet?"

"Yeah. He's our man, all right. He must have really hated that family."

"Damn," said the sergeant, dropping into a chair. "The evidence was here all along."

Dennis blamed himself. He blamed himself even more for what could have happened to Melody. From the very beginning he'd had a gut feeling that Pfeifer might have been behind the burglaries, maybe even Quinn Fosh's death, but since he couldn't prove either, at least to a judge's satisfaction, he'd been waiting for the two men he'd assigned to the case to come up with something concrete. He needed probable cause to get a search warrant.

"What's this?" said Dennis, noticing a legal pad sticking out from between the pages of a book. *Endburg's Explosives Manual.* He removed it carefully and placed it on the bed. Bending over to get a closer look, he said, "It's the beginning of a letter."

"To who?"

"To whom."

"Yeah yeah yeah. Give me a break, for crissake. I didn't have Eddy Dumont for senior English."

Dennis smiled, then read quickly through the contents. "It's addressed to Quinn Fosh. I'd say, by the looks of it, Pfeifer hated the guy's guts big-time."

"Why?"

"I don't know. But this letter clearly threatens his life." He twisted his head around and looked pointedly at the sergeant. "Did we pick up any of his prints on Fosh's boat?"

"Not that I remember."

"Well," he said, standing up straight, "at least this establishes a motive. And since we've got a bunch of stolen property here, it forms a pattern. The gun used to kill Fosh was stolen by the Lake Burglar. If we're lucky, we might be able to link it to one of these burglaries. If we can, I think we may have found our man."

"It would sure take the Dumonts off the hook."

"I never really thought they were on it. I just had to

cover all my bases." He hoped they understood the position he'd been in. He couldn't ignore their potential involvement, just because they were his friends.

"What about the bedroom screen?" asked the sergeant, wiping the sweat from his forehead. "It looks like it was cut pretty recently."

Dennis placed a hand over his gun. "Hard to tell. It could be Pfeifer forgot his key and cut it himself."

"True."

"Get a couple more men over here right away. I want this place gone over from top to bottom. Make sure they dust the windowsill for prints. You never know, we might come up with something interesting."

"Roger," said the young sergeant, heading out to the squad car.

Dennis grimaced. "One more thing."

"Yeah?" he said, stopping near the front door and checking his look in the front hall mirror.

"Stop saying 'Roger.' I feel like I'm in a bad John Wayne movie."

37

"So, what's on today's agenda?" asked Cordelia. She was sitting at the kitchen table in the cottage, finishing her breakfast. "I'll do anything except get in a boat."

"What a pity," said Jane absently. She was lying on the living room couch, paging through the morning paper.

"Why is it a pity?"

"Oh, I thought we might try some waterskiing later." Cordelia shuddered.

"If you don't get right back on the horse, you'll never ride again."

"Thank you for that wonderfully concise pop-psychology analysis." She stabbed a piece of ham with her fork.

"It's true."

Chewing resentfully, Cordelia muttered, "We've been here for nine days and *now* she wants to play." She rolled her eyes at the moose in disgust.

"I had other things on my mind before."

"Right. Tramping around the woods. Going off to visit nursing homes."

"We learned a lot from Angela McReavy." She felt around on the coffee table for her coffee mug. "Just not enough."

"So, you're finally going to stop this snooping binge. I'd say it's about time." She took a last bite of toast and then mumbled into her glass of milk, "I figured we'd have to visit Robert Weintz before you'd be satisfied."

"What did you say?" said Jane, adjusting her reading glasses as she flipped to the next page.

"Nothing. I shouldn't have brought it up."

"No, I'm listening. I just didn't hear you right. You didn't make sense."

"I *always* make sense." She sniffed, glancing at the moose for support.

"Okay, then explain to me how I can go visit Robber's Wine, Cordelia. You don't *visit* a drink."

"Not Robber's Wine, dearheart. *Robert Weintz*. That friend of Belle's mother. The old lawyer. The one Angela McReavy said you should go talk to if you wanted to get more poop on Fanny Adams."

Jane put down the paper and sat up. After staring at Cordelia for a moment she said, "You know, that's really weird. I was sure you said Robber's Wine."

"Robert Weintz!" she persisted. "My classical pronunciation and dramatic projection have always been and continue to be perfection itself." Her eyes rose again to the moose, which stared straight ahead in silent agreement. "See? Even *he* agrees. It must be your ears, Janey. Face it. At forty, you're starting to disintegrate."

"Just be quiet for a minute."

"Why?"

"Let me think this through." It was too close to be a coincidence, wasn't it? "Cordelia, what if—" She ran the scenario through her mind one more time.

Cordelia finished her milk in several noisy gulps and then set the glass down with a crack. "What if what?"

"Well, I mean, what if the words Anne heard her grandmother say that night so long ago . . . what if it wasn't, 'The only thing protecting us now is Robber's Wine,' but instead, 'The only *one* protecting us now is Robert Weintz.'"

Cordelia stifled a burp. "Yeah, they do sound a lot alike."

Jane tapped her fingers impatiently on the arm of the couch. "I wonder if he'd see us?"

"He's got to be in his nineties," said Cordelia. "Who knows what kind of shape he's in—or more important, what kind of shape his mind's in."

"Well," said Jane, slapping her knees and standing. "As I see it, it's either Robert Weintz or waterskiing. What's it going to be?"

"Neither," huffed Cordelia. "I'm going to the Judy Garland house. I have to pay my respects at least once before we leave, spend a few minutes in quiet meditation about the vicissitudes of fame and the price we glitterati pay for success."

"We?"

"Yes, Judy and I. We're a lot alike. Both sex symbols. Both intensely talented, and both with a tragic flaw."

"And that would be?"

"Our self-deprecating spirit, dearheart. I should think that would be obvious."

Two hours later, a full-time private nurse ushered Jane and Cordelia into the rear study of Jeff Weintz's home in Grand Rapids. It was a two-story white house, with a wraparound porch and lots of Victorian gingerbread.

"He's expecting you," said the nurse, keeping her voice low as she flowed quietly down a darkened hall. "As I think about it, Belle Dumont was his last visitor. To think she died so suddenly."

Cordelia poked Jane in the ribs.

Jane put a finger to her lips.

The main part of the house was decorated with an unattractive and somewhat jarring mix of modern Scandinavian furniture and well-cared-for antiques. The den, however, showed no such war of tastes. It was much like stepping back in time to an earlier part of the century.

"We don't want to tire him now," whispered the nurse. "So I hope you'll keep it short."

Jane nodded her understanding as she walked into the study. Cordelia inched in behind her.

Robert Weintz sat in a wheelchair next to a window overlooking a garden. Resting next to him on a low table was a wicker birdcage containing two chattering blue parakeets. Even though the room felt warm, the elderly man had a blanket over his lap. He was also wearing a gray sweater, one that almost matched his hair.

Sensing that someone was in the room, he turned toward them, fiddling with the controls of his hearing aid. "You must be Jane and Cordelia," he said, his voice hoarse and faint. With two hands that were almost literally skin and bone, he maneuvered the wheelchair away from the window and rolled toward them, pointing at a couple of Queen Anne chairs in front of the desk. "Please," he said, his voice growing a bit stronger, "have a seat. This used to be my office, you know." He gazed somewhat wistfully at the leather desk chair. "I met all my clients in here. As a matter of fact, I had this house built back in '36, two years after I was married."

Jane was glad he was in a talkative mood. She knew his professional relationship with Fanny Adams might preclude much of what she wanted to talk about, yet she hoped the years might have mitigated some of the necessity for that. She sat down, waiting until Cordelia had made herself comfortable next to her, and then said, "I'm glad you could see us today."

"You say you're a friend of Fanny's?"

Jane smiled at the misunderstanding. "Not Fanny's, Belle's."

"Oh, that's right," he said, a little embarrassed. "What am I thinking? I saw her a few days ago, just before she died."

Jane was curious what they'd talked about but thought it would seem too intrusive to ask a question like that right off the bat. She might be able to approach the subject later. "My friend Cordelia and I are staying out at the Dumont house on Queen's Bay right now."

"Did you come up for Belle's funeral?" He looked from face-to-face, the words spoken matter-of-factly, with no trace of sadness or sentimentality.

"I suppose we did," said Jane, not wanting to go into everything that had happened.

"I'm afraid I couldn't make it. I've outlived most of my contemporaries. After a while, it begins to feel like one endless stream of funerals. I'm not being morose, mind you. It's just the way it is." It was clearly a strain for him to talk, yet at the same time he seemed eager for their company. "Belle was much too young to die. She was in the prime of her life."

Jane was pretty sure most people wouldn't consider sixty-five their prime, although perhaps she had a lot to learn about aging. "The day before she died, Belle called a family meeting for the following evening. She was finally going to tell her children everything she knew about the great Dumont family secret."

"Is that right," he said.

By the tone of his voice, Jane assumed he already knew.

"How did you know about that?" he asked. He seemed intrigued, but cautious.

"She told Helvi Sitala, the woman she lived with."

He stroked his chin. "I suppose she would have."

"But," chimed in Cordelia, "she died before she could tell anyone the whole story. We were wondering if you could shed any light on it for us."

The only part of Robert Weintz seemingly untouched by age were his eyes. Cool and sharp, they surveyed Jane and Cordelia with a keen intelligence born from many years of dealing with people—all kinds of people. "Forgive me for being rude, but I'm not clear why you're so interested. You're not family."

"She was our friend," insisted Cordelia somewhat defensively. "We're not just being prurient, you know."

One of the parakeets let out a squawk.

"Certainly not," he said, the crinkly skin around his mouth smoothing into an amused smile.

"We were close friends," said Jane. "She helped me through a pretty rough time once. And Anne and I have been friends for years." Continuing on, she said, "I understand you were Fanny Adams's lawyer."

"And her friend. Yes, I do understand the bonds of friendship." He sat forward in his wheelchair and once again readjusted the controls on his hearing aid.

"Why do you suppose her daughter, Belle, picked now to talk to her family?" Jane felt it was a critical question, one she hoped he could answer.

He shifted in his chair and shook his head. "I wondered about that myself. I'm sorry to say I don't know. We didn't discuss it."

"Was Quinn Fosh really her half brother?" asked Cordelia, her voice a little too eager for good taste.

Robert Weintz rested his arms on the sides of his chair and took a long, slow breath. "You know," he said after a deliberate pause, "Belle and I just talked about all this. It's funny, but it seemed like such a big deal sixty years ago. So wicked and so immoral. Today, it's just more of the same. Just more gossip for the mill. Still, the point is, back in the Thirties, this information could have ruined lives."

He looked over at Cordelia, his expression both weary and sad. "To answer your question, yes, Quinn was indeed Belle's half brother. She knew about it, but he didn't. Fanny told her when she was in her early teens. When Belle first found out, I think she was intensely curious. Quinn was a beautiful boy. Went to a private school. Spent his summers sailing with his father and traveling with his mother. Belle had only seen him from a distance. But Fanny nixed her desire to get to know him better. For one thing, she was still too frightened of Quinn's father to allow any contact between the two families. Also, Quinn was a spoiled kid. Fanny didn't want her daughter to form any opinions about life based on the way the Foshes ran their affairs."

"But was that the secret, or just part of it?" asked Jane. Perhaps she shouldn't be so direct, but it just fell out of her mouth. "Look, I know this may not seem like it's any of our business, but . . . we brought Anne up here for the family meeting Belle called last week. She died before she could talk to her kids and tell them what was on her mind. I think you know what that was. Am I wrong?"

He drew his hands together in front of him. "No," he said, his voice growing hoarse again. "You're not wrong."

Her confidence buoyed by his admission, she forged on. "I'm not convinced Belle's death was an accident." She stopped, giving him a second to mull over the implications of what she'd just said.

The elderly man's expression changed slowly from one of wariness to stunned horror. "How do you know that?"

"Did you know Quinn was murdered on his houseboat last weekend?"

He nodded. "My son told me."

"I can't prove this, but I think the two deaths may be related. If we just knew what Belle was going to tell her family the night she died, we might be able to make better sense of what's happened since."

He rubbed his hands together, thinking it over. "You know," he said finally, easing back into his chair, "before Belle came to me two weeks ago, I hadn't thought about any of this in over thirty years—not since Fanny died. I thought it had all died with her. I don't really understand how the knowledge of what happened back then would help you, but since virtually everyone involved is dead, I can't see any reason to be silent any longer. However, first you have to promise that if I tell you, it will remain a secret. Other than Belle's family, no one must know."

"Agreed," said Jane.

"Good. Actually, I've been wanting to tell the story. I half expected to find one of Belle's kids knocking on my front door with some very pointed questions. But since no one came, I assumed they either didn't know about our professional relationship, or they didn't care. Oh, they knew we were friends, but even that was a long time ago."

He looked down into his lap and shook his head. "Then again, kids don't pay much attention to their parents. Don't get me wrong, I love my son, but we're just a given to them. Instead of seeing us as real people, we're just Mom and Dad. My own son has never asked me much of anything about my early life. It's not as simple as saying he doesn't care. I don't think it enters his mind that I've had a life apart from the one he knows about. I'm sure Belle's children are no different.

"The truth is," he continued without pause, closing his eyes and tilting his head back, "the story you've come to hear isn't very unusual. It's what we see around us every day, if we can believe the morning paper. Yet, back in the Thirties, cheating on your wife was still considered a sin and it carried a harsh stigma. Unfortunately for Herbert Fosh, and for his family, he was a big-time cheater. He usually carried it off pretty well, but with Fanny Adams, his luck ran out."

"She got pregnant." Jane knew she didn't need to coax him anymore. The story was his now. And he seemed more than willing to tell it.

Robert Weintz opened his watery blue eyes wide and stared at her. "That's right. Bad luck all around. Fosh had used that age-old line on Fanny that his wife didn't understand him. He was hopelessly trapped in a loveless marriage. Since Fanny was only nineteen at the time, she believed every word he said, even went so far as to think he'd marry her after he got up the courage to ask his wife for a divorce. Oh, Fanny loved him, all right. And she was willing to wait. But as soon as she went to him with the news that she was going to have his baby, he changed. He didn't want anything more to do with her. He called her a slut, accused her of getting pregnant by some other man just to trap him.

"Fanny left Earlton a month later. She didn't return for almost two years. When she did, she told everyone she'd met a man, but he'd died shortly after their marriage. Of course, people may not have known the truth of the matter, but everyone knew it was a lie. From that moment on, Fanny lived with the disgrace of having had a baby out of wedlock. Times were different back then. Having an illegitimate child was a terrible mark against both the mother and the child.

"It took persistence, but Fanny finally found a decent job. She became a telephone operator. She handled the entire Earlton–Fosh Lake area. If you wanted to make a call, you picked up the phone and asked Fanny to connect you to your party. She worked as an operator until the spring of 1938. That's when she finally saw her chance to get back at the man she'd once loved and now hated. And believe me, when she saw her opportunity, she took it. Fanny Adams was nothing if not resolute. Resolute in her love, and now in her vengeance.

"Even though she'd asked Herbert for money many times, often in desperation—Fanny's father had died just two years before and she was now all alone in the world—Herbert steadfastly refused to give her any financial help with the child. Belle was growing into a beautiful little girl, the spitting image of Fosh himself. She was dark, small, intense. His own son looked more like his wife—fair-skinned and blond, with a tendency to overweight. Fosh was never much for kids anyway, so it was probably all to Belle's good that he didn't have anything to do with her. Even so, it galled Fanny that he refused to take any responsibility for what he'd done, galled her that he drove an expensive car, had his suits specially tailored in Minneapolis, and lived in a huge new house with a woman he supposedly loathed and a son the entire town knew he never talked to. Fanny loved her daughter fiercely and knew that his money could make the difference between just scraping by, which is what they were doing, and having the kind of life she saw him providing for his legal wife and son.

"Her chance at revenge came in the winter of 1938. Fosh and two other friends, both doctors, took a trip down to the Cities that year. They said it was for a convention, but whatever the case, they spent most of their time in a hotel room in downtown St. Paul with a couple of prostitutes. These two women had a slick scam going. Through a tiny hole in the wall, they had an accomplice take pictures of the men they had sex with—pictures of them in, shall we say, extremely compromising positions. When the unsuspecting johns got home, the women phoned and told them what they'd done, offering to sell them the photos.

"Needless to say," said Robert Weintz, smiling at some memory plucked from the dusty archives of his mind, "Fosh was hysterical. He promised to pay what they asked—a few hundred dollars—but he demanded that they not only turn over the photos, but the negatives. Unfortunately for him, Fanny was the operator that put the call through to his house. Instead of hanging up, she listened to the entire conversation. After they were done talking, she called the women back and offered them twice the price if instead of sending the photos and negatives to him, they'd mail them to her. Well, of course, they jumped at the chance. Once she had it all in her possession, she approached Fosh. But unlike the women, she didn't ask for money, at least not right away. She wanted him to sign a legal document that she had me draw up. It stated that he was Belle's father. It was short and sweet. And, of course, lethal.

"Fosh sputtered and spit his usual vitriol, but in the end, he knew he didn't have much choice. So he signed it. Once she had his name on the dotted line, witnessed and notarized by me, she had two huge swords to dangle over his head. Pathetic man, really. He was a pretty good doctor, but he wasn't much of a schemer. Fanny had it all over him when it came to cunning. Two weeks after he signed the document, she went to him and demanded ten thousand dollars, saying that if he gave her the money, she'd leave town and take Belle with her. She promised to destroy the negatives and give him the original photos."

"Did she?" asked Cordelia, her eyes wide.

He nodded. "But first, she made another set of prints which she gave to me. They were placed in a sealed envelope marked 'Confidential.' At the time, I wasn't privy to all the particulars, though everything came out years later. Fanny told me the whole story before she died, made me promise I'd watch over Belle and her children. Early on, I had to stay in the dark about what the envelope contained because, as an officer of the court, I couldn't be party to blackmail. I just knew it was important information that she wanted kept safe, information that if need be, would protect her and her daughter. Since Fosh had little choice—if the dirt she had on him ever came out, he'd have lost face in the community, probably even lost his livelihood and his family—he paid her immediately. Ten thousand dollars was a lot of money back then, but his bank account was fat. It wasn't a hardship.

"As soon as she had the money in her hand, she and Belle left Earlton. I thought I'd never see them again. Fanny was about five years younger than me, but we'd known each other since we were children. I might even have proposed marriage if matters had gone differently."

He sighed, bringing a shaky hand up to smooth back his hair. "She invested the money with a family friend when she got to Chicago. I don't know this for a fact, but I believe this man was dealing in the black market. There was a lot of illegal profit to be made during the war. Whatever the case, when she came back to Earlton in 1945, she was a wealthy woman. Oh, Fosh threw a fit when he saw her. They had an ironclad agreement. She'd broken it. But by then, she was older, and he couldn't intimidate her quite the way he once had.

"So, she built the log house out by the lake and moved in. That was also the year she had me write Fosh a letter demanding child support payments, although we didn't call it child support back then. Again, he didn't have much of a choice. By 1945, he was really dug in around here. He had everything to lose and nothing to gain by refusing the demand. Over the years he'd become an exceedingly wealthy man, far more than Fanny, though he had a terrible time hanging on to it.

"Eventually, he agreed to a small allowance each month. I don't think Fanny cared one whit about that cash. She just wanted some further admission from him that he knew he was Belle's father and was taking care of his responsibilities. She also wasn't above wanting to see him squirm. They both hated each other with a virulence I've seldom seen in my life.

"Once, about five years before she died, Fosh actually threatened her. He said he'd made friends with some rather nasty people in Las Vegas. He used to go there several times a year to gamble, which was where I understand he lost a great part of his fortune. Anyway, he said that if she ever pushed him again, she'd find herself inside a box at the bottom of Pokegama Lake. That's when she told him she still had the photos. If anything happened to her, an envelope would mysteriously appear to show the world the motive behind her disappearance, as well as the kind of man he really was.

"Until the day she died, she was scared to death of that man. She passed that fear on to Belle, with the proviso that if he ever tried to hurt her or her children, she was to come to me. He died about three years ago, taking all his sleazy secrets with him." He said the last sentence with an air of finality.

Jane wished it could have been the final stroke of the pen. But it wasn't. "Did you know Quinn had demanded money from Belle's estate? He said that since he was her half brother, he should receive some of the family inheritance."

Robert Weintz drew his lips together angrily. "He was so much like his father. That family was a cancer in this town. Fanny wasn't the only young woman Herbert Fosh seduced. There were others. But Fanny played as rough as he did. And Quinn," he said, uttering the name with distaste, "was no better than his father. Perhaps I'm being blunt, but I say good riddance to both of them. I'm only sorry it's created problems for the Dumonts. What came out about Belle recently—" He hesitated, then began again. "What she does in private with that woman friend of hers is her own business. I knew her to be a good and honorable woman, and nothing she's ever done has changed my mind. I don't know what this information can do to ease her children's pain or help you or the police to find out what happened to her on the night she died, but there it is. The Dumont family secret. It's sad, but no one can go back and change it now, no matter how much we might want to."

His body seemed to sink inward under the strain of the telling. Even so, he appeared content in his exhaustion, as if he'd been waiting a long time to lift this particular burden off his shoulders.

"One more question," asked Cordelia, raising her finger.

"Yes?" he said, lifting a weary hand to his forehead.

"Do you still have the photos?"

He nodded. "Would you like to see them?"

Cordelia and Jane both answered at the same time. Jane said, "No," and Cordelia said, "Yes."

Jane shot, Cordelia a pained look.

"They're in my safe."

"And that's where they should stay," said Jane firmly.

Cordelia looked crestfallen, but bit her lip and remained silent.

"I think you're right," he replied seriously. "Belle was going to take them with her the last time she visited, but before she left, she said they were part of the past and should remain there."

A soft knock drew their attention to the door as the nurse stuck her head inside. "It's time for your nap, Robert."

He shrugged and then gave a resigned sigh. "My keeper," he said, smiling at the woman.

"Thanks for your time," said Jane, rising quickly. She didn't want to tire him any more than they already had. "We can show ourselves out."

"I suppose I can't exactly say it was a pleasure," said Robert, pulling the blanket up over his stomach, "but it's been on my mind ever since Belle died. I'm glad I finally had the chance to tell someone the truth before my time's up."

"Don't talk such nonsense," scolded the nurse, slipping behind him and making sure the locks on his wheel-chair were off.

"It was nice meeting you," he called as she wheeled him down the hall. "I'll be seeing Belle and Fanny soon. I'll tell them someone cared enough to come by. It will make them both happy, I know that for a fact."

38

Cordelia stuck her head into the cabin's refrigerator, rummaging around for dinner ideas. It was her turn to cook. "There's a dirigible in here," she muttered, removing a jar of peanut butter and some grape jelly from behind it.

"It's a musk melon," said Jane, walking out of her bedroom and stretching her arms high above her head.

After a leisurely lunch in town, Cordelia had browsed the afternoon away while Jane spent some much needed time walking along the lakeshore, thinking. The story Robert Weintz had told them, while a fascinating piece of social history, seemed to have little to do with either Belle's death or Quinn Fosh's murder. Sure, Jane might have cleared up a small family conundrum—where the name Robber's Wine had come from—but in the overall scheme of things, it didn't bring her any closer to the truth behind Belle's and Quinn's deaths.

And that's where she was stuck when she finally returned to the cabin around five o'clock for a short nap. As she dozed on the bed waiting for Cordelia to get back, she tried to relax and empty her mind. Yet, no matter what she did, the same vivid image kept reappearing, almost as a taunt. It was the interior of Quinn's boat on the night he died. There was the smell of pine cleaner—used in making the Robber's Wine. She understood its significance now. And the messy cupboards and dirty dishes. The counter was wiped clean except for the powder circle. What was that all about? The Robber's Wine sat on the floor on the other side of Quinn's La-Z-Boy. Quinn was sprawled on the floor; the gun, compliments of the Lake Burglar, lay in his hand. What did it all mean? What was she missing? She'd fallen asleep, still wrestling with those questions.

When she awoke several hours later, she lay very still, keeping her eyes shut. In her sleep, she knew she had grasped something important, but she couldn't quite bring it into her conscious mind. It was just a taste, a flavor, but it was the key, she knew it. If she didn't move, if she stayed in this in-between state for just a moment longer, perhaps it would come back to her. Almost instantly, an image reappeared inside her mind. Yes! That was it. She understood now. Of course, it was just a theory—she had no proof—but it all fit.

As she entered the living room, the phone started to ring.

Cordelia answered it in the kitchen. As she chatted away, Jane flipped on the TV and curled up on the couch. A local fishing program was on. She stared incuriously as two portly men in plaid shirts discussed lures and bait. Finally, Cordelia hung up and sauntered into the room, plunking a P.B. & J. sandwich down on the table next to her.

"Why do I feel like a dog being served its dinner?" said Jane, taking a bite. She was hungry, or she might have refused such a pathetic offering.

"I'm tired, dearheart. This was the best I could do on short notice. We can have some sliced dirigible for dessert."

"No raspberry trifle with custard sauce?"

Cordelia closed her eyes and gave a wistful sigh. "What a lovely thought. It reminds me of that magical world we left behind in the Twin Cities. Ah, the delis and the late-night bistros. The car exhaust and concrete are calling to me, Janey." Her rapturous smile faded as her eyes flicked scornfully to the television set. "Do we have to listen to this crap?"

"Kind of *goes* with peanut butter sandwiches, don't you think?"

"One more day," Cordelia sighed again. "Maybe we can find something fun to do tomorrow." As she chewed her sandwich, she glanced outside. "It's beginning to get dark."

"You stayed in town pretty late. By the way, who was on the phone?"

"Helvi."

"What's up?"

"Well, she called to tell us Lyle's oldest boy was taken to the hospital yesterday afternoon. He tried to smoke Freon, or whatever one does with it, and he nearly died."

"That's awful!"

"Yeah. Lyle just stopped by up at the main house to give Helvi and his sisters an update. Seems the lad's doing fine. He'll come home in the morning."

"I'll bet Lyle's relieved."

Cordelia nodded, wiping a bit of jelly off her chin with a paper napkin. "Helvi said he wanted us to know that he's still planning on coming to our good-bye dinner tomorrow night, though Carla will be staying home with the kids."

"He doesn't have to do that. We'd understand his absence."

Cordelia shrugged. "Helvi said he insists on coming. He promised us last week that he'd pull that raft out into the deep water beyond the dock so we could all take a moonlight swim together. He wants to keep his promise. Tomorrow night will be our last chance."

A local news bulletin interrupted the fishing program.

A young man, sans suit coat, read from prepared notes:

"We interrupt your regular program to bring you a special news report. Earlier this evening, police in Earlton released a statement giving the name of the man they believe to be responsible for almost a dozen break-ins around Pokegama Lake. The man was identified as Pfeifer Biersman, thirty-six, a short-time resident of Grand Rapids and husband of Melody Dumont, daughter of Belle Dumont, the owner of Northland Realty. Biersman died yesterday in a boating accident. His estranged wife was also injured, though not critically. Police found evidence at his residence linking him to the burglaries, as well as information that may lead to further charges in the recent murder of Quinn Fosh. We'll bring you more details about this breaking story on the nightly Ten O'clock Report."

Cordelia whistled. "No shit. That's great news!"

"But it's not right!" said Jane, erupting from the couch. She raked a frustrated hand through her hair.

"What do you mean? If the police found proof, that's good enough for me. This is the best news we could get, Janey. It means the entire Dumont clan is innocent."

"But it's wrong," said Jane, switching off the TV. "Pfeifer had nothing to do with Quinn's death. And unless I'm badly mistaken, he wasn't the Lake Burglar either."

"Then who *was*?" asked Cordelia, her voice impatient.

"You're not going to believe me. Maybe I should just keep it to myself until I have more proof. Or maybe I should go talk to the police right now."

A loud crash drew their attention to the porch.

"What was that?" asked Jane, her voice dropping to a whisper.

Very soberly Cordelia replied, "I don't know."

"We better check it out."

"Good idea. I'll wait here."

Jane gave her a nasty look as she crept quietly to the

front door, peering carefully onto the screened porch. Near the corner, an empty vase had fallen off a stool and broken in pieces on the floor. It hadn't happened by itself. Scanning the room, she saw that nothing else was out of place. Even so, the implications were obvious. "Someone was out here," she called, racing outside into the deepening twilight. In the distance, she could just make out a figure as it darted into the woods.

"Who was it?" asked Cordelia, rushing up behind her.

"I couldn't tell." She watched for a minute longer, but the only visible movement came from leaves rustling in the evening breeze.

"But what do you think it means?" persisted Cordelia.

"It means that someone was listening to our conversation. And that someone now realizes I know the truth."

"Oh this is dandy. Just dandy." She sank down on the steps.

"This person is a killer, Cordelia. I have no doubt they'd kill again if they felt pushed."

"I think you just pushed them," she whispered, her eyes rising to Jane's and then dropping again to her lap.

"The problem is," continued Jane, sitting down next to her, "I can't prove what I know, at least to the satisfaction of the police."

"It's one of the Dumonts, isn't it?" she said, her voice low and full of defeat.

Jane nodded.

"Who?"

She whispered the name.

Cordelia's head snapped up in surprise. "That's incredible . . . I mean terrible! But . . . what are we going to do? Maybe we should pack our bags and shove off tonight."

"No, I can't leave it like this."

"So, what then? Do we go buy a rifle and take turns standing watch?"

Jane looked up at the house on the hill. Lights were on in almost every room. After that news bulletin, they were probably celebrating, breaking out the champagne and dancing in the hallways. All except the person who'd been standing on their porch, eavesdropping. Undoubtedly, it wasn't the first time they'd been watched. "You know, maybe we should find a motel room and stay in town tonight."

"But what about tomorrow?"

Jane mulled it over. "As I think about it, a plan does occur to me. First thing in the morning, this is what we're going to do."

39

After Jane and Cordelia's good-bye dinner the next night, everyone took their coffee out on the back deck and sat down to enjoy the sunset. In the aftermath of the storm several days ago, the weather had turned cooler. Yet tonight, temperatures had once again risen into the low eighties. A perfect evening for a swim.

Even though Jane wanted to tell the Dumonts everything she and Cordelia had learned yesterday while talking to Robert Weintz, she decided it was probably not politic to bring up the subject of Fanny Adams or Robber's Wine tonight. She couldn't chance another upset. She'd sworn Cordelia to secrecy and, reluctantly, Cordelia had agreed.

Anne seemed friendly enough throughout dinner, though Jane could see she was still angry. The only mention made of their heated conversation the other day was Anne's comment that she was glad the police had finally discovered the truth, no thanks to anyone other than Dennis Murphy. Once Jane had been duly put in her place, Anne's disposition altered considerably and she began to enjoy herself.

Now, relaxing after the delicious meal Helvi had prepared, they all leaned back and talked companionably. Lyle spoke for a while about his decision not to run for public office. He had to put his family first. If, one day, he did choose to run again, it wouldn't be as some made-up public image. It would be as himself, the real man, warts and all.

Cordelia wished him luck and everyone laughed.

For the next hour or so, the conversation turned to the future. Melody spoke eagerly of her plans for the baby. Helvi wanted her to stay on at the house, and Melody had agreed—at least temporarily. Anne said she was planning to sell her catering business in Minneapolis and move back up to the lake. It was time. She had nothing more to prove, either to herself or to her mother. And again, Lyle spoke of spending more time with his children. Neither Helvi nor Eddy said much, though both seemed content to listen to their children's plans, allowing their dinners to settle as the brilliant coral sunset faded into night.

Around ten, Lyle got up and went inside the house. When he returned, he was wearing his swimming trunks, a beach towel slung over one shoulder. "Last one out to the raft's a rotten big-city bum," he proclaimed, giving Jane and Cordelia a challenging grin.

"I'm too old for that sort of thing," groaned Anne, folding her arms over her stomach and stifling a yawn. "Besides, our friends have a long drive tomorrow. I'm sure they want to turn in early."

"Oh, come on, sis," said Melody, coaxing her. "If a pregnant woman with a damaged arm can do it, so can **you**." Poking her playfully in the ribs, she said, "This will be just like old times."

"I'll meet you out on the dock," said Lyle, taking off down the outside steps. "I'll get the inner tubes ready."

Eddy and Helvi exchanged amused glances. "You kids go ahead and have fun," said Eddy. "We'll just sit up here and watch."

"You're sure?" said Jane. "We're not going to do anything particularly athletic."

Eddy shook his head. "It's one of the prerogatives of age. I do what I want."

Helvi nodded her agreement, but said nothing.

After gathering up the empty glasses and depositing them in the kitchen, Jane and Cordelia followed Anne and Melody into the back bedrooms to change. It was now or never. Jane felt her stomach churn with anticipation.

Lyle had sunk the raft's anchor about twenty yards off the end of the dock. A good six feet away a reflector buoy bobbed gently in the darkness. Even though the raft looked small from a distance, as Jane swam closer, she realized there was plenty of room for five people.

Before they all dove in, towels were tossed on top of a board placed across an inner tube. Lyle pulled it with him as he sidestroked out, hooking it to the edge of the raft before he climbed on.

"Pretty great place, huh?" he smiled, as he lay down flat on the bare wood planks.

After drying herself off, Cordelia spread her towel out next to him and then lay down too, looking up at the stars. "I could get used to this."

"Yeah, except for the sharks, this lake is perfect," offered Melody, glancing at Cordelia out of the corner of her eye.

Cordelia raised herself up on her elbows. "Sharks?"

"She's kidding," said Jane, dangling her feet in the water. Her eyes rose to the moon. She wished it weren't quite so full and bright.

Anne shook her head at them, reaching for the flask she'd brought with her. Normally, she didn't drink all that much. Tonight, however, she seemed to have thrown her usual caution to the wind. "Sharks are everywhere," she mumbled. Losing her balance, she nearly slipped off the edge into the water.

Lyle caught her arm. "Be careful, sis." He grabbed the flask.

Anne yanked it back. Her mood had soured again.

Jane found it interesting that not once during the course of the evening had anyone mentioned Pfeifer or Quinn Fosh by name. Perhaps Helvi had set the tone. She wanted this dinner party to be relaxing and fun. She didn't want to dwell on tragedy. But even so, it seemed a strange omission.

Over the next half hour, everyone except Anne took a turn in the lake. Melody paddled around the raft splashing water on everyone's feet. She was clearly not a great swimmer, but she seemed to be having fun. Lyle floated away on his back, allowing the waves to pull him in toward shore. And since the lake was fairly deep under the raft, Jane and Cordelia took turns doing fancy dives. Finally, around eleven, Lyle said he was pooped. He wanted to catch a little of Jay Leno's program before he drove back home.

Anne and Melody agreed. It was getting late.

"Would you mind if I stayed out here for a while longer?" asked Jane. "It's so beautiful, and this is our last night here."

"Sure," said Melody. "Why not?"

"Stick one of those reflector flags in that hole over there," said Lyle, pointing toward the end of the raft.

Jane found several attached to the side.

"Great. That way our ass is completely covered and I won't have to come out and drag it back in before I leave."

"I think I'll swim in too," said Cordelia with a big yawn. "Will you be okay out here all by yourself?"

"Fine," said Jane, one hand slipping protectively over the other. The ring Julia had given to her had already begun to feel like a good-luck charm. And tonight, she needed all the luck she could get.

"If you aren't back in half an hour, we'll send someone down to check on you," said Lyle. He stood and dove into the water. He was a powerful swimmer and was nearly to the shore by the time Anne and Melody dropped off the side.

Before diving in herself, Cordelia bent close to Jane and said, "I'm scared."

"Me too, but we've got no other choice. You're clear on what you're supposed to do, right?"

Cordelia gave a guarded nod. "What do you think?" She flicked her eyes to the house on the hill.

"I think," said Jane, watching her friends' retreating wakes, "that with me as bait, we may just catch ourselves one of those sharks."

After drying off and changing back into her clothes, Cordelia joined everyone in the living room, taking a chair near the back. *The Tonight Show* droned on as she waited for the real show to begin.

Not five minutes later, Anne got up to go to the bathroom. While she was gone, Lyle went into the kitchen to rustle around for a bag of chips. When they both returned, Helvi said she was bushed and was going up to her room to read a bit before turning in. She said her good nights, telling Cordelia she'd see her again in the morning. Then, selecting a book from the coffee table, she headed up the stairs.

After a few more minutes, Melody began complaining that she was cold. Since she didn't think it was good for the baby, she excused herself to go take a hot shower.

During the next commercial, Lyle turned to Cordelia and said, "I suppose you and Jane will want to get an early start tomorrow."

"Yes, I suppose so," said Cordelia. "Actually, I'm pretty beat myself."

"You do look tired," said Eddy Dumont from the easy chair in the corner. "Best to get a good night's sleep before a long drive."

"I'll probably see you in the morning then," said Lyle.

"Carla and I are taking Melody to the doctor. Carla's thinking she might offer to be Mel's Lamaze coach."

"Really?" said Cordelia, trying to sound interested. It was a struggle. All she wanted to do was get outside.

"Yeah. I suggested I'd do it, but Carla thought it would be better if she did."

"Right. Good idea." She inched toward the door. "Well, see you in the morning then." Without further comment, she turned on her heel and left.

Once outside, she retrieved the binoculars she'd hidden in the bushes just under the deck and took up her position. She felt like General Patton surveying the battlefield. It wouldn't be long now. She crossed her fingers, hoping nothing would go wrong.

Out on the water, Jane could barely see the dark figure move cautiously down the hill toward the dock. She felt as if she'd waited for hours, but in reality, it had been less than fifteen minutes. The moon had drifted behind a cloud, making identification impossible. Not that it mattered. Jane knew who it was. As the form eased into the water, careful not to make a sound, Jane could see a long, narrow weapon held tightly in one hand.

All her muscles tensed as she waited, her breath growing rapid, her heart pounding inside her chest.

The swimmer moved steadily toward the raft, closer and closer until just a few feet away it sank silently beneath the surface.

For several seconds, all was silent.

Then, roaring up out of the water, the figure slammed a crowbar down heavily. A stream of red burst upward. The figure scrambled quickly onto the raft, ready to hurl the hideously maimed body over the side. As the moon emerged from the cloud, the woman gasped, realizing she'd been fooled. "What the hell?" she said, almost inaudibly, her hand fingering the bathing suit covering a plastic mannequin.

Bright lights slashed through the darkness. Catching her breath, Melody covered her eyes, hearing a loud-speaker say, "This is the police. Stay where you are."

Jane watched from behind the marker buoy as a small police boat blasted into the lake about a hundred yards away. It sliced through the calm water, heading straight for the raft.

In all the commotion, Melody seemed dazed. She looked down at the mannequin lying on the wood planks, touching the wig that had once covered the balloon face, the one she'd just destroyed.

Looking back up at the house on the hill, Jane saw that Cordelia had done her job well. All the Dumonts had been herded onto the back deck in order to watch the scene unfold. From this distance, Jane couldn't see their faces, but she could imagine their feelings, and her heart went out to them all.

Returning her attention to Melody, she could see the young woman slump onto the base of the raft, her eyes dropping to the red paint covering a good part of the wood planks as well as most of her upper body. As Melody looked around, her gaze was drawn to the buoy and the familiar face floating next to it.

For an instant, Jane's and Melody's eyes locked. In that one intense second, Jane felt the young woman's fury, and her desperation.

Jane watched as the police boat reached its destination. There could be no doubt in Dennis Murphy's mind now. Even though Jane couldn't see him up on the hill next to the house, the lights from his squad car pulsed and burned into the darkness. Melody was guilty. She had attempted to murder Jane to cover her tracks. It was the act of a woman who had gone over the edge, a woman

who felt she had no other choice. Even though Jane
didn't understand it all, she prayed she would soon.

It was painful to watch Melody being taken away by
the police. She seemed to have lost all her fight. Jane felt
herself shiver as she realized she could swim back to
shore now. What would she say to the Dumonts? They'd
all be there waiting for her, demanding answers. There
were no words to express how sorry she was. And yet,
she'd done what she had to do. She would never have felt
safe again, not until Melody was caught.

Perhaps, thought Jane, pushing away from the buoy,
feeling her muscles release some of her pent-up tension
as she stretched into her stroke, the nightmare for this sad
young woman was finally over. Yet in a very real sense,
another one had just begun.

40

At ten the following morning, after a virtually sleepless night, Jane drove to the police station in Earlton, where she was ushered into a small room at the back. She sat down at the long table, her eyes rising anxiously to the clock. Ten minutes later, the door opened and in walked Melody Dumont. She looked pale and tired, her eyes puffy from crying and from lack of sleep. The paint stains on her body had been removed with turpentine, though some of the bright red was still visible on her knuckles and around her fingernails.

Melody sat down across from her. Folding her hands on the table, she said, "Thanks for coming."

"I wanted to come."

"I hope Cordelia understands. This is between you and me, Jane. I wanted to speak to you alone."

"Don't worry about Cordelia. She's back at the cabin, packing. We're planning to leave as soon as I get back."

Melody nodded. After a moment she said, "I confessed to Quinn's murder."

"I know."

"You may not believe this, but I had to tell you I was sorry about what happened last night. I know it's too little too late. I've been out of control for so long now, I feel like a stone hurtling down a mountain. I knew I was going to crash, but I just couldn't think about the consequences."

Jane could well imagine it. She'd had some out-of-control moments in her own life. Yet she wanted to know more. She needed to hear the whole story.

Regarding Jane somewhat coolly, Melody asked, "How did you know? How did you figure out it was me?"

Jane's throat felt suddenly tight and dry. "Well," she began, "there were a couple things I noticed that I couldn't explain any other way."

"Like what?"

Leaning into the table, she said, "For one, there was the plastic wineglass. The police never saw it, and never would have. One of you made sure of that. Even if they had, I doubt they would have understood its significance. I guess you could say I stumbled on the name Robber's Wine kind of by accident. It came up in a conversation I had with an old friend of your grandmother's. Angela McReavy."

"Really." Melody seemed surprised. "Why'd you go talk to her?"

Jane shrugged. "I wanted to know more about your grandmother's early life. Since Angela had been a friend, Helvi suggested I go see her. I never believed your mother's death was an accident. I thought the answer might lie in the Dumont family secret—and to know more about that, I had to find out about Fanny Adams."

"Jeez," said Melody, leaning back but continuing to look straight at Jane, "you have been a busy little snoop, haven't you?"

Jane ignored the sarcasm. Under the circumstances, she understood it. "Tell me," she continued, "when you left the wineglass on Quinn's boat, it was as a symbol, right?"

She gave a slow nod.

"Was it done on a whim?"

Her mouth curled into a smile. "Yeah. Stupid, huh?"

"I never would have assigned any meaning to it if it

hadn't been whisked away so quickly and you hadn't all lied about it."

Melody gave a weary nod. "Yeah, I know. Big mistake. But what was it about the wineglass that made you think I'd put it there?"

"Well," said Jane, "the interior of Quinn's cabin smelled like pine cleaner because that's what you'd used to make the Robber's Wine. You'd even found some cleaning powder to top it off, just the way it should be, except you didn't just sprinkle it around the rim; you did what any trained bartender would do, you turned the glass upside down, dipped it into the sugar or salt—in this case, the cleaning powder you'd spread out on the counter—and then you filled it. That's what created that powder circle. I'll bet it was almost a reflex. You didn't even think about it. Since you were the only trained bartender in the group, the finger pointed to you."

Melody shook her head in amazement. Then, her shoulders sinking in defeat, she said, "What else did I do wrong?"

"Actually, nothing. But the day Pfeifer died, I ran into him over at the Fosh Lake Country Club. He gave me a message to deliver to you. He said that he loved you, and that he missed you, not just your mother's money. Sure, he liked having the extra cash, just like any other guy, but you were the most important thing to him—or words to that effect. The problem was, as I thought about it later, it didn't make sense. I knew Belle didn't subsidize her kids financially. If I recall correctly, the Dumont dictum was that you all make it on your own. So, what was he talking about? The more I thought about it, the more certain I was of my theory. You were the burglar, weren't you, Melody? The cash you'd stolen, and the money you received from selling stolen property—you told him it came from your mother."

Melody smiled. "You're clever, Jane. That's exactly what I did."

"But why? Were your finances that strained? Did you have debts?"

The smile faded. "You have no idea what was going on in my life. No one does."

"But I want to understand. That's why I'm here, Melody. Why did you steal? And what made you kill Quinn Fosh?"

Melody tilted her head back and closed her eyes. After almost a minute she said, "I've been going over this all night. I'm not sure I can do it again."

Jane waited. She couldn't force Melody to talk. Yet, as far as she was concerned, Melody owed her an explanation.

Finally, Melody said, her voice intensely weary, "What do you want to know?"

"Start with the burglaries. That's as good a place as any."

She opened her eyes and leveled her gaze. "All right. I'll try." Taking a deep breath, she began, "When Pfeifer and I were first married, we were pretty happy. But as time went on, and our financial problems grew, Pfeifer became more and more frustrated. Two years ago, the abuse started."

"Physical abuse?" asked Jane. This was the first she'd heard of it.

"That's right. At first he was smart enough to hurt me where it didn't show. Later, he stopped caring. I was terrified my family would find out—that they'd all think it was my fault."

"But why?" said Jane. "Nobody deserves to be beaten."

"I know that, but while it was happening, Pfeifer kept saying it was my fault, that I drove him to it—and I believed him. Maybe in a way, I still do. He harped on my mom's refusal to help us financially. Why couldn't I get her to understand? There weren't any decent jobs up here. Mom had all the money in the world—what was the problem? I tried to explain why she'd taken such a hard line, and when I did, he thought I was taking her side against him. That I was calling him a failure.

"I begged Lyle to give me a job at the real estate office. It brought in a little extra income, but not enough. I was often late for work, or missed days completely because Pfeifer had beaten me the night before and I couldn't get out of bed. It made me look like a rotten employee, which in turn made me feel even more like a screw-up. In the meantime, Lyle was putting pressure on me to take my job responsibilities more seriously. By coming and going when I felt like it, I was making him look like a fool in front of his other employees. It looked like he was playing favorites—letting me get away with stuff just because I was his sister. Lyle didn't understand what I was dealing with, and I couldn't tell him.

"One night, after a particularly bad blowup, I took my car and left. I drove along the beach road trying to figure out what to do to save my marriage. By that point, I wanted out, but felt *that* had been part of the destructive pattern of my life. When faced with a problem, I usually ran away. This time, I ordered myself to stay and work on it.

"That same night I robbed my first house. I saw a car back out of a drive and take off toward town. I knew the people who owned the place. It was an elderly couple. Both were in the car, so I felt pretty confident the house was empty. I just strolled up to the door, rang the bell and knocked, and when no one answered, I walked in. It wasn't even locked. I took all their jewelry, found about two thousand dollars in cash in a bedroom drawer, and also grabbed a couple handguns from a gun case. It was easy. Later, by asking around a couple of the sleazier bars in the area, I found a guy who said he'd fence the property. He paid pretty well too—said he'd take anything else I got.

"The next day, I told Pfeifer I'd gone to see my mother the night before, and she'd finally relented. I showed him the two thousand dollars. Well, as you can imagine, he was thrilled. But I told him Mom had sworn me to secrecy. I wasn't supposed to tell anyone. Not even him. So he had to keep his mouth shut about it. He agreed so fast I felt my head spin. It was the first time in months that he'd treated me with any love or respect. It lasted about as long as the two thousand dollars took to spend, and that was a little less than a month. After that, we were right back to where we started, with one exception. The crummy job Pfeifer had found at that filling station was now history. He'd been fired. So, I committed another robbery. From then on, I took my new life of crime more seriously, scouting out possible targets ahead of time. I was successful in every home I robbed. My last theft was in late May."

"The burglaries stopped when you moved into your mother's house, right?" said Jane.

Melody nodded.

"But . . . what about Quinn Fosh? That note he sent to your mother, the one in which he says he has some important information about one of her children that she needs to know. Was he talking about you? Did he know you were the Lake Burglar?"

Melody gave a short, angry nod.

"But *how* did he know?"

"Let me backtrack a minute," she said, lowering her eyes and staring at a nick in the tabletop. "After Mom's will was read, I came back to the house with the rest of the family, but I knew I had to get away from them. They were getting on my nerves, driving me crazy. So, I hopped in my car and drove into Earlton. I wanted to

simply sit by myself at the local bar and sip a Coke. I
wasn't in the dump for five minutes before Quinn Fosh
sauntered up. He sat down at my booth uninvited and
proceeded to bitch at me about the way he'd been treated
at the lawyer's office. He was pissed as hell that his new
family had rejected him." She gave a bitter laugh. "He
was such a liar. He said he wanted to be an uncle to me.
To all of us. That he'd help protect me from Pfeifer."

"Is that when he mentioned the meeting he had with
Belle?"

"Yeah. He kind of whispered the entire story to me
over his fourth Scotch and soda."

"But why would he tell you something like that?"

"He was drunk and he felt like whining. Also, because
of what he knew about me, he thought he could count on
my silence. Oh, and he was also setting up another blackmail attempt. It was my turn this time. Apparently, he
first approached Mom about a year ago, shortly after his
father died. On his deathbed, his father told him that
Grandma Fanny had been blackmailing him for years. It
was a lie, of course, but Quinn didn't know that. His dad
told him he'd find the canceled checks in the wall safe.
Not being terribly original, Quinn decided to organize a
little blackmailing scheme of his own. He came to Mom
with the canceled checks and said he'd make them public
unless she gave him money. Since she didn't want him
running around town with a lot of wild accusations, she
gave him several thousand dollars on three different
occasions. It was nothing to her, but I guess it was
enough for him to buy that used Cadillac.

"From then on, I suppose Quinn figured he'd found the
golden goose. When he came to her again several weeks
ago, demanding more money, she told him she'd changed
her mind. She didn't care if he published the checks in
the Congressional Record—or words to that effect. That's

when she called the family meeting to tell everyone the truth behind the Dumont family fortune.

"The day of the meeting, Quinn stopped by just after sunup and pushed that note you found in Mom's purse under the porch door. When Mom found it, she called him right away and they agreed to meet around ten. That's when he told her about me. It just so happened that the guy I was selling the stolen property to was a good buddy of his—they got drunk together regularly. One night, Quinn happened to mention to him about the problems he was having with my mom, so the idiot up and tells him about me. So much for honor among thieves. Anyway, Quinn knew he really had some juicy blackmail material now. The morning Mom died, he presented her with the bad news. I guess she begged him not to tell the police. He said he wouldn't, but his silence would cost her.

"Well, she got pretty upset—you know how excitable Mom could be sometimes. She started screaming at him that he didn't understand. If he told the police, he'd be turning in his own niece! Quinn didn't have a clue what she was talking about, so she whipped out that signed statement Grandma Fanny had gotten Herbert Fosh to sign—the one where he admits he was Belle's father. I guess Mom had finally gotten her fill of the Dumont family secret and, since she'd called that meeting later in the day to come clean with us, she'd brought proof along to show him as well. Needless to say, Quinn was pretty shocked. As he read through it, Mom told him those canceled checks he was going to offer as proof that Fanny had blackmailed Herbert Fosh were in reality child support payments. Mom and Quinn were half brother and sister. Didn't that mean anything to him? As far as she was concerned, she was bringing out the biggest guns she could imagine. Family was sacred. How could he even think of hurting his own niece!

"Well, of course, Quinn just laughed at her. I meant nothing to him—neither did Mom. I suppose when she saw that, she got even more upset. She pushed him. He pushed her back. Somewhere in there, he pushed too hard and she tumbled over the side of the ravine. He said he saw her get up, but when he yelled down, she didn't answer. He was so angered by her silence that he just grabbed the proof of paternity and took off. He figured he'd talk to her later."

Jane could hardly believe her ears. "You mean, he just left her there? He didn't try to help?"

"If you can believe him, he said he didn't realize she was injured. He just thought she was refusing to talk to him." Melody closed her eyes. "Mom wouldn't have been there if it hadn't been for *me*. If I hadn't robbed those houses, she'd never have been out there alone with that bastard."

Jane massaged her right temple, letting it all sink in. "When he came to you that night at the bar, what did he want?"

"My help. He wanted me to convince the rest of the family that he wasn't such a bad guy after all and should be allowed to inherit a share of the estate. I didn't stop laughing until he told me he had proof that I was the Lake Burglar. I could have killed him right then and there, Jane. I've never hated anyone so much in my entire life. I felt trapped. By him, by Pfeifer, and by my own actions. I didn't know where to turn. I had no one to talk to, no one who understood.

"The next night, I drove back to my home, the one Pfeifer and I had rented together the year before. I was desperate. I made sure he was downstairs at his work-table, then tried the front door. He'd apparently changed the locks. So, I ran around to the bedroom window and cut the screen. I was in and out in a matter of seconds. I know it was stupid, but I'd kept some of the stolen property. Mostly jewelry, but a couple of the guns too. I'd hidden them in one of my dozens of shoe boxes on the top shelf of the closet. Pfeifer never touched my clothes, so I figured it was safe. Anyway, I took one of the guns, grabbed a couple of personal items from one of the dresser drawers, and left. I don't think he even realized I was there.

"Before the fireworks the following evening, I'd agreed to meet Quinn on his houseboat. I was supposed to bring several thousand dollars with me to show my good faith. As you may already realize, I didn't have several thousand dollars just lying around. I knew Dad and Helvi had gone for a walk, so I borrowed Dad's boat and raced over to meet Quinn. His houseboat was moored in a fairly deserted part of the lake. We talked for a while. Since he'd been drinking, he moved quickly into his uncle mode. You know, all chatty and friendly. God, but he made my skin crawl. He asked why I'd brought my camera bag along. I told him I wanted to take a picture of him in his captain's hat. You should have seen him, Jane. He puffed up like a blowfish. He had his back to me when I took out the gun and shot him. It was just that simple. I had to protect both my future and my baby's future. I knew what I'd come to do and I did it. I'm not saying I acted nobly. I wanted to save my skin. That's a pretty strong motivator. It's a small consolation to me now, but the truth is, I saw no other way."

"But . . . then why did you confess?" asked Jane. "Since the police don't have an eyewitness, any evidence they might find would only be circumstantial. I'm sure your lawyer explained all that to you. You might have gotten away with it."

Melody stared down at her hands, touching the red paint that still lingered there. "I was terrified," she said, her lower lip starting to tremble.

"Terrified of what?" asked Jane.

"Terrified of *me*. Frightened to death by what I'd just tried to do to you. You have to understand. I don't hate you. I don't even dislike you. When the police turned that spotlight on me after I'd tried to kill you, I looked down at what I thought were my bloody hands and completely freaked. I disconnected from time and space. At that moment, I don't think I even knew who I was anymore. I had no idea I was capable of such violence against someone I considered a friend. I couldn't let it go on any longer. I had to stop ... *myself*." She clamped a hand over her mouth, squeezing her eyes shut against the pain.

The silence in the room pressed down on them. Under other circumstances, Jane would have tried to find some words of consolation. But Melody had phrased it accurately right from the beginning. It was too little too late.

Finally, struggling to find her voice again, Melody said, "And also, I figured I owed Mom that much. Just once in my life, I wanted to do the right thing. Just once," she said, her voice breaking, "I wanted to do something to make her proud of me."

As Jane watched her, she realized how immensely weary she felt. There was nothing else she could do now but listen to Melody cry. It was a terrible sound. Like a dying animal. Deep, guttural, and utterly hopeless. "I'm sorry," said Jane finally. After another minute she asked, "What's going to happen to your baby?"

Melody bent forward, wrapping her arms around her stomach as she began to rock. "I'll probably have her in prison," she said, her voice thick with tears. "I suppose it depends on how long the trial takes. Anne says she'd like to take care of her for me. Raise her until I get out, if I get out. I just don't know what's going to happen. But I've already got a name for her."

"Her?"

Melody nodded, taking out a tissue and blowing her nose.

"What is it?"

"I want to call her Eileen. It was Mom's middle name. I just hope to God she doesn't grow up to be like me."

After wiping her eyes, she pushed away from the table. As she got to the door, she turned, taking one last look out the window. It was a beautiful summer morning. Not a cloud in the sky.

Freedom, thought Jane, following her gaze. Everyone took it for granted. Yet for this tragic woman, the window had just been closed and locked.

"Thanks for coming, Jane. I hope you'll find it in your heart to forgive me one day. But . . . I'll understand if you don't." Lowering her head, she stepped into the corridor where two guards were waiting to escort her back to her cell.

Jane sat motionless in the empty room, too overwhelmed by Melody's sadness, and her own, to leave.

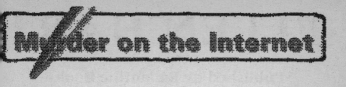

ELLEN HART

Published by Ballantine Books.
Available in your local bookstore.